Theresa disappeared down the narrow hall and returned with a small red book stamped PRIVATE in gilt letters. "Mary Jane's diary. Oh, I know—a daughter's sacred privacy and all. But I *had* to read it. Look." Theresa passed the book to Holly, her finger marking a line. Holly saw that Theresa's hand was shaking.

> *Today I took the Citibank papers into the conference room. Ned was having Bruce on the carpet. Bruce was absolutely white. I felt terribly sorry for him. I thought of the time by the elevator when EDK gripped my arm so tightly I cried out. I think he could be dangerous.*

Holly stared at Theresa her face blank as an erased blackboard. "I think he killed her, Holly."

MOST WANTED

MARGRET PIERCE

PUBLISHED IN HARDCOVER AS *WILD JUSTICE*

St. Martin's Paperbacks

The characters and events in this book are fictional, and any resemblance to real people and situations is strictly coincidental.

Most Wanted was published in hardcover under the title *Wild Justice*.

Copyright © 1995 by Margot Peters.

All rights reserved. No part of this book may be used or reproduced in any manner whatsoever without written permission except in the case of brief quotations embodied in critical articles or reviews. For information, address St. Martin's Press, 175 Fifth Avenue, New York, N.Y. 10010.

Library of Congress Catalog Card Number: 95-1035

ISBN 0-312-95759-9

Printed in the United States of America

St. Martin's Press hardcover edition / June 1995
St. Martin's Paperbacks edition / May 1996

10 9 8 7 6 5 4 3 2 1

For Uncle John

ACKNOWLEDGMENTS

Grateful thanks to Mary Boileau Bailey; to Quintin Peterson of the Washington Metropolitan Police Department; to the many Washingtonians who answered my numerous questions; to Audrey Roberts and Ray Ruehl, who critiqued the manuscript; and to my editor, Jennifer Weis.

Revenge is a kind of wild justice.

—FRANCIS BACON

MOST WANTED

CHAPTER ONE

I don't know why you invited me," she sobbed. "Why did you?"

It was her first real experience with the cruelty of the world, and she was devastated. She crouched in the white leather chair next to the fireplace, her head in her hands. Her hair, falling forward, made a childish part down the back of her head, dividing her scalp neatly except for the pale wisps curling into her neck like delicate ferns. "You haven't looked at me all night." She groped for Kleenex in a cheap sequined bag. "Why did you bother? You don't care about me, do you? You don't give a damn!"

"I thought you might enjoy the band and the pool," he said coldly. His blunt, capable fingers fiddled with a malachite-handled paper knife. "Obviously I made a mistake. They don't amuse you."

She blew her nose into a wad of tissue. "You said you'd introduce me to people. You said it would be all right." She lifted her head. Tears failed to damp the hurt in her forget-me-not eyes. "You know what one woman did when I sat down next to her? She just stared me up

and down and said, 'Who are *you*?' As though I was a
worm or something. And you said you'd take care of me.
My God, you've never even looked at me all night."

"So you've said." He went to a cigarette box on the
long library table, lifted the lid, and changed his mind,
remembering that he had given up cigarettes six months
before. "You don't seem to realize there are seventy
guests downstairs who also need my attention. Important people."

"And I'm not!" Her voice broke. She shook her head
disconsolately. "I know I'm not."

"I didn't say that." With a frown, he lit a cigarette
after all and drew smoke deep into his lungs. "Let's con-
duct a little test. Look at the painting over the fireplace.
Now tell me: Who is the artist?" The question was not
quite fair, since he cared little about art; and the moment
he asked it, he realized that he himself had forgotten the
name of the painter. He shrugged. After all, he owned the
damned thing.

She turned her head to stare at the large canvas she
had not noticed before and hated it immediately. It
wasn't a picture at all, as she understood pictures, just an
orange blob here, a blue zigzag there, yellow splashed
like egg yolk everywhere, and a line, thick and black as
death, slashing the painting in two. She thought it crude
and intrusive in a room that otherwise seemed romanti-
cally rich.

"I don't know," she said defiantly, "and I don't care. I
don't like it!"

"Of course you don't. Because you don't understand
it. You are ignorant, I'm sorry to have to tell you—abys-
mally ignorant in every way."

"You mean I'm stupid? I'm not!"

"I didn't say that," he said wearily, realizing the futility of argument with someone who couldn't grasp the basic terms.

"You don't have to." She stood up, gripping the wing of the white leather chair, swaying a little on her high silver heels with anguish and the six or seven glasses of champagne she'd tossed down recklessly since ten o'clock that evening when she'd begun to realize that she was having an awful time. She hitched up a thin sequined strap that kept slipping off her slightly rounded shoulder. Her wide eyes accused him. "What do you take me for, Ned?" She gasped at her use of the first name of a man who now seemed a stranger, yet the shock dared her on. "A nobody, don't you! Just some dumb blonde you picked up one night when you'd had too much to drink. What you don't realize is that I can *learn.* I want to learn! You looked at me, you paid attention—why did you bother?"

He studied the tip of his cigarette, then spun it into the grate. "I don't know," he said honestly, as though considering the question for the first time.

Yet on her feet and angry, she was pretty again. He didn't mind anger; he was used to it. You had to be in a business like his. He didn't mind hardball, not that she could pitch it if she tried. He smiled.

"Now, now," he said soothingly. "As for having too much to drink, you've been hitting the bubbly pretty hard, haven't you?" He circled her shoulders and began to lightly massage her upper arm, gradually increasing the pressure until his fingers bit into her flesh. The simple trick, he knew, made women quite pliable. "I think you'd better run along home now, *Ms.* Jones." His tone mocked the neutral title. "We'll talk about it sometime when you're calmer." His lips tickled her ear.

She felt herself melting because she loved him. Oh, she loved him so terribly, this graying man with the suave smile and melancholy brown eyes, this man who could not be teased about a slight thickness around his middle, this man who could kill her with a word, yet had wept— yes, actually wept on her shoulder that first night, that magical night when she'd pulled his head down on her breast and rocked him like a child. But at the same time, she knew it was all wrong. All wrong for him to be treating her like this. Decent people didn't behave this way, and she knew what decent people were. Her mom. Her kid brother, Matt. Holly Bauer next door. Her dad, even though he'd left them when she was fifteen; it wasn't his fault, she knew that. This was a bad, frightening world that she didn't know.

"Don't," she said, ducking away from him, though not very far. Her voice sounded thin and hollow in her ears. Oh, why couldn't she get a grip on herself? Where was her pride? She'd made straight A's in school, she was good at her job and certain to get a promotion. She had great friends.

His caressing hand moved coaxingly down her spine. Yet he was profoundly, monumentally bored. How had he gotten involved with this kid anyway—this Mary Jane Jones? He grimaced, trying to remember. The Christmas party, it must have been. Strange, even in the international banking business, you had to throw the old office Christmas party. It had not been a good night. There'd been that scare about the Tokyo stock exchange, and he'd had too many scotches, an indulgence he rarely permitted himself.

But there had been these two tellers or programmers or

whatever, and they'd listened to his pronouncements
with big eyes and glossy pink lips pouting as they sucked
spiked eggnog through straws. Little to choose between
them—one dark, the other blond, good tits and asses,
both wet behind the ears—but somehow he'd ended up
driving the blond one home and they'd parked in front of
her family's small house in Silver Spring and she'd listened to a lot more about the dirty divorce he'd lived
through—two, three years ago, but it seemed like yesterday—and maybe he'd rambled on a bit, what with the
five scotches, and then she'd said, "I'll let you kiss me if
you'd like."

Let him—that was rich!

Hadn't given her a thought until one day by chance
he'd met her on Pennsylvania Avenue running for the
subway. He'd taken her for a drink at the Four Seasons.
Her awe at the big, swank hotel lobby, her childish pleasure when he'd asked the man at the gleaming grand
piano to play her favorite song had curled his mouth contemptuously, yet had somehow saddened him too, so
that he'd driven her home again. Not a bad kid; anyway,
she listened. Maybe he'd opened up too much. Unlike
him to do that.

But then she'd started to stick. Calling him at home.
Wanting to see him more often. Inviting him to her twen-
tieth birthday party, for chrissake, and not having a clue
why he roughly refused.

That's why he'd invited her to his fancy Georgetown
bash tonight. To show her just how far out in left field she
was playing. To put her in her place. Of course it was
cruel: Sometimes, as the old saw went, you had to be
cruel to be kind.

She'd told him she was madly in love with him, not seeing that this was the sure way to turn him off. Another woman had pushed him once, roped him cunningly in ivy. He'd married her and regretted it for twenty-five years.

He moved adroitly away from her at a knock on the door. A woman with sleek, thick, honey-blond hair caught back in a black velvet bow put her head into the room. She looked at Mary Jane's face and raised little circular eyebrows. "Am I interrupting something, Neddy?" she said ironically. "I thought you should know that some of your guests are talking about leaving."

"Come in," he said. His voice was curt. Caught in the library upstairs like this by Nancy Wylie, wife of Bill Wylie, whose friendship was one of the gilt-edged securities you couldn't buy in Washington, and Nancy herself a pearl, yes, the rarest of pearls. "You're not interrupting. This young woman isn't feeling well. Wants to go home."

Mary Jane looked at him with astonished blue eyes.

"Better fix your face first, honey." Nancy Wylie pulled a lacy handkerchief from her beaded bag and held it out to Mary Jane. "Mascara down to *there*. Don't tell me this old man's been bullying you!" But she was only teasing because she turned and laid a slim hand ornamented only by a plain gold wedding band lightly but familiarly on Ned's sleeve. "Shall I make your excuses downstairs, darling, or are you coming?"

"In a minute."

In a flash Mary Jane saw it all. Of course Ned Kaplan wasn't in love with her, Mary Jane; he was in love with this cool, elegant woman, whoever she was. Whoever she was, she was somebody very important, important to Ned Kaplan, the man causing her such pain. The way this strange woman had laid her hand on his arm, the way she'd said "darling."

She handed back the handkerchief, glad she'd smudged the delicate white square, wishing she'd used it to blow her nose. She couldn't say thank you because she hated this cool, dainty, porcelain woman so hard.

"Not at all," said the woman with a kind, pitying smile that Mary Jane did not see. The door closed behind Bill Wylie's wife.

"You have to go now."

She said in what she thought was a calm, reasonable, grown-up voice, "It's her, isn't it?"

"What the hell are you talking about!"

"That woman. Nancy, whoever she is." Oh, she was going to die! She felt actual wrenching pain as though someone was driving a sharp knife into her belly.

"Have you gone crazy?"

Mary Jane sank back into the chair, hiccuping with sobs. It was clear to her now: He'd told the woman to come upstairs and interrupt them. "This little nobody's a pain in the neck; come rescue me, darling"—that's what he'd said, imprisoning her small hand in his for an instant before he'd let her go. Mary Jane threw back her head and moaned.

He yanked at his collar, jerking his neck back and forth as if for air. Suddenly he was fed up. Completely, absolutely. "None of that," he said harshly, pulling her to her feet. "This has gone far enough."

"What do you mean?"

"You're going home."

Feeling like a fool, he grabbed her arms and frog-marched her out the door into the long upstairs corridor. Below, he could hear laughter in the front hall.

"Please," she cried, digging her sharp silver heels into the thick carpeting, writhing like a snake, *"please.* You're hurting me!"

He clamped his hand over her mouth, forcing her along the hall toward the back stairs, past somber paintings of long-ago people lit by rosy lamps that flushed their dead faces with life. Detachment numbed him. He could see their struggling progress down the hall as though he stood behind them with folded arms, a ballet master ironically watching a grotesque pas de deux. Fools, he thought again dispassionately. Both of you, fools.

At the top of the back stairs he threw her roughly against the post. They must be out of earshot now, with the racket of the dance band and all the chatter. Let her howl.

"Look," he said between clenched teeth. But he was still curiously detached, still looking on coldly from far away at the fools playing this charade. "Tell them to get you a cab in the kitchen. Tell them you've got a head-ache—tell them anything! And don't call me tomorrow. Don't call me ever again. That's a warning!"

The keen blade made a final twist in Mary Jane's stom-ach and she grabbed the banister for support. She saw his face recede from her like the long strip of shore that day she'd been caught by a wave at the beach and sucked in-exorably out to sea, scraping the razored ocean floor, while the rest of the children played happily with shovels in the sand. She was losing him; she was drowning.

"You can't do this to me. I know too much," she said desperately. She'd read that in a book somewhere, or maybe heard it on TV, and, despite the iridescent green eye shadow and flashing earrings that trembled in the hollows of her throat, she was very young.

Yet as soon as she spoke the words, she knew they were absurd. Suddenly she knew she was getting over him. Miraculously, the wave had flung her back on dry shore. He had been too cruel, too dangerous. He wasn't her sort at all. And suddenly she thought what fun it would be to laugh tonight with her roommate, Chris, about the whole crazy evening. The snooty butler, the way she'd almost taken a header into some old man's lap in her new high heels, the big scene in the library. So why not go for broke, get him for once the way he'd got her? She took a deep breath. "Besides," she said recklessly, "I'm pregnant!"

He heard this, he thought, in a perfectly detached way. She's lying, he thought, very detached. But he must not have been as detached as he imagined because suddenly he seized her shoulders with both hands. He shook her back and forth silently, watching her silly head snap on its thin white stalk of neck, hating her. He shook her hard and flung her away. When he finally looked over the banister, he saw, clearly yet remotely, as through the wrong end of a telescope, a broken silver shoe on the landing, and, at the foot of the stairs, quiet on the black-and-white tiles, something broken that had been Mary Jane Jones.

CHAPTER TWO

Automatically he backed away, straightening his silk tie, a drum of fear beating in his ears. He walked noiselessly back down the long corridor, paused for a moment, and, drawing a deep breath, ran lightly down the sweeping main staircase with his chin in the air. It was a trick he had; it gave the impression of youthful fitness. The knot of guests below looked up.

"Sam," he said heartily, crossing the foyer famous in Georgetown circles for the purity of its soaring lines. "Elsa. Not leaving already?" He extended his arm, meaning to fling it fraternally around the stooped shoulders of the Chairman of the Joint Finance Committee, and at that moment saw the brand of red lipstick on his right palm. His arm dropped to his side.

"You deserted us," pouted Elsa Frazier. She was a plump, beautiful, copper-haired woman with an astonishingly small waist and a vulture's beak in all the latest gossip. Her doting husband, much older and growing deaf, bent his bald, freckled head to catch her words. She lowered her voice. "I was wondering, darling, whether you were having a little *distraction.*"

He sensed danger. Elsa was ruthless. "One of the guests," he said easily. "Franchot told me someone was in the library feeling unwell, and I went up to see." Dammit, why had he dragged in Franchot? "She decided to slip out the back way."

"If she's sick, shouldn't someone be driving her home?" said Bob Cohn acidly. Bob was the current lawyer of choice among politicians indicted for conflict of interest, and very rich. His wife, Sally, taller than he by two inches, chimed agreement as she always did, though rumor whispered that she was both the brains and the power in that marriage.

So like Cohn, thought Ned with deep, deep irritation. Doesn't give a damn about any "sick guest," just wants to make trouble. That was his courtroom technique: haggle over everything, especially when it doesn't matter; wear them down. He doesn't like me even though he is my lawyer, Ned realized suddenly, shaken. Aloud he said, "They've called her a cab in the kitchen. She preferred it that way." He suppressed an insane desire to laugh. Mary Jane, lying in a sauce of blood from her own cracked skull, had certainly not preferred it that way.

"We're leaving; we can take her." Cohn examined him with small, gray, close-set eyes.

Again! "Seems she lives out in Silver Spring," he said, still easily. The Cohns lived across the Potomac in McClean, not that they would have driven their grandmother across the street. "Besides, she's gone by now."

He escorted the Cohns and the Fraziers to the front door. "Band's too damn loud, Ned," said Sam, digging a powerful finger in his ribs. "Other than that, great show, great show."

He smiled automatically, watching the four of them recede down the lamplit walk into the thick night. If only
he could follow! The house at his back seemed like a gap-
ing mouth ready to swallow him. He looked up at the
sky. A starless, black-velvet September night, crickets
shrilling. Nights of his youth. Then remembering the red
stain on his palm, he wrenched off a handful of cool,
thick magnolia leaves from the ancient tree fronting the
house and scrubbed furiously until his palm stung. He
could not see the result. He turned back to the relentless
throb of the band and above it the peacock screams of
guests from the patio around the pool. Why the hell did
every party these days, including his own, have to oper-
ate at five thousand decibels?—though on second
thought, tonight the din was a lucky thing. He checked
his watch. One-forty. The party might racket on for another hour, yet it was only a matter of minutes before one
of the help discovered Mary Jane and came running. For
a moment he considered breaking up the party on some
pretext or another, then discarded the notion—suspicious as hell. He became aware that sweat had plastered
his fine cambric evening shirt to his back. Surreptitiously,
he thrust his hand under a lamp, and saw no stain.

He poured himself a stiff scotch at the sideboard as he
struggled to formulate his reaction to the inevitable news.
Shock. Concern—Bob Cohn's kind of concern. Of
course he knew the girl, they'd been out together a few
times. No use denying it. Someone might have seen them.
So he'd invited her tonight to the party—casually, very
casually. About half an hour ago Franchot had told him
she was upstairs in the library feeling unwell.

He set his glass down with a crash. Damn the Franchot
slip! Maybe it wasn't too late to scrap. No, why not—the

Cohns and Fraziers had had enough to drink, even Sally—they wouldn't remember. All right, then. There'd been this unimportant girl—no, for chrissake, not unimportant because everybody, especially the scum, was important these days, and not a girl either. This guest. He'd seen her run upstairs and followed her. She'd said she was unwell. Much better. The ever-solicitous host. He'd offered to call her a cab. She'd insisted on slipping down the back stairs and phoning from the kitchen, didn't want to interrupt the party.

He groaned. No good. Insignificant little Mary Jane Jones couldn't interrupt a party if she tried. He doubted anyone had even noticed her.

Of course. She'd heard people in the hall downstairs and hadn't wanted to face them. Shy, very shy. Knew she looked a sight. He let his breath out slowly in relief.

"Hate to break things up, Ned, but Myra's playing breakfast bridge at the crack of dawn. Ever hear anything so crazy? Three no-trump in cold cream and hair curlers. Thank God they don't invite their husbands! Great party, but don't bother. Franchot will show us out."

He started. The Schiers were leaving.

"Lovely, Ned. Wonderful food, wonderful entertainment. As always." Hating her husband, Myra Schier detached herself and offered her mouth. Last year she'd had a terrific *schwarm* for Ned Kaplan, which her marriage had unfortunately survived.

"It wouldn't have been the same without you," he said gallantly, kissing her dry hand instead. He clapped George on the back. "Talk next week, old man."

"Right," said George affably, grinning at his wife's disappointment.

If they all would just follow the Schiers out the door. How the hell was he going to get through this!

"Darling." Nancy Wylie slipped her hand into his. "Jesse is flying high in there. You know how he gets. Better come lasso him."

Milo "Jesse" James, the senator from Texas. Sweat broke out on Ned's forehead. The last thing he needed now was a scene with Jesse. He took a deep breath—breath control, that was it, deep breathing; it slowed the rush of blood to the brain. Act normal, he told himself for the hundredth time. You don't know that anything has happened. You can't know it because you weren't there. That's how you have to behave—as though this party is exactly like any other.

Nancy's narrow hand was cool in his. Dear Nancy. She'd stuck after the divorce. Had been his unofficial hostess half a dozen times over the years. Did her husband mind? If so, Bill never gave a sign. Aloud he said with jovial irritation, "Why does anyone invite Jesse anywhere?"

"I suppose because for at least two hours out of the twenty-four he's the most entertaining man in Washington."

Jesse's bass boomed over the band's New Age rendition of "Yesterdays." His arm was draped over the shoulders of a helpless State Department official occupied in protecting his shirt front from the contents of the senator's glass.

"He's had poor Lee Tyler pinned against that wall for half an hour. Bill tried to pull him off and almost got tossed into the pool."

"I'll handle it," said Ned. "Jesse, old man—"

But at that precise moment he became aware that

Franchot was speaking to his housekeeper Mrs. Marty in the next room. Uncanny! He could not possibly hear anything over the band, the raucous chatter, and Jesse's bellow—yet he did. He caught Franchot's low murmur, Mrs. Marty's urgent whisper. They were consulting how best to break the news to him. He stiffened as he felt Franchot moving swiftly among the guests toward the crowded patio. He felt suddenly naked, like a buck who senses the muzzle of a shotgun trained at his heart. Both paralyzed and aware.

When Franchot touched his arm, it was all he could do to keep himself from leaping like a shot animal.

Chapter Three

"What's the matter, Franchot? Running low on booze?" He thought his voice sounded natural. It had better. Because this was a big moment. Every move he made now must seem spontaneous. He could feel Nancy and Bill watching him, was aware of Nancy's smooth blond head tilted like a curious ferret's to one side. He could not look at her.

"In private, sir."

"Of course."

Mrs. Marty stood waiting just inside the drawing room doors, her plain round face the color of cold potato.

"Looks like the study is deserted. We can talk in there. Now, Franchot, what's the problem?" He believed his voice to be steady, his manner composed.

"Apparently it's quite serious, sir." Franchot had borrowed his style from butlers in 1940s Hollywood movies. He was not Ned Kaplan's exclusive butler—few people in Washington boasted one these days—but divided his services among three or four houses. "There's a young lady, sir, lying in the back hall at the foot of the stairs. She seems to have fallen."

"Young lady? What young lady!"

"I don't know her name, sir. One of your guests. At least I noticed her wandering about during the course of the evening. I've never seen her before, and I wondered."

"You mean—"

"I mean she's dead, sir."

Oddly enough, though he'd been bracing himself for just these words, his shock was quite genuine.

"Dead? Impossible! Have you called a doctor?"

"Nobody's called a doctor, Mr. Kaplan." Mrs. Marty spoke for the first time, with authority. "There's no need."

"Where is she?"

"In the back hall, like I said, sir. One of the help found her."

He flung back the kitchen door. No one had turned off the small television on the counter, which was showing an old movie starring, he noted automatically, Cary Grant. The three girls hired for the evening were huddled together against the sink as though for protection. Their eyes were round, like Mary Jane's when he'd told her she was leaving. He must not think of that now.

He pushed through the swinging door that led to the back hall, Franchot and Mrs. Marty at his heels. The rear quarters on the west side housed the butler's pantry, the kitchen, and the laundry room. Straight ahead, down a shallow flight, the back door. To the right, along a marble-tiled floor, past a dumbwaiter inactive since the 1836 basement kitchen had been abandoned, the old servants' stairs, and at the bottom—

"Impossible," he said again. He was almost sincere. In

the long minutes since the episode at the top of the stairs, he had somehow discredited Mary Jane's corporeal existence even while waiting for its discovery. She wasn't important enough to still be there.

She was lying as though asleep, her mouth slightly open, one arm caught beneath her body. Asleep, except for the broken look of her neck, the finality of her position, and the blood. He knelt briefly over the body, avoiding the dark pool congealing under the pale matted hair. He rose. Careful.

"One of the guests, I'm afraid. Poor kid! We'll have to have someone look at her. Mrs. Marty, ring Dr. Phillips. Home number. It's in the book." He turned to Franchot. "What the hell are we going to do about all those people out there?" He felt as though he had been assigned a part in a play with very bad lines.

Franchot bowed his head in thought. "If I were you, sir, I'd announce that one of the staff has been taken ill and that under the circumstances you'd appreciate their leaving." He shot his cuffs. "High time, too, if I may say so. I'd be glad to do it, sir."

"Thanks, Franchot."

He stood alone in the hall for a moment, his back toward her because he couldn't bear the sight of the skewed young body, the pathetic pool of blood. Well, that was the whole story, wasn't it? He'd turned his back on her.

Don't think of that now, he told himself firmly. Don't think of anything but behaving like a host who's breaking up the party because one of his staff is ill.

In the dining room he met Nancy coming to look for him. She was drawing on gloves.

"What's happened, Neddy? Franchot says—"

Did anyone but Nancy still wear white gloves? he

thought inconsequently. Surely they belonged to the innocence of another age. He focused with difficulty on the matter at hand. "I know I can tell you," he said, glancing over her shoulder as he drew her farther into the room. "It's difficult because it's not one of the staff at all. You know the girl upstairs—"

"That poor unhappy girl in the library?" Nancy's crescent eyebrows climbed almost to her scalp.

"Yes. Mary Jane Jones, works at the bank, nice kid. She's had an accident. Fallen down the back stairs. I'm afraid . . . she's dead."

He was amazed to see quick tears. "Dead! Oh, God, no! Oh, Neddy, how awful."

"Why the fuss? You didn't even know her!" he said roughly.

"Yes, but *still.* Poor kid! I felt sorry for her tonight. She seemed so—so dismal and lost. What on earth was she doing on the back stairs? Won't it look—"

What the hell did she mean! Thank God Elsa Frazier had left. Nancy was bad enough. "Look what?" he said brutally.

She studied his face, then managed a smile. "Nothing, darling."

"It's a hell of a thing," he said, thrusting his hands into his pockets and moving restlessly about the room, "but I can guess how it happened. She was upset—not feeling well. Too damn much champagne, probably. I told her Franchot would get her a cab, but she said she wanted to slip out the back way. I suppose she was in a hurry and—"

He stopped, struck by an unpleasant thought. Suppose Nancy had lingered outside the library door, suppose she had heard the argument. Mary Jane saying she loved

him, him saying, "This has gone far enough." He had
said it, hadn't he—*"This has gone far enough."* Suppose
she took that to mean what in fact it had turned out to
mean.

He looked at Nancy's small kid-gloved hands clutching her purse and dismissed the idea. Nancy Wylie did
not listen at doors. Her manners were impeccable. Always had been. One of her greatest charms.

Mrs. Marty appeared in the entrance, stout and efficient, color back in her cheeks. "The doctor's on his way,
Mr. Kaplan. I was lucky to get him; he'd just come in the
door."

"Good. Thanks, Marty. Now, Nancy." He kissed her
lightly on the cheek, reacting, even in his fear, to the
warmth of that scented curve. "You and Bill trot on
home. There's nothing either of you can do here." He
liked the sound of that—casual yet firm.

"I'll ring you tomorrow."

"Do that. Good night to Bill."

Dr. Brian Phillips met the Wylies on the front steps.
They were old friends and he struck Bill lightly on the
arm.

"What's going on in there?"

Bill Wylie, towering over his wife by a foot and looking
down at Phillips from six inches, shrugged. "Nancy says
it's not one of the staff at all; it's a young lady. Name,
Mary Jane Jones. Fell down stairs and broke her neck,
they say."

"Who is Mary Jane Jones?"

Bill caught a look from his wife. "Nobody," he said
drily, "quite seems to know."

* * *

The first thing Brian Phillips noticed was that she was
wearing only one shoe. He knelt over the body. Dead an
hour, he guessed, two at the outside. Fractured skull,
broken neck by the look of it, multiple contusions. He
squinted up the stairway—steep, nasty hairpin bend at
the landing, dimly lighted, no carpeting—you wouldn't
catch him living in one of these damned Georgetown
mausoleums. Something gleamed on the landing. Stepping over the girl's body, he mounted two stairs at a time.
A silver shoe, heel torn off. Heel must be—yes, there it
was, five steps up. He stared at the shoe and the silver
spike in his hands. Flimsy sandal, nothing but straps. So
she'd started down, tripped, broke a heel, and pitched
headfirst to the bottom. Easy to break a neck coming
down, and that cold marble floor—the real thing, none of
your marbleized vinyl—could crack a skull. He frowned.
Trouble was, why would one of Kaplan's guests be leaving by the back stairs? He stood looking at the girl, the
silver shoe in his hand.

Ned was in the study smoking. He rose when the doctor came into the room. They had known each other socially for years without being particular friends.

"Well?" Ned said, feeling again that this play had rot-
ten lines.

"Seems fairly straightforward," said Phillips. He held
out the shoe and heel, then set them carefully on the big
square teak table next to Ned's leather chair. He sat
down gingerly on the edge of the cushion, hitched up
black trousers. He hadn't stopped to change his tux.
"No, thanks, nothing for me."

"Sure?" Somehow he'd feel better if Phillips accepted a
scotch.

"Hell, yes, it's time for breakfast!" Phillips looked at

him coldly as though he was talking to an alcoholic. "About the girl— What's her name, by the way?"

"Mary Jane." It sounded improbable now that he'd said it. Girls were all Courtney, Jennifer, or Tiffany these days. "Jones." More improbable.

"Nasty fall. Multiple contusions, fractured skull. Neck broken." He jerked his thumb at the sandal on the table. "Heel snapped. Seems to tell the tale." He sighed and raked his thinning hair, thinking not of breakfast but of the sybaritic pleasures of his warm, undulating water bed. "Not the kind of thing one wants to happen at a party."

"Hell no." But as Phillips's words sank in, Ned felt a huge gust of relief like morning air sweep through him. The shoe, of course. Told a tale indeed! Jill fell down and broke her crown—all because of those damned silly high heels women wear. And Phillips, brilliant son of a bitch, had seen it immediately.

". . . may wonder what she was doing leaving by the back stairs."

"What?"

"I said, of course someone may wonder what the hell the girl was doing here in the first place and why she had to sneak out the back way. I take it she wasn't exactly out of your drawer."

"I think I can explain that," said Ned, ignoring the sarcasm. He felt he had arrived, finally, at the crucial point of the evening. Phillips was not a friend, but maybe he could be talked to man to man. Not complete frankness, of course; just enough to weight the scale of credence in the doctor's mind. "The girl works—worked—at Security American. I've seen her a few times, nothing serious—she understood that. She heard about the party tonight, said she'd never been to a real Washington bash. I thought she might get a kick out of it, so I invited her. Told her to bring a friend, guess she didn't. Later in the evening I saw her head upstairs. Seemed strange, so I went up after her. She was in the library complaining she didn't feel well. Obviously she'd been hitting the champagne. I told her Franchot would get her a cab. She said she didn't want to see people, could slip down the back and call a cab in the kitchen. I protested, but she was determined to do it her way and very embarrassed about the fuss. So I excused myself and went back down to my guests. End of story."

"So that's the last you saw her, upstairs in the library?"

"What is this, a fucking exam?" He grinned, trying to mask the fear and hatred he felt.

Brian Phillips yawned widely. "Okay, okay. But just out of curiosity, how does a stranger happen to know about the back stairs and the kitchen phone?"

"Standard equipment in a house like this." Ned studied him, then threw up his hands in surrender. "All right. She's been here once or twice before. But there was nothing between us. How could there be? She was a nice kid— on the make professionally, but who the hell isn't? I didn't hold it against her. And now she happens to be dead."

"You've notified the next of kin?"

Another blast of wind, not pleasant this time. Why was he so damned off balance all the time!

"I never thought of it," he said honestly.

"Looks like it's up to me. Well, I'm used to the game." Phillips consulted his watch. "Not the best time to call someone with this kind of news." He yawned again and his eyes watered with fatigue. "I suppose you've got her number."

"You suppose wrong."

"You must know where she lives, for chrissake. Or do I call every Jones in the book?"

"She had an apartment with a friend, somewhere near the Cathedral, I think." He decided not to mention the Silver Spring house, not that he remembered the address in any case.

"What's the friend's name?"

"I honestly don't know. I told you, Phillips, she wasn't important."

"I can see that." The doctor's voice was cold.

"I'll call my secretary. She'll know, or she'll find out." He went to his desk and lifted the phone. Through the French windows, he saw that the dark was bleaching into dawn. I've made it, he thought. After all, Phillips could have called the police. God damn it, I've made it!

Phillips's hand on his arm arrested him. "There's another call we'd better make first," said the doctor. He grimaced slightly, as though apologizing for the intrusion. "MPD Headquarters may be interested in Mary Jane Jones."

CHAPTER FOUR

Yet apparently Mary Jane Jones was as insignificant in death as she had been in life. The police came—and left. Ned threw down the papers in relief. Nothing about an accident at a fashionable Georgetown party, only a routine mention on the local Channel 7 news. Of course, he and Phillips had quietly pulled a few strings. He realized, again with that curious detachment, that he had almost begun to think of it as an accident.

He'd gone through the last forty-eight hours in a dream. Dorothy Swerdlow had finally got hold of the girl's father at six A.M. He had driven right over, apologized profusely for his jogging sweats, then broken down in tears over his daughter's body. There'd been a bad moment when he asked to talk to the police, but Phillips, the bastard, had come through after all, assuring Mr. Daniel Jones that it was nothing but a tragic mishap, showing him the broken shoe, laying a sympathetic hand on his shoulder, suggesting tactfully that his daughter had been recklessly imbibing too much champagne, implying that it would not be pleasant if that fact were bruited about.

Eventually Mr. Jones had left and then the body was called for and taken away, and the dried black stain in the back hall eliminated by Franchot.

Always the chance of a lawsuit, of course; today people sued on principle. He'd have to deal with that when, and if, it came. Today, walking along the corridors of Security American and into the office as though nothing had happened, he had met dozens of guardedly curious eyes. The news had swept through Security American, he knew, like a firestorm. And four visiting Saudi bankers and a sheik to be given the red carpet treatment—a nightmare, but no getting out of it. At least the Saudis knew nothing about Mary Jane Jones. He'd excused himself from dinner; Bradley could handle it, thank God. And tomorrow a board meeting and the damned Saudis again. He got up and poured himself another scotch.

Mrs. Marty knocked and entered. He saw her glance quickly at the *Post*.

"Supper on a tray as usual, Mr. Kaplan?"

He looked at her sharply. There was something odd about her tone. "Yes," he said, "in here. I've got a load of work as usual."

She nodded, but turned at the door and stood there uncertainly.

"Well, Marty?"

Her round, pockmarked face reddened. "This is hard for me to say, Mr. Kaplan; in fact, I don't know how to begin, but you know how I've been talking about retiring?"

He set down the glass of scotch on a thick brass-rimmed glass coaster designed as a compass. The needle, he observed inconsequently, swung to the northeast. He sat very still in his chair.

"No," he said coldly. "I don't remember any talk of retiring."

"Oh, yes." Mrs. Marty approached the chair, emboldened. "Remember after the divorce how I said I'd stay on a year if you really needed me, seeing as Mrs. Kaplan was moving to the house at the shore and didn't need me, though my husband was nagging at me night and day to quit housekeeping and stay home with him now that he's retired? Well, it's going on three years now, isn't it, Mr. Kaplan, and last night Frank and me sat down and had a long talk, and Frank says, 'Hilda, you've got to tell Mr. Kaplan straight out it's time to quit, no matter how bad you feel about letting him down!' And I said, 'I don't know if I can bring myself to do it, Frank, but I'll try.' And so, I am." She drew a deep breath and pressed her lips together.

He did not answer immediately, but got up and slowly poured himself another drink. She's lying, he thought, and there's nothing I can do about it. Retirement, hell— she was *grateful* when I kept her on after the divorce! At the same wages too, for half the work. Dammit, how is this going to look to people? To Nancy and Bill, the Fraziers, the Cohns, the Schiers. I can answer that one. They'll say my own housekeeper suspects me of murder.

He leaned forward confidentially. You had to reassure subordinates like Marty. They didn't like scandal; they didn't like change; they lacked imagination. You had to persuade them that everything was ticking along in the regular groove. "I realize," he said, "that what happened Saturday night must have upset you very badly. But you're not the only one, you know. My guests, Franchot, the kitchen help—we're all still in shock. And what we all need is time to get over it. The great healer, after all, isn't it—time? I realize it's against your principles, but I seriously want you to consider taking the rest of the week off."

Mrs. Marty hesitated a moment, tilting forward on thick-soled jogging shoes with hands clasped across her round aproned stomach as though she might literally tumble to the proposition. But she said, "Thank you, Mr. Kaplan, that's very kind, but really, my mind's made up, and so's Frank's. He won't have it any other way but that I quit. After all, I'm sixty-three and I've been cleaning and cooking for people in the big houses forty years. That's long enough for anybody."

Yes, he thought bitterly—and the urgency for leaving struck you just now.

"I'll require two weeks' notice," he said stiffly.

"That's understood, Mr. Kaplan."

He was too angry to say more. When she brought in his tray ten minutes later, he did not look up. He left his favorite boned chicken breasts in lemon-tarragon butter untouched.

"I've sent flowers to the funeral home, Mr. Kaplan."

He looked up from a folder of securities he'd been studying, pulling off glasses with heavy black frames.

"Pink roses. I think plain flowers are so much more tasteful than a wreath."

"Good," he said abstractedly, massaging the bridge of his nose. "Thank you."

"But if you don't mind my saying so, Mr. Kaplan, I think you ought to go to the funeral. A simple graveside ceremony, I understand." She consulted a large wristwatch. "One o'clock today."

He flung the glasses onto the desk. "Why the hell—

pardon my English—should I! I hardly knew the girl."

"We all understand that," said Dorothy with consummate tact. "But it's good public relations, isn't it—good for the bank. One can't be too careful these days. And it would mean a great deal to the parents, I'm sure."

"I can't go," he said. His head had begun to throb. "I've got the Intertrust people at one."

Dorothy flipped open a red notebook for inspection. "We rescheduled that meeting for eleven tomorrow. You've got nothing this afternoon until three."

He sighed, beaten. "All right. Where is it?"

"The Gates of Heaven Cemetery."

"Jesus. Where is that?"

"Georgia Avenue and Main Street, Silver Spring. At least I think it's still Silver Spring out that way, though it may be Wheaton." She handed him a map.

Nancy agreed to go with him. "It's been ages since I've been to a funeral. Do people still wear black?"

She was more than ten minutes late, and not in black, but in elegant coffee-colored silk. "I'm sorry," she said through the opening elevator doors, "but Liz just called from San Francisco. Such wonderful news! She's expecting next April. Just what Bill and I have been longing to hear—not that we dared breathe a grandparently word."

He felt a sick jolt in the pit of his stomach. "I'm pregnant," she'd said, and then he'd seized and begun to shake her. Had she been? Or had she been lying? "Wonderful," he said mechanically, opening the passenger door. "Give Liz and Ted my congratulations. Though obviously it's impossible, since you're not old enough to be a grandmother."

They hit every red light on the endless drive. Nancy

peered anxiously at her small gold watch. "I'm afraid we're going to be late. My fault."

"It certainly is." He was fighting a curious sense of dread. Relax, he told himself roughly; it's over—or will be over in a matter of minutes. This is the end.

It was nearly fifteen past one before Ned swung the hunter green Mercedes between the white stone pillars of the Gates of Heaven.

"A Catholic cemetery. Was she?"

"I have no idea."

"Do you know *where?*" Nancy peered anxiously right and left. The cemetery was heartlessly green, curiously empty and flat, and she realized that the gravestones must be sunk horizontally into the ground.

"Haven't a clue."

"There's a lodge. We'll ask."

By the time they got directions, it was one-twenty. Ned headed in the direction of a golden row of maples the guard had pointed out as a guide.

"There! I see people. The next road over."

Ned swung the Mercedes right, then left, pulled over, and turned off the ignition. "Too late."

The group of about thirty was breaking up. Ned avoided looking at the raw earth. He recognized Daniel Jones, though he looked very different in a black belted raincoat, dress shirt, and tie. He was talking to an older couple, grandparents, perhaps. The woman pressed a handkerchief to her eyes; the man tugged at the jacket of his dark pinstriped suit as though unused to the fit. There were young people of both sexes—friends, he supposed. He thought some of the girls might be from Security American, though he couldn't swear it. One or two were still obviously in tears.

"I'd better say a word to the father," said Ned, his voice rasping. His jaws seemed locked. "And there must be a mother somewhere. You don't have to get out."

His hand was on the door when a tall woman with dark blond shoulder-length hair broke away from the group and came along the grass toward them. A bright scarf at her neck fluttered defiantly. She seemed unconscious of her surroundings. Her head was thrown back, her face transfixed with grief—not passive sorrow, but wild hurt and outrage. A young boy of thirteen or fourteen walked self-consciously at her side; their hands were locked. Strangely enough, he saw this pair not in detail but as a kind of vision, out of focus, felt rather than observed. When she was a yard or so from him, she turned toward the Mercedes and stopped, and for a frozen moment they stared at each other through the glass before he bent over the wheel and turned the key. Nothing had passed between them but a look; yet he felt suddenly and unreasonably as though the psychological armor in which he had carefully encased himself since "the accident" had been pierced. He pulled away, tires squealing.

Nancy grabbed at the leather strap above her head as they took a corner. "I thought you were going to talk to the parents," she said in surprise.

"They don't need me. It's over." He took his foot off the accelerator.

She sighed and shook her head as the Mercedes coasted between ranks of pines. "So terribly sad. Such a brief life. And such a—a *cold* death. Among strangers. So anonymous."

"Life is brief, sad, and anonymous," he said harshly.

"Yes, I suppose it is. But I'm glad I came today. Obviously there are people who care." She was looking at him curiously. "Can you drop me at Dupont Circle or is that out of your way?"

"Of course I'll drop you," he said, shaking off her gaze. He was sorry he had asked her to come along. She knew him too well, and he was having a hard time acting the appropriately concerned boss.

"You know—darling, that was a red light you just ignored!—I wonder if that was the girl's mother. Back there. That tall blondish woman walking on the grass, holding on to the young chap for dear life."

"I didn't notice."

"Oh, but you must have. She looked right at you."

"No."

Nancy snapped the large leather purse she'd been rummaging in with a click. Her famous tact seemed to have taken a holiday. "Apropos, darling, whether it was the mother or not, and I suppose it really doesn't matter, don't you think it's time you came clean about little Mary Jane Jones? You can tell Nancy, you know. *Something* was going on between you two up there in the library. I could feel it the moment I walked in the door." She turned to him with clear, curious gray eyes.

His hands tightened on the wheel. He could not look at her. He said finally, his voice rasping as it rose and tightened, "There was nothing. It's over. I don't see any point in discussing it."

She stared at him in surprise.

"Of course, darling," she said long blocks later.

He double-parked just off Dupont Circle, ignoring the bleat of angry horns behind him.

"Close enough?"

"Yes, thanks." She sounded hurt and her small round chin was tilted in silent argument.

They looked at each other across the luxurious, private, leather space and found that it could not be bridged.

"Neddy, I know you must be feeling responsible—"

"Some other time."

She pulled down the corners of her mouth. "All right for you, I'm going home. I used to say that when I was a kid, did you? When I wasn't getting my way with other children's toys. Good-bye."

Reproach hung in the air with her delicate floral perfume. In the mirror he watched her neat-suited figure recede until she turned a corner. He did not head back down Connecticut to Security American; he was hardly aware, in fact, of his direction or purpose. He only knew finally, certainly, that Mary Jane had been lying, and his hand pounded the wheel in time to his furious "Stupid bitch, stupid stupid little bitch!"

It wasn't until the following Friday that Ned remembered his current housekeeping crisis, little wonder with the ten-hour days he'd been putting in at Security American as President of International Divisions in charge of SA's projected expansion into Kuwait, Japan, Mexico, and Australia, as well as in his capacity as vice-president of the board. Endless meetings, endless international phone conferences, all a case of cautiously moving pawns here to trap a bishop there while pretending you had only the bishop's welfare at heart. He'd welcomed the overload, as conscience-numbing as a hit of speed to the vein.

He flipped the intercom and called back Dorothy Swerdlow, his personal secretary of more than eighteen years. Though he pointedly ignored Secretaries Week, a fresh rose on her desk every day, a year-end bonus, and an annual three-week, expenses-paid vacation kept her content. She had said nothing about the previous Saturday night except, "I'm very sorry, Mr. Kaplan." He'd resented her pressing him to go to the Gates of Heaven, yet he acknowledged that her reasoning had been sound. Hers was the kind of loyalty and discretion you couldn't buy.

"By the way, ring Elsa Frazier for me, will you?"

"Yes, Mr. Kaplan." Dorothy Swerdlow's prominent eyes behind round wire-rimmed glasses brightened. Elsa Frazier, perhaps the most feared and admired woman in Washington, was her *culte.* The only time she ever indicated disapproval of her employer was when he omitted La Frazier from his guest list.

"Tell her Mrs. Marty's leaving—retiring. Ask her if she can recommend someone else. Somebody totally sound, of course, all the right references. Handle Elsa with the usual velvet gloves. Better ask her to ring me back."

"You prefer not going through an agency?"

"Elsa *is* an agency. But you might as well cover all bases. Oh, and run an ad in the *Post.*"

He didn't realize until later that evening when he eased his taut body into his leather chair with a scotch in one hand and a report from Mexican Bank Central in the other that Elsa had not returned his call. He sat up. Elsa always returned his calls. Perhaps she and Sam had left early for the country; that must be it. Yet in that case, her social secretary would have rung him back.

He felt that stab of apprehension he'd felt earlier when Nancy had said good-bye. The kind he'd felt as a child when his perfumed mother allowed him to kiss her cheek very carefully before she rustled out the door, or when his roommate at Princeton told him in his senior year he'd found someone else to bunk with. Suddenly the evening seemed to stretch endlessly in front of him. He frowned, got up, went to his desk, dialed a number. After five rings, an answering machine clicked in. He hung up abruptly. These days Diana Maynard was often out when he called.

The next morning after a fifty-minute workout with weights, the Nordic Track, and the Stairmaster in the bedroom he'd converted into an exercise room, followed by a quick dip in the pool, he rang the Wylies. Bill himself answered. The millionaire building contractor and his wife lived simply in a two-floor condo overlooking Rock Creek Park. No regular maid or housekeeper, no cook except on special occasions, just a chauffeur because both Bill and Nancy hated city driving.

"What's the good word, Ned?"

"Hell of a week, Bill. Haven't had a chance to catch my breath."

"Heard you had the Saudis. Did you sell 'em Washington?"

"That's your job, mate. Anyway, we did our best to send them home happy. Look, what about you and Nancy and I getting together tomorrow for dinner, just the three of us, like old times? The new restaurant, La Forza, is supposed to be fairly spectacular."

"Sounds good, but you know better than to ask me. Refer all invitations to the social secretary. Nancy!"

Rather breathless, Nancy came on the line. "Stretches on the balcony," she explained. "Tomorrow night, dinner? Lovely, Neddy, I've been dying to try La Forza; you know Bill never takes me anywhere, but tomorrow evening is the Cohns, remember? The monthly Sunday. Can we have a raincheck?"

"Of course. Any time."

"Wonderful. See you at the Cohns'."

Ned hung up slowly. Bob and Sally Cohn entertained at a casual five o'clock cocktails and buffet at their neo-colonial McClean, Virginia, home once a month on Sunday. The guest list varied, but certain people were regulars, including Ned Kaplan. In the pressure of events, he had not given the Cohn Sunday a thought.

He stood there rubbing his chin thoughtfully. Through the tall French windows he could see that it had begun to rain, a fine September drizzle coaxing down the first amber leaves from the towering maple that dominated the brick-walled backyard. He would have to have Mario drain and cover the pool one of these days soon, store the patio furniture, prime the fireplaces with the birch logs that cost him three hundred and fifty a cord.

He opened the doors and walked out onto the patio, cursing as he lost his footing momentarily on the rain-slicked flags. The seat of each white chair had turned into a miniature pool; the furled table umbrellas drooped dis-piritedly like unfired rockets. The pool had been Carol's idea; she was the sunmaiden, the worshipper of chlori-nated waters. He much preferred the old Georgetown backyards—walled, bricked, tangled with holly, azalea, rhododendron. Private. Lush. Secret.

Yet the pool had been a hit with their friends, perhaps for its incongruity. Was it only two weeks ago, tonight, that the place had been swarming with people laughing, dancing, drinking? Today it seemed abandoned.

He would not see Nancy and Bill at the Cohns tomor-

row evening. There was a simple reason. For the first
time in more than ten years, he had not been invited.

Sundays at the Cohns ended promptly at eight and,
ahead of all the other cars jockeying for position in the
circular drive, the Wylies' old black chauffeur, Morrison,
had the silver Lincoln limo ready and running. In the
gray-plush backseat, Nancy shivered in her white fur
wrap and snuggled closer to Bill, still in the process of
collapsing his tall frame comfortably. He took her hand.
Ever since the children had left home, they'd held hands
behind Morrison's tall, straight back, feeling daring and
a little risqué.

"Well?" demanded Nancy, still waving over her shoulder though the Cohns had disappeared inside.

"Well what?"

"You know exactly what I mean. I couldn't get Sally
alone for a minute. What's the matter about Ned?"

"Funny, his not being there. Actually I did manage to
have a few words with Bob."

"And? Oh, darling, you *can* be maddening."

"Bob was close; you know the way he can be. Says he's
zeroed in on something he calls 'slightly fishy' about this
Mary Jane Jones affair. I don't pay it any mind. Lawyers
always smell something fishy, it's their job."

Nancy prayed for patience. "Might I know what this
'slightly fishy' something is?"

"Hell, Nancy, *I* don't know. Something about Ned
telling Bob and Sally it was Franchot who told him to go
up and check on the girl. But then it seems Bob talked to
Franchot, who said he did *not* see the girl go upstairs and
certainly never spoke to Ned about her."

Nancy pondered a moment, nibbling a gloved finger.

"Is that all? The difference between Franchot alerting him and Ned going up on his own? I may be rather thick, but it doesn't strike me as particularly sinister."

"Frankly, me either. But Cohn says, 'Why the lie?' You've got to admit he's sharp as hell."

"Ruthless as hell! So you're saying that because of some, some *flimsy* slip of the tongue—it could be just that, you know—the Cohns refused to invite old tried and true Ned Kaplan tonight?"

"Look, Nance, I'm as surprised as you are. But I don't think it's a big deal. I think Bob's just turning things over in his subtle, Machiavellian mind, and Sally's going along. Though, come to think of it, this is probably her idea. Always on the side of the underdog, as long as it pays."

Nancy giggled, then sighed. "But darling, something like this could ruin Ned socially."

Bill Wylie tucked the lap robe more securely around his wife's sheer-stockinged knees. "Surely not!" He hesitated. "Well," he said doubtfully, "I suppose it could."

CHAPTER FIVE

I don't believe what I'm hearing! And give up your new job? Terry, baby, you're crazy!"

Theresa Foley got herself another Perrier out of a fridge almost camouflaged by the cute magnets her children had given her for Christmas and birthdays. Three weeks ago she had been a rather pretty woman of forty-two, not remarkable in any way but with good skin—fair with a sprinkling of childish freckles along the bridge of her nose—high cheekbones, deep-set dark blue eyes, and a quirky, generous mouth. This evening there were lines around the mouth, a cleft between her eyebrows, brown smudges under the eyes. Privately her friend Holly Bauer thought she'd aged ten years.

"I don't think I'm crazy," she said defiantly, pulling up a chair opposite Holly at the small kitchen table painted dark green. "Want to split this?"

"Actually, Perrier has never turned me on."

"Suit yourself. But read it, will you? I want to hear it again."

Holly sighed deeply and flapped the pages of the *Post*.

"All right, here goes: 'WANTED: Experienced house-keeper for large Georgetown residence. Five-day week, flex hours, salary competitive. Live-in pref. Light cooking, cleaning. Refs required. Apply in writing: P.O. Box 7195, Washington 20007.' Holly threw down the paper in disgust. 'Experienced, Terry, *experienced*. Why isn't that getting through to you?"

"But I am experienced. How long have I been keeping house for people? Fifteen years!"

Her friend groaned. "You know that running a vacuum for people like the Murrays and the What's-'ernames isn't the same thing. This is the big time. You've got to know how to run a Georgetown mansion. This place could be twenty rooms. Mrs. Danvers, remember? With all those keys on a ring!"

"The ad doesn't say *mansion*. Besides, I catch on fast."

"Oh, sure. From little old Knox Circle to Georgetown in one easy lesson. Anyway, how can you even think of giving up a job you were raving about a month ago?"

Theresa pushed back her wooden chair and crossed her long, greyhound legs. "It's not such a great job—selling wildly overpriced properties to young couples I know are mortgaging themselves to the grave. Three-hundred and fifty thousand for a 'starter' home? I feel like a mugger."

Holly was unconvinced. "Besides, how do you even know it's him? There's only a box number."

"I'll show you." She disappeared down the narrow hall and returned with a small red book stamped PRIVATE in gilt letters. "Mary Jane's diary. Oh, I know—a daughter's sacred privacy and all. But I *had* to read it, after. Look." She passed the book to Holly, her finger marking a line. Holly saw that her hand was shaking.

" 'Edward Devereaux Kaplan, P.O. Box 7195.' Why'd she write that in there?"

"I don't know. I suppose she thought every bit of information about him was diamonds and gold, you know the way it is when you're young and in love. But it's the same, isn't it? 7195." Inadvertently she turned a page, but she hardly had to look at it. She knew the diary almost by heart.

> *February 13. I'm beginning to think I must have imagined that magical night of the Christmas party and the Friday after. I never see EDK any more except when he comes in mornings, and then he just nods and says "Good morning" to the staff, me included. Today I was asked to take a portfolio to Meeting Room A. Knowing he would be there tied my stomach into knots. I had to knock three times before someone said "Come in," and then walk all the way down the room to hand him the folder. He didn't stop talking or even look up, though our fingers touched for a second and I felt his eyes following me as I left. Though I admit I might have imagined that. It's terrible carrying this burden around with me. I can't tell anyone about it, not even my best friend, Chris. The only good thing is, I've lost five pounds.*

Holly had gotten laboriously to her feet and was staring out the window, hands on hips. Theresa's small suburban backyard was graced by a broken fence, two plastic lawn chairs collecting leaves, and a pile of bricks intended, long ago, for a patio. Terry certainly had no gift with gardens. In contrast, Holly's trim green backyard flamed with borders of purple asters and gold chrysanthemums.

But then Theresa was a superior cook and Holly often traded flowers and cuttings in order to dine (Theresa called it *dining* even when they ate in the kitchen) on her chicken breasts Florentine and veal Provençal. Her eye fell on the African violet on the sill above the sink, its fleshy arms collapsed over the sides of the pot; automatically she ran tap water into a glass and drenched the soil. Then she sat down again and planted her plump elbows on the table.

"Terry, look me in the eye. Tell me you're not serious, because this is the craziest thing I've ever heard, and you *know* the stuff I hear every day at La Beautique. I feel like I'm in a bad movie, a *real* bad movie, and it's not going to be a couple paddling into the sunset at the end. Look, why would he hire you in the first place—the mother of the kid who died in his house? I mean, she *died* right there at the bottom of his stairs! Okay, I'm sorry—but it happened. It's something he wants to forget, not remember. Unless you're telling me he's into S and M."

Theresa winced. Holly could be cruel. "What makes you think he'll know I'm the mother?"

"Of course he'll know." Holly frowned, marshaling arguments. "Those flowers he sent. He knows who you are."

Theresa laughed harshly. "They were sent to the funeral home addressed to 'the Jones family' by his secretary—who else would inscribe a card, 'So terribly sorry about Mary Jane.' Apparently I didn't even exist in Mary Jane's world. Dan said the secretary called him because Mary Jane had listed him as next of kin to be notified in an emergency."

Holly's dark eyebrows drew together sympathetically. "That's tough. I know how you feel, Terry. Maybe taking back your maiden name last year—she might have resented that. But you know what I really think; I think Mary Jane *wanted* to believe her father still cared about her. Listing him as next of kin was wishful thinking. She took the divorce awfully hard."

"But he hasn't been there for her, and I *have*."

"You don't have to sell me. Anyway, you said Kaplan saw you at the funeral and knew who you were. What happens when he recognizes you?"

Theresa shook her head. "I've changed my mind about that. He couldn't have known who I am, though I recognized him all right—that big green Mercedes that Mary Jane talked about. Besides, men never really look at women over forty."

"That's the truth."

"Besides, I'm not going to look much like the person he saw." Theresa felt confidence flowing back like a tide. "My hair, after you cut and perm it tonight, is going to be dark, not light—and curly. I'm going to be wearing comfortable flat shoes and horn-rim glasses off a dimestore rack. I'm going to look fatter around the middle." She sighed. "Anyway, I'm not the same woman he saw at that cemetery. I look in the mirror and don't know myself any more."

Holly was tracking a different scent. "But would it matter if he did? Recognize you, I mean. After all, why the secrecy, why the disguise?"

Theresa reached for the small red diary, opened it, and leafed the pages. "I want you to listen to something. Wait, here it is. 'March 3. Today I took the Citibank papers into the conference room. EDK was having Bruce from our office on the carpet. Bruce turned his head away when I came in; he was absolutely white. I felt terribly sorry for him. I thought of the time by the elevator when EDK gripped my arm so tightly I cried out. I think he could be dangerous. The trouble is, I love him too much to care.' " Theresa passed the book to Holly. "Read it yourself."

Holly shrugged. "What do you want me to say? Mary Jane interrupted a boss taking down one of his employees. It must only happen a million times a day."

" 'I think he could be dangerous.' What about that?"

Holly sighed. "Terry, even you have to admit that Mary Jane had a flair for the dramatic. Sounds like something right out of a Harlequin romance to me."

"Mary Jane did not read Harlequin romances," said Theresa coldly.

"Oh, no? Remember that Meryl Streep movie and how for weeks she went around sucking in her cheeks and talking through her nose? That's what this sounds like to me."

"Not to me. Listen, Holly. A young woman falls in love with her boss. Falls much too hard, but not so hard that she can't see that *he could be dangerous.* Still, she pursues him, makes a fool of herself, gets under his skin. The boss invites her to a party. The young woman dies *on his back stairs.* An accident. Nobody questions. The boss goes on with his life—minus the inconvenient intrusion."

Holly stared at Theresa, her face blank as an erased blackboard.

"I think he killed her, Holly."

"Oh my God."

They sat in silence. The splat of water onto the counter from the overflowing saucer under the African violet became deafening.

Holly shook herself into speech. "Terry, have you told

your analyst about this?" She spoke slowly and kindly, as though to a disturbed child.

Theresa's eyes narrowed. "Why should I?" she said coldly.

"Because, frankly, it's morbid."

"Is it?" Theresa was on her feet, pacing. "My daughter dies mysteriously in a millionaire's house and *I'm* morbid? No, thanks; I don't buy that. Don't you ever listen to the news? Neighbor hauled away in handcuffs for poisoning his ninety-year-old mother. Kid arrested for torturing his sister. Teenager OD'ing on speed. *Our world's* morbid. I'm not!" She didn't realize she was shouting.

"Okay, okay, calm down! All I asked was, have you talked this over with your analyst? After all, that's what you're paying her for."

"Wrong. I'm not paying her anymore. I canceled my last appointment. And I'm not going back. I don't need to hear that I'm suffering from my father's rejection and acting out his destructive side. I don't need to hear that I'm clinging to my daughter's 'absolutized innocence.' I don't need to hear that my rage is really guilt. And I don't need to hear you telling me to talk it over with my psychologist!"

"Jesus, Terry. If you want me to get out, just say so." Holly was hurt, even frightened at Theresa's vehemence. There were limits to putting up with a friend's suffering.

Theresa sat down again and blew her nose. "I'm sorry, I've got a terribly short fuse these days. I guess I thought you'd understand."

"I understand that you're still grieving for Mary Jane. That's natural. But this idea that he might have . . . *killed* her! What proof do you have? Where's the evidence?"

"That's what I've got to find." She got up, went to a

small telephone desk next to the fridge, took out a sheet of paper, and handed it to Holly Bauer.

"What's this?"

"A copy of my application. I mailed it this morning."

Holly stared at her in disbelief, then scanned the page. "Widow, twenty-five years experience, excellent references—oh, boy, I think I need a drink!"

"You know where the bourbon is. Help yourself."

"You're not having one?"

"No."

"Now I'm *really* worried. Those Muslim terrorists, they don't drink either." Holly filled half a juice glass, passed it under the tap. She was almost back in form. "Excellent references, that's a laugh! You know, Terry, you never cease to amaze me. Tell me, where are these 'excellent references' supposed to come from—the Pope?"

"I've already taken care of that. The Murrays and Carters were happy to oblige. And that's not all. Washington society women order their engraved stationery through Woodward and Lothrop. Yesterday a friend of mine in the stationery department mailed out boxes of Eatons Select to Mrs. Samuel Frazier and Mrs. Oban Cummings minus one sheet and envelope apiece. She doesn't think they'll be counting."

"You're faking recommendations from Mrs. Frazier and Mrs. Cummings?" Holly followed Washington society like a London beautician might follow the Royals; there was respect in her voice. "And what happens when this Ned Kaplan of yours checks in with them?"

"That's a risk I'll have to take." She spoke confidently, but suddenly she felt dead tired, hammered into the ground by her friend's strenuous disbelief, her own faith in her plan faltering. Holly was right. She was acting on nothing more than gut feeling, vague suspicion. As for the references, Ned Kaplan would promptly call the two women for confirmation and then the game would be up before she'd moved her first pawn. It was hopeless; she should have seen that from the beginning.

"Look, maybe he won't check." Holly stopped, appalled at what she'd said. Because she *did* think the whole business not only morbid but slightly crazy.

But Terry always did that to her. She couldn't stand to see her unhappy, always wanted to protect her. Because there was something . . . a little finer about Theresa than about most people Holly knew. You could tell she'd had money once; no, it wasn't just money, it was something more subtle, like, maybe, taste—or sadness. Little things, nuances. Holly lacquered her talons bubble-gum pink, Theresa's small ovals were clear. Holly liked beer, Theresa preferred the champagne she couldn't afford. There was something kind of . . . *still* about Theresa, something quiet, so that you didn't really know what she was thinking, whereas you knew *she* knew everything that was going on in *your* dumb mind.

She sighed and picked up the want ad again. There must be some argument she hadn't tried. *Live-in.* The words lept at her. "Look," she said, shoving the paper under Theresa's nose. "You can't live in; you've got Matt." Somehow she knew Theresa would have an answer.

"That's where you come in. I'm not worried about living in; he just says 'live-in preferred.' Nobody can expect live-in these days; help's too hard to get—you realize that? But I could have irregular hours, so I thought since you're right next door, maybe you'd keep an eye on Matt. As a favor. Of course I'll pay."

Holly snorted. "I'll say you'll pay! Come on, Terry, you don't mean 'keep an eye on him,' you mean 'take care of him like a mother whenever I'm not around'!"

"He's fourteen, after all."

"Don't I know!"

"All right." Theresa pushed back her chair. "I realize it's a lot to ask, even of a best friend. It's just that nothing seems important to me anymore but this. Nothing else seems real. It's like a big black thundercloud has blotted out the sun."

Holly groaned. "Take it easy, Terry. I didn't say I wouldn't, did I? I don't mind if Matt comes over to my place after school, I guess. He's a good kid. I could fix him dinner once in a while if you're not around, see he does his homework—"

The two women stared at each other, then drew closer like conspirators. Holly leaned across the table and squeezed Theresa's slim hands.

"Listen. I don't think there's a chance in the world that you'll get the job. But if you do, there's just one thing I've got to say." She hesitated.

"Well?"

"You don't *know* anything, remember that. Myself, I think it happened just the way they said it did: dark stairs, high heels, too much champagne. But the main thing is, Mary Jane is gone and you're alive. Working in that house every day is going to be constant pain. Someday you're going to have to say, 'It happened and it's over.' You're going to have to put it behind you, Terry— for *your* sake."

Theresa tossed back the ash-blond hair that was about

to become short and brunette. "Mary Jane wasn't the kind of person to leave a party by the back stairs. Dammit, Holly, don't you see that? *My* life got derailed somewhere along the line, but *hers* was going strong. Second in her class, a promotion coming up at the bank, a nice young man interested in her. And then this older man seduces her. Coldly and deliberately uses her to pass the time of night. And because she's young and inexperienced, she thinks he cares. All right, maybe he didn't kill her. But I hold him responsible and I'm going to make him pay. She was a *good girl.*"

CHAPTER SIX

B y two P.M. the usually stoic Dorothy Swerdlow was out of temper. In the last three days she had interviewed four women applying for the position of Ned Kaplan's housekeeper, was expecting a fifth in ten minutes, and had fallen almost a whole day behind with her work. So when Chris Stacio stuck her head in the door and said, "Another one to see you about the job," Dorothy said snappishly, "Let her simmer awhile. I'm busy!"

Sitting in a glassed-in outer office next to an enormous rubber plant with leaves like rafts, turning unseeingly the pages of the *Washingtonian,* Theresa Foley felt calm. There had been a bad moment when the young woman at the computer terminal, lifting her head, said, "May I help you?" and Theresa recognized the girl with whom Mary Jane had shared an apartment. But Chris Stacio had shown no flicker of recognition, and gradually her heart had stopped racing. The encounter braced her: She felt determination settle over her like a fine net of steel, a resolve—for her own sake—never to be shaken so badly again. So that when Chris finally said, "You can go in now," Theresa slung her purse over her shoulder, threw back her dark, curly head, and walked firmly into the inner office.

"Please have a chair," said the woman behind the desk. She did not look up but continued to hit computer keys with terrific speed. Theresa sat down again and looked about her. A large, strictly functional office—no personal photographs, no paintings, nothing except, on the secretary's desk, in a crystal vase, a single amber rose. Traveling around the room, her eyes fastened on a closed door to her right. Just a perfectly plain dark wooden door, no nameplate, no ornament, but she suddenly felt sure that Ned Kaplan was behind it. She stared at it, fascinated. . . .

> *Saturday, June 10. EDK asked me yesterday in the hall whether I'd like to come and have a swim Sunday morning in his pool. I was so surprised—I never expected to meet him—that I said I couldn't! Actually, we're going to Baltimore to see Gram Sunday, but I could probably have got out of it somehow. I've got to get my own apartment like Chris—I can't do any living at home. Mom would never approve of EDK. He looked so handsome Friday—beautiful light gray suit and red silk tie—so elegant and important I could hardly say a word. I felt stupid afterward. I acted like a child.*

"I said, 'You must be Theresa Foley.' "
Theresa understood that the woman behind the desk was speaking. "Oh, yes. Sorry."
"I am Dorothy Swerdlow, Mr. Kaplan's personal secretary." The personal secretary opened a folder on the

desk in front of her, and Theresa recognized the pilfered pale lavender sheet of Eatons Select. "You come very highly recommended, Mrs. Foley—it is Mrs., isn't it?"

"Mrs., yes."

"How long did you work for Mrs. Cummings? She doesn't say."

"Five years, 1984 to 1989."

"What sort of duties did you have?"

Theresa cleared her throat. In the past days, with the help of a lavishly photographed article on Washington's social aristocracy in *Connoisseur,* a recently published memoir by Gloria Vanderbilt's personal maid, and a vivid imagination, she had tried to think her way into the gilded lives of the Cummingses and the Fraziers. "I supervised the house, generally. It's a very large establishment, as you probably know. Mrs. Cummings had two cleaning women who were responsible to me. I saw to special things like the good china, the silver, and the bed linens myself. Mrs. Cummings also had a cook, and I was the liaison person between them—I mean I consulted with them both about menus, ordering the food, and so forth. Mr. Cummings took care of all the liquor and wine. On the cook's day off I often fixed light meals, though sometimes Mrs. Cummings preferred to do that herself. Of course, I was responsible for locking up last thing at night—unless the Cummingses were going to have a very late evening—and opening up in the morning. And I saw to the flowers. Mrs. Cummings was extremely fussy about having fresh flowers in all the rooms, even the bathrooms, every day."

"I don't know if you realize it, Theresa—may I call you Theresa?—but Mr. Kaplan's situation is not exactly like the Cummingses? For one thing, he lives alone; for another, the house isn't as large. I believe there's a woman who comes in twice a week to clean, but Mrs. Marty, his present housekeeper, keeps things going on a daily basis. She also does the cooking and the laundry, except for shirts and table linen. Mr. Kaplan has those sent out. Of course, when Mr. Kaplan entertains, Mrs. Marty gets in extra help, including a caterer and a butler. And there's a yardman, Mario, who comes two afternoons a week."

"It certainly sounds like a heavier job than I'm used to," said Theresa boldly.

"Yes and no." Dorothy Swerdlow leaned forward encouragingly, but she'd probably done that, thought Theresa, with all the candidates. "Mr. Kaplan travels a great deal, and I'm sure there's relatively little to do while he's away. Only your own meals, to get, for instance, and some light maintenance and cleaning. On the other hand, I understand from Mrs. Marty that the hours can be rather irregular."

"Yes, I see."

"Tell me, if you don't mind, why you left your last position with, let's see, the Fraziers?"

"I needed to be at home. My son was having some personal problems adjusting to a new school, and I wanted to be available for him. All that's straightened out now and he's almost independent, but I should say frankly that I still prefer not to live in."

"I'm afraid no one wants to these days. Mrs. Marty is one of the old school." Clearly Dorothy Swerdlow regretted, for Mr. Kaplan's sake, the old school. "Now, about salary. Mr. Kaplan is offering $29,500. All benefits, of course: social security, health insurance, and so forth. And I believe Mrs. Marty received fairly regular raises and a two-week vacation every year. I trust that's satisfactory."

Theresa nodded. She found it incredible that the shrewd-looking Dorothy Swerdlow had swallowed her story whole. But then an expert secretary did not necessarily have to be an expert in the housekeeping line. At the thought she smiled confidently.

"That seems to be about it, then. Do you have any questions for me?"

Theresa hesitated. Her eyes went to the dark wooden door. "Could you tell me something about Mr. Kaplan himself? I mean, what he's like to work for?"

Dorothy Swerdlow smiled in a rather superior way. "Oh, I should think you'd find him very fair. I don't think he and Mrs. Marty get in each other's way much. Mr. Kaplan often works a nine-hour day, comes home, then just takes a light supper on a tray in his study. And as I said, he travels a great deal. From what I understand, he leaves Mrs. Marty pretty much to herself—but then she's been with him seventeen years and knows all the ropes. You know, of course, that he used to be married. To Carol Bigelow Paine." She waited for the surnames to register. "He and Mrs. Kaplan divorced three years ago."

"No, I didn't." But Theresa did know, for Mary Jane had told her.

Dorothy Swerdlow stood up, pencil-tall and efficient in a regulation tailored navy blue suit and crisp white blouse. "Then if there's nothing else—"

"When would I start?"

"Mrs. Marty leaves the end of next week. The new person would want a few days with her, breaking in, then be

ready to take over—let me see—yes, the first Monday in
October."

"I see. That's fine with me."

"Good. You do understand, I hope, that there are
other applicants."

"Oh, yes."

"Good," Dorothy Swerdlow said again. She came
round the desk and held out a large, capable hand.
"You'll be hearing from us one way or another in a few
days."

"But," said Theresa, surprised. Her eyes went again to
the closed door which had never been out of her mental
vision throughout the entire interview. "Doesn't Mr. Kaplan want to see me?"

Dorothy Swerdlow patted her sleek gray head. "Oh,
no," she said. "Mr. Kaplan is in Rio de Janeiro. He's left
the hiring to me."

Ned Kaplan's secretary was famous in certain Washington business circles for working straight through her
lunch hour. She was less famous for, though equally
dedicated to, drinking two margaritas after work with
friends at Chico's, where free tortilla chips and salsa were
supplied along with discount drinks during the happy
hour, from five to six. She found the bar noisy and
crowded, and Maggie and Ruth, crushed against the wall
at a table for two, already sipping their first.

"You're late," said Maggie accusingly, neatly whip-
ping a third chair from under an adjacent table, toward
which three young men with briefcases were struggling,
and shoving it at Dorothy Swerdlow. "Person could die
of thirst."

"It's been that kind of day," said Dorothy, dropping

into the chair and imperiously signaling a cocktail waitress decked out in cowboy boots, hot pants, and a huge spangled sombrero. After all, they were regulars. Though, she thought again, if Chico's didn't serve such superior margaritas, I wouldn't patronize a place where the waitresses run around half naked.

"More interviews?" asked Ruth sarcastically. She was a senior accountant for an insurance firm and privately thought Ned Kaplan overworked her friend.

"The last, but I'm still buried from yesterday. I don't really think I'm enjoying this responsibility. After all, what if he doesn't like the person I choose?"

"That's his problem."

"Wrong, darling, it will definitely be mine. But I liked the woman today." Dorothy leaned forward confidentially. "Sensible type, right age—two of the others are really too old. Good references—Frazier and Cummings."

"*The* Mrs. Cummings?" Maggie wiggled her eyebrows. "I'm impressed."

Dorothy licked at the salt-encrusted rim of the cold margarita glass and took a large, appreciative gulp. "Unfortunately, I can't get a hold of the Cummingses; they're in Houston visiting their daughter who's ill, and I don't want to bother them. And Mrs. Frazier hasn't returned my call." She lifted her glass again and swallowed, feeling a warm sense of assurance stealing through her. "But I think I'll go ahead and hire this Foley person anyway. After all, the references can't be forged."

CHAPTER SEVEN

Theresa stood on the brick sidewalk looking up through the gate at the white portico of a massive three-story brick house rising above enormous hedges of yew and holly guarding a front yard doubly enclosed by a spiked iron fence. The roof seemed all chimneys. Twelve tall windows flanked by dark green shutters faced the street, as narrow and exclusive as the streets of Georgetown themselves.

She shivered in the wet, clinging October air that smelled of age and decay and sewage, and tried the gate. It was locked; belatedly she noted a glaring white eye announcing that these premises were PROTECTED BY PRO-GARD and in fine print that the consequences of violating that protection were dire. Eventually she spotted a small buzzer embedded in a pillar topped by an eagle brandishing a stone branch in its stone beak; she pressed it, and after a few moments the gate clicked open. She shoved at the heavy bar and started up the walk, hearing behind her the gate swing slowly on its hinges and clang shut. Entering—if not breaking—was not easy.

It had occurred to her only this morning, clinging to an overhead bar in the crowded Metro, that all the housekeepers in social Washington might know each other. There was even the dreadful possibility that Mrs. Marty and her counterparts at the Fraziers and the Cummingses were the best of friends. In that case, the only response she could imagine was to turn tail and bound through the shrubbery like a deer.

She hesitated, wondering whether there was a tradesman's entrance like the kind one read about in English novels, but decided to dare the broad white front steps. At the door topped by a fanlight, a choice between a bell and a massive brass lion's head knocker presented itself; but the snarling knocker repelled her, and she rang. Waiting, she was fixed by another sign; stepping back she saw that all the first-floor windows, Argus-like, sported watchful eyes. She waited, hands clenched, then rang again. Suddenly a voice hummed electronically in her left ear.

"Is it Mrs. Foley?"

"Yes, it is."

"One minute."

Bolts shot back, a chain scraped, and the door was finally opened. Looking down, Theresa met the shrewd eyes of a short, stout woman wearing an enormous flowered apron and lavender Reeboks.

"Mrs. Marty?" Theresa waited tensely, watching Mrs. Marty's pleasant, pockmarked face for signs of surprise or dismay.

"That's right," said Mrs. Marty comfortably. " 'Scuse me for not shaking hands, I'm all black from polishing. Come along in. You'll be wanting to use the back entrance from now on. If you don't mind, I'll finish up what

I'm doing before we get down to business."

The enemy, thought Theresa, is within the gates. Feeling grimly triumphant, she followed Mrs. Marty's rolling gait through a series of high-ceilinged, elegantly furnished but gloomy rooms. Every window, she noted, was shrouded by foliage, every room was graced by a fireplace, and there were dozens of large paintings on the walls. She tried not to stare because, after all, she was used to houses like this, but Mrs. Marty must have rearview vision because she suddenly turned and planted herself beneath a painting of a Spanish matador in a hundred-pound gold frame.

"I see you're eyeing the pictures. I just want to say that *she* took the best of them with her when she left—a genuine Renoir and a van Gogh—not because she's greedy but because she cared about Art. *He* don't care for any of this"—she jerked her stocky arm—"at least as far as I can see. He's all business, he is." Her tone was not disapproving.

She flung open a swinging door and motioned Theresa into a high, narrow galley lined to the ceiling with darkwood cabinets. Theresa stared about her.

"Butler's pantry," explained Mrs. Marty, reattacking at the sink an ornate silver candlestick with polish and, Theresa noted for future reference, a toothbrush. "Most of these old Georgetown houses have 'em. Handy it is, too. I'm going to miss it. I do all the silver and glass here and you'll find all the table linens and china and glassware in these cupboards as well as a couple sets of everyday dishes. I use the everyday for breakfast, which Mr. Kaplan takes in what we call the morning room, looking out at the pool. You'll want to remember he takes only skim milk and Sweet'n Low in his coffee and drinks at least two big glasses of orange juice every morning, fresh squeezed. That and whole wheat toast with honey, no butter. Sundays I make him an omelet with green peppers and onions, and he likes that."

A man of habit, thought Theresa. She would remember that, though she wondered how much else of the information pouring forth she could retain. Aloud she said, "Have you always lived in, then?"

"Yes, always, except for two nights a week. At first Frank, that's my husband, threatened to divorce me for desertion, but now we both think my living-in's what's kept us happily married all these years. To tell the truth, I'm a bit worried about us being cooped up together like rabbits in a hutch when we've both been used to our freedom. Who knows, maybe we'll find we can't stand each other!" Her laugh did not sound particularly worried. "There!" She wiped down the candlestick, then buffed it with a soft cloth until it gleamed. That finished, she washed her hands at the tap, dried them, then applied lotion lavishly from a bottle next to the sink.

"Some people wear those rubber things when they work. Not me, can't stand 'em. Hands sweat in 'em and I'm all clumsy. Jergen's Lotion for me, and you can't say my hands have suffered, can you?" She held out plump white hands for inspection. Despite her nervousness, Theresa smiled. Obviously, Mrs. Marty's hands were her particular vanity. "Now, I expect you'd like to go over the house to get yourself acquainted?"

"If you have time, yes, I'd like that." Steady, Theresa, she warned. Upstairs there would be the library where Mary Jane had spent some of the last moments of her life. And there would be the back stairs.

"Oh, I've got plenty of time. Mr. Kaplan isn't due

back till Sunday evening and there's not much to running the house while he's away, you'll be glad to know. It's all a matter of what I call 'keeping things on the go.' We'll start in here with the kitchen—"

Theresa followed, but her mind, less obediant, slipped back to the telephone call two days ago:

"Mrs. Foley? Dorothy Swerdlow, Mr. Kaplan's secretary."

"Dorothy Swer—? Oh, *yes!*" She had just come in, arms loaded with groceries, and was in the process of deciphering a code from Matt that seemed to say not to worry, he'd be getting a ride home after football practice.

"Congratulations, Mrs. Foley. You have the job."

"The housekeeping job?"

"As I recall, that is what you applied for."

"Sorry, it's taking awhile to sink in—"

"Mrs. Marty is expecting you Thursday morning promptly at ten. I hope that's convenient?"

"I'll be there," said Theresa. She had already mapped out her route: Park the car across from the Silver Spring station in a sixty-dollar-a-month lot; take the Metro to Dupont Circle; walk or take a P Street bus from there. "It's Q Street, isn't it?"

"Between thirtieth and thirty-first. You can't miss the house. Well, congratulations and good luck with everything, Theresa. Of course we'll be in touch."

She'd just hung up when Matt had come roaring in, flinging books and football equipment right and left, knocking into perfectly obvious chairs and doorways.

"I've got the job, Matt!" She didn't dare kiss him these days, though she would have liked to.

"What's for supper? Not pizza again! *Gee.*"

"Aren't you glad? About the job, I mean?"

"What's to be glad about? You'll never be home."

"That's not true. And I'll be making lots more money—well, quite a bit more. That's good, isn't it?"

"Do I get my allowance raised?"

"We'll see."

Matt sighed deeply. "Then could we hurry up with supper? There's a show I've got to watch."

"Matt, you know you can't—"

"For *homework,* Mom! I can show you the assignment right here!" He thumped his notebook in frustration.

"All right, darling. I believe you."

She watched him as he stowed away in the fridge milk, a wedge of Parmesan for making Alfredo sauce, ground veal, a dripping plastic bag of romaine, tomatoes, three bags of carrots (the only vegetable he would eat), and a six-pack of Coke. He was helping. His shoulders under the flannel shirt were still knobby, too young for football pads; his long brown hair curled tenderly between the tendons of his young neck.

She sighed. He was his father's child to the bone. She had been close to Mary Jane, but somehow she and Matt had never been comfortable with each other. They were always wrangling uselessly about eating the right foods and doing his homework—uselessly because he ate only what he liked and because since third grade he'd always done just enough in school to earn mediocre but unpunishable C+'s and B−'s. "If Matt only buckled down, Mrs. Foley." She was sick of hearing it. She couldn't force—or inspire—him, apparently, to buckle down, and now when she longed for comfort, she could not even put her arms around him and hold him, for courage, to her breast. Could only argue about the four basic food groups and television. Futilely, eternally. As though a mother and son didn't have the world to discuss.

Later that evening she'd taken a bottle of cold champagne next door. Holly, fundamentally the most unsurprised of human beings, clutching a bowl of popcorn to her stomach, suspended her hand halfway to her open mouth. "You *got* the job? I don't believe it! You mean he fell for those references?"

"His secretary did at least. He's in South America. Can't we have that damned thing off?" She shot a hostile glance at the TV, feeling unreasonably jumpy.

"Why not. Nothing on anyway. Forged references—and they worked? Boy, it sure makes a person believe in the good old American way! Anyway, why the champagne? This isn't exactly something to celebrate."

Theresa set the bottle down firmly on the coffee table. "I think it is. How about some glasses?"

She'd spent an exhausting hour repersuading her friend that she was not a candidate for the mental hospital. "Look at it this way, Holly: He's paying thirty thousand, all benefits, with regular raises."

Holly clinked glass. She looked relieved. "So, Terry, you're not going to make too much of this, are you? I mean what you said that afternoon, all that 'dangerous' stuff in Mary Jane's diary. Mary Jane—rest her dear soul—was just a kid after all. You are definitely not. You're a professional and you're starting a new job tomorrow. Period."

"Exactly. Starting a new job. Don't worry." She refilled her glass lavishly. "I'm not going to brood."

". . . not much used except for breakfast, like I said, and once in a while in summer if someone comes for luncheon and a swim." They were standing in the morning room, a light pleasant space with a white-and-green tiled floor; ferns, fiscus, and rubber plants in big white ceramic pots; and a round glass-topped table and white chairs. Glass doors opened onto a flagged patio surrounding an oval turquoise pool. Mary Jane had told her about that patio and pool; that meant she'd been invited to use it. Had she also shared Kaplan's bed? Even while confessing her love for him in the pages of her diary, she had been curiously circumspect, as though she'd imagined someone peering over her shoulder. All the great plans were for the future *when I get my own apartment;* what actually had taken place between them was largely unexplained. She'd asked her once outright whether they were having sex, but Mary Jane had just laughed in a dismissive kind of way and said not to worry, she was old enough to take care of herself. At the memory of those words, Theresa felt the rush of rage that had become her familiar since her daughter's death. Take it easy, she told herself again. You've got one job today and one job only: to find out how to run Ned Kaplan's house.

"Might as well take a look at the upstairs next. This way." Mrs. Marty rolled through the long formal dining room with its massive central chandelier and smoky gold Chinese wallpaper, then through another of the seemingly endless living or drawing rooms out into the large front vestibule, its parquet floor washed by light filtering through ribs of the fanlight cresting the front door. "Up these stairs. You go first. Takes me a year and a day."

Theresa mounted the broad staircase that arched, she noted with eyes that appreciated the graceful, in a classic curve of white balustrade, rose carpeting, and polished wood to the second floor, Mrs. Marty huffing unappreciatively behind. Mary Jane had run up these stairs feeling unwell, the doctor had said, the secretary had said. What had she really been feeling? Why had she left the party downstairs? A prearranged meeting with Kaplan in his bedroom? No: EDK, as Mary Jane had described him in her diary, would not commit folly at his own party. Besides, she hadn't gone to his bedroom; she'd gone to the library. Had the library been familiar? A place of refuge? But how, and why?

"How many bedrooms?" she asked Mrs. Marty. Anything to wrench her mind back to the job.

"Five on this floor, plus three baths, a walk-in linen closet, and the library. Servants' bedrooms on the third floor, not that they're used for anything but storage anymore. People used to have a dozen servants in the old days. Here's the library." She led the way into a tall, handsome green room lined to the ceiling on the left wall with well-stocked bookshelves. There was a fireplace with a fluted mantel painted white, a large cream and coral Oriental carpet, and comfortable-looking leather chairs. A long mahogany table stood in front of floor-length windows hung with green velvet draperies that had whitish nap. On the table lay a huge magnifying glass with an exotically carved ivory handle, a leather-bound blotter, an impressive-looking block made of a huge chunk of some greenish stone (malachite, she decided), and a paper knife with the same green stone handle. It was the kind of room that to this moment had existed for Theresa Foley only in the movies or the pages of *House Beautiful* and *Architectural Digest*. She tried to imagine Mary Jane in this room, and failed.

"What does Mr. Kaplan use this room for? I mean, you showed me his study downstairs."

"Oh, it's mostly for looks these days," said Mrs.

Marty, flicking a speck of dust off the long table with the corner of her flowered apron. "Actually Mrs. Kaplan, not Mister, used to use this room a lot. She liked to curl up with a book or magazine in that chair." She pointed to a white leather wing chair with matching hassock near the fireplace. "Used to wrap herself up in a big pink afghan I crocheted her one year for Christmas, soft as down. Took it with her when she left. Said, 'Marty, this is the last thing I'd leave behind.'" Mrs. Marty sighed with pride.

Staring at the leather chair tucked next to the fireplace, Theresa felt again the surge of rage. Mary Jane might have sat in Mrs. Kaplan's chair that night, just to see how it felt—because Mary Jane had longed for their own fireplace. They had never had one, but the Kaplans could afford a fireplace in every room. And suddenly the futility of trying to invade this world overwhelmed her. When could the poor ever touch the rich, the little people get back at the big? Useless, hopeless. If Ned Kaplan had cracked open *his* skull in one of their houses, they might all be in jail. But since it was only Mary Jane who had died in Ned Kaplan's house, the death hardly mattered. She couldn't hope to understand people like him. She was weak and he was infinitely strong.

"Tell me," she said, pulling herself up with an effort from despair. "It's none of my business, I realize, but why are you leaving after all these years? You're not— well, of course I don't know your age—but you certainly don't look old enough to retire."

The small eyes blinked. Mrs. Marty went to adjust the position of a blue-and-white Chinese vase on the fireplace mantel. "Thanks for the compliment," she said with an abrupt laugh. "But I'm not young, neither. And

I've been with the Kaplans—and now Mr. Kaplan—seventeen years. Before that three other families. My husband's retired from the Post Office, sits home twiddling his thumbs in front of the TV all day. Gets ideas about traveling, maybe buying our own RV. After all, there's a limit to working for other people. After a while you get wanting a life of your own."

"I can understand that."

"There's not much work to this room." Mrs. Marty seemed glad to change the subject. "Mr. Kaplan likes a fire laid and ready to light because sometimes when there are just a few people I serve after-dinner coffee up here, but that's Mario's job, not yours. Though I'm warning you, you'll have to get after Mario." She led the way out into the spacious corridor and paused with more ceremony than she had shown thus far at another door. "This," she said, as though about to reveal the treasures of the Vatican, "is Mr. Kaplan's room."

Theresa realized that her face was burning, yet at the same time she was controlled by that detachment, that fine net of steel that had protected her in Dorothy Swerdlow's office. She followed Mrs. Marty, unbearably curious yet feeling like an intruder not only into Kaplan's but into her daughter's life. What kind of monster inhabited this den?

A big, darkish room, conservative as a banker's suit: soft gray carpet, gray silk spread covering a simple double bed. Strange, somehow she had expected opulence. A new wall of closet spoiling the original classic proportions (she felt them) of the room; a plain bureau with a few gentleman's toiletries neatly arranged; another fireplace, dead; dark mulberry silk draperies on east windows pulled back over gauze.

"Is Mr. Kaplan Catholic?" She went to study a trip-tych dominating a handsome dressing table made of rich inlaid woods to the right of the door. In the center panel a madonna with a pale oval face gazed down at the child in her arms with a half-smile on her lips. Except for a small filigreed cap, her blond head was uncovered, as was her long white throat, and the blue of her gown cast cool shadows in the hollows of her delicately modeled cheek. To the left and right shepherds and magi bowed their heads as they proffered gold and spices, but the dream-ing blond madonna was unmoved. Theresa bent closer. Mrs. Marty was not such a paragon after all: drops of white wax marred the table's surface. "Is he Catholic?" she asked again.

Mrs. Marty plumped bed pillows vigorously and re-smoothed the silk spread. "Not Catholic, no," she said at last. "Kaplan can be a Jewish name, of course, but Mr. Kaplan's mother was a Devereaux and his wife a Bigelow Paine. I don't know that he's anything, really. After all, it's Mr. Kaplan's business, not mine. A housekeeper isn't paid to ask questions." Her voice rebuked Theresa's curi-osity. "Now, this is the master bath."

Theresa stared, forgetting that she was supposedly ac-customed to luxury. The bathroom was large and lavish, twice the size of her own kitchen. Wrap-around mirrors, a marble lavatory with gold-plated faucets, a glass shower stall, a small Jacuzzi sunk into a tiled platform, palms in tubs grouped under a skylight, a heated towel bar, the kind of big velvety royal-blue towels that the ads call "thirsty," a gleaming marble floor punctuated here and there by thick fleecy rugs like white clouds floating across a deep blue sky.

"I must say that Mr. Kaplan can be fussy," said Mrs.

Marty. "He's told me more than once, 'Marty, I don't care how much dust you sweep under the rug, but I want this bathroom spotless. I do it up special every day."

She had already "done it up" this morning. Their reflections gleamed in a dozen polished surfaces.

Mrs. Marty opened a connecting door. "This used to be Mrs. Kaplan's room." She shook her head disapprovingly. "Pity to have spoiled such a lovely room like this. It don't seem natural to me, working yourself into a lather on a machine, but I guess it's what people do nowadays."

Theresa looked around. No trace of the former lady of the house remained except, incongruously, the charming pale yellow wallpaper spattered with big bunches of pink roses. The room had been turned into a gymnasium, outfitted with half a dozen grim-looking machines, sun lamps, and other arcane paraphernalia with which, she decided immediately, she had no desire to be more intimately acquainted. She herself scrupulously avoided all opportunities of "working out."

"Does Mr. Kaplan actually use all this?" she asked doubtfully.

"He *thinks* he does," replied Mrs. Marty rather mysteriously. "Of course I can't say what goes on up here weekends. We'd better be moving on."

Dark paintings lined the walls of the long upper hall; a rose carpet patterned with gold fleur-de-lis ran down the center. Theresa tensed involuntarily. Mary Jane walked down this hall, she thought. She found herself, as she had in the library, searching for some trace of her daughter's presence, knowing at the same time that three weeks and Mrs. Marty's competence must have erased any sign. They briefly inspected two more blankly unused bed-

rooms, the huge, well-stocked linen closet, several bathrooms, but Theresa could think of one thing only. And
finally they came to it, opposite the room Mrs. Marty indicated was her own. The back stairs.

Theresa clung to the square post top, looking down.
Steep, narrow, dark. A bad twist halfway down. Lethal.
She closed her eyes, sickened, dizzy, seeing it all at last—
Mary Jane hurrying in her high silver heels, the stairway
poorly lighted, her heel catching on a rubber tread, the
headlong plunge. She opened her eyes.

Yet why had Mary Jane left by the back stairs? It made
no sense: invited to a party, then sneaking out the back
way. All wrong. Unwelcome, Mary Jane's diary entry for
September 21 swam into her head:

> *My own place at last—though it still feels more like
> Chris's apartment than mine. But at least I'm out from
> under. Free! Actually I wanted to tell Mom about
> EDK's party. We used to talk about my dates, what I
> was going to wear. She even used to wait up for me.
> But I'm 20 now and EDK is no date and she wouldn't
> understand. I can just hear her: "What's his real mo-
> tive for asking you?" Actually Chris said the same
> thing. Is there any law against a party being just a
> party?*

She still hadn't gotten over the hurt of reading those
words, as though she'd been living her life through Mary
Jane's romances. Had home really been that repressive?
Maybe someone who could sneak to a party could also
sneak out the back way. But no, she repeated stubbornly,
she knew Mary Jane, and Mary Jane really wasn't that
kind of girl.

Mrs. Marty flipped a switch.

"Dark even in daytime," she said. "Not that these stairs are used much except by the help. Convenient for me because the laundry room's right below and my bedroom's at the top."

Theresa looked at her imploringly. Was she really going to say nothing of what happened here three weeks ago? Nothing about the young woman who tragically fell to her death at Edward Kaplan's party? Nothing?

Mrs. Marty coughed and lowered her eyes. "I expect you heard about the accident at a party Mr. Kaplan gave a few weeks ago. A real sad thing it was—a young lady, one of the guests. We all felt terrible, I can tell you. But you can see for yourself how something like that could happen, can't you?" Mrs. Marty started rolling cautiously down the steps, leaning heavily on the banister. On the small triangle of landing, she stopped and looked up at Theresa several steps above her.

"To tell the truth, if the Kaplans ever had to use these stairs themselves, they'd have seen the danger long ago and had them widened or straightened or better lighted. But because it's only the help, they don't care."

Theresa met Mrs. Marty's eyes. It was the first sign of disloyalty the housekeeper had shown toward her employer, the first hint of complaint. Mrs. Marty had resigned shortly after Mary Jane had died here, she reminded herself; were the two events somehow related? But as she herself started down the steep steps, she tripped and lunged for the banister.

"Oh, my stars!" gasped the housekeeper. "Are you all right? What a scare you gave me! For heaven's sake, hang on to the railing. You'll be wanting a pair of sensible shoes, like mine." She arrived heavily at the bottom.

"Well, we're back where we started. Kitchen's through that swing door and the laundry room's just off here. We'd better have a look at it, because you'll be doing the washing and the ironing, not that there's a lot of it. I send out Mr. Kaplan's shirts and the linen tablecloths and napkins. They don't get used that much."

Theresa stood at the bottom of the stairs, hands clenched, staring down at the black-and-white floor. Mary Jane had died here, her skull cracked on the cold marble tile. She could almost see the pressure of the young body on the tiles, almost smell the blood she imagined so vividly. Almost.

I was wrong to come here, thought Theresa, wrong to think that I can change what has happened. It's over. I can't bring her back, I can't get close to her here. She's gone. It's all over. She flung back her head to keep hot tears from spilling down her cheeks.

"Frankly, Mrs. Foley." Mrs. Marty's voice was dry. "If you can't give more of your mind to this job than you've been giving me this morning, I don't see how you're going to manage! I suppose this house don't look like anything to you after your other places, but I can tell you it takes a bit of doing to keep it up."

"Sorry." Theresa willed herself to walk away from the bottom of those stairs down the back hall to the laundry room. She listened respectfully to Mrs. Marty's explanation of the equipment and her methods, dogged her to the back door where she breezed through the instructions for a very complex set of security locks and switches that Theresa doubted she quite understood, followed her now-familiar rolling gait back to the kitchen, accepted the offered cup of tea, and sat down opposite Mrs. Marty at the kitchen table. She tried to look attentive.

The kitchen itself was big and square with lots of old-fashioned cupboards painted white, red-topped counters, and an old red-tiled floor. It looked comfortable despite the formidable array of state-of-the-art appliances. Theresa had never seen a refrigerator like the industrial steel monster behind Mrs. Marty's back or a stove with so many glass-doored ovens. The place smelled of new wax and warm yeast, and she noted with dismay two covered loaves on a board on the counter. She did not plan to bake bread. "Did Mrs. Kaplan cook?" she asked.

"Couldn't pry the lid off a can," said Mrs. Marty with grim satisfaction. "I did all the cooking—and remember, Mr. Kaplan don't like a lot of garlic, hot spices neither. Don't you hit him with any of those jalapeño things. And none of this tofu and lentils. He's a meat eater. Old-fashioned that way. But to get back to business. I told Mrs. Swerdlow I thought you should come back tomorrow, actually help me out, at least for the morning. Settle up any other questions you're bound to have." Mrs. Marty clanked her teaspoon vigorously, as though expecting an argument.

"Oh, yes, I'm planning on that. I need as much time with you as I can get."

"I should think so! As for Sunday evening, I'll stay until Mr. Kaplan gets home. It's the least I can do, my last time. And I'll lay the table for breakfast. After that, you're on your own."

"What time does Mr. Kaplan usually take breakfast?"

"Like I said, he expects it at eight. That means getting here half-past seven at the very latest."

Theresa thought of Matt eating his cornflakes, scribbling at last-minute homework, getting off to school alone. But no, Holly had promised to look in mornings.

"I don't know how you wangled getting off at four. I certainly don't! I've always made dinner and served it, and washed up after, let me tell you."

"This is a different arrangement," said Theresa soothingly. "I'm not living in. I'm working by the hour. It wouldn't make much sense to finish up with the house midafternoon, then sit waiting for Mr. Kaplan to come home evenings—when he does eat at home. Mrs. Swerdlow agreed that if I have dinner all made, Mr. Kaplan can easily heat it up in the microwave. The dishes I'll do the next morning."

"I don't know what Dorothy Swerdlow has to do with it!" Mrs. Marty was still testy. "It's sacrilege, that's what it is, Mr. Kaplan having to do for himself after a long day. He'll never heat up anything; he'll eat it cold. I know him!"

"Then perhaps you'd better stay and take care of him yourself, Mrs. Marty," said Theresa sweetly. "I can see you've spoiled him terribly all these years!"

Even so, they parted fairly amiably, and Theresa returned for further instruction the next day. She spent as much time that weekend with Matt as he would allow. She waited with eager dread for Monday.

CHAPTER EIGHT

Monday morning, Theresa let herself in the back door of the Kaplan house on Q Street with a list of complex instructions and her own key, one of many on a brass ring inherited from Mrs. Marty. She hung her coat on a peg in the hall. She had no idea what genuine housekeepers wore on duty, but hoped that a plain white blouse, a dark skirt, and a clean apron would pass.

The house was silent, the big kitchen expectant, as though waiting to pounce on her inexperience. She quickly checked the morning room; the table was laid with the blue everyday dishes. Mrs. Marty had kept her word. Back in the kitchen, she marshaled her equipment: the big Krups coffeemaker, the sleek eight-slot Toastmaster, the Cuisinart Juice Extractor, the silver coffee Thermos for the table. So much heavy metal for such a light breakfast! This is easy, she told herself. Her hands were clammy.

At quarter to eight, he had not yet come down. She returned the orange juice to the refrigerator, watched the seconds blink away on the digital stove clock. He must be

tired after such a long flight, that's it, she thought. I think
I hate you, EDK, she thought. Would he know it?

"Mrs. Foley?"

She spun around. He was standing in the kitchen, a
newspaper tucked under his left arm, his right extended
toward her. She saw that she must shake his hand. She
had not expected it to begin like this.

"Welcome aboard. Mrs. Marty's been saying good
things about you, so you don't need to be nervous. I see
you've plunged right in—fine. I suggest you go ahead on
your own, see how the game plays for a week, then we
can huddle and sort out whatever needs to be discussed.
Unless you've got questions right now you'd like me to
field."

"No, Mr. Kaplan." The flood of metaphors amused
her.

"Good. Frankly, at this hour I prefer coffee to
quizzes."

He talks and looks like any ordinary businessman,
she thought as she loaded a tray: about five-feet-ten
or eleven; carefully combed dark hair clipped short
around the ears and graying slightly at the temples; well-
maintained physique, thickening just slightly around the
middle; face too broad and heavy to be handsome; deep
vertical line between dark eyebrows; heavily lidded dark
brown eyes; faint expression of dissatisfaction tightening
the mouth; regulation charcoal pinstripe three-piece, discreetly patterned red tie. Boring! Yet Mary Jane had
found this man fascinating. She shook her head.

When she came in with the tray, she found he had buried himself in the newspaper; clearly, conversation was
not on the menu. It wasn't until she was clearing away
that he raised his head.

"You know that Mondays and Thursdays are Mrs. Sweeney's days to clean?"

So he kept track of such things, even when he was just back from South America.

"Yes, sir. Mrs. Marty copied out the schedule for me."

"And that on Wednesday the plumbers are coming to replace the shower head in the master bath?"

"I have it on my calendar, Mr. Kaplan."

"And that Mario comes to do the yard and whatever other outdoor work needs doing Monday and Friday afternoons?"

"Yes, sir."

"All right, all right!" Laughing, he threw up his hands in a gesture of surrender, and suddenly, reluctantly, she felt the charm. "I can see I'm not needed around here. You women as usual have everything under control. Incidentally, what do you prefer to be called—Mrs. Foley or Theresa?"

"Theresa is all right."

"Theresa, then. A saint, wasn't she?" He picked up the newspaper. " 'The Little Flower of Jesus'?"

"Yes," said Theresa, eyeing him steadily. "She believed in the 'little way'—getting to heaven by performing the humblest tasks."

"Rather like a housekeeper."

He did not think of her again until Dorothy Swerdlow, handing him some papers to sign, said deferentially, "I hope Mrs. Foley will work out, Mr. Kaplan. It was quite a responsibility for me, but she seemed the best of the applicants by far."

"Mrs. Foley?" He looked at her blankly, then remembered the new woman. Foley, Theresa Foley. Midforties, he guessed. Plain, though rather a good figure still. Sensible looking, yet there was something lurking in those deep-set eyes. Distrust? Unhappiness? Never mind, not his business. Seemed to have things under control. That's all that mattered. "Of course, the new housekeeper. Don't worry; I'm sure she'll work out very well. And I appreciate, believe me, all the trouble you took." He glanced up, his eighteen-carat gold Mont Blanc pen poised over a page. "Frankly, I don't know what I'd do without you."

Mrs. Sweeney, a tall bony woman with a dead-white face and fiery dyed hair, arrived before Theresa had finished clearing up breakfast. She stood looking at Mr. Kaplan's new housekeeper, hands on hips. "Well, you're *young,* I'll say that," she announced ungraciously.

"I can't help that, you know," said Theresa with a smile, "and I'm not, really."

"Don't matter to me, might to some," Mrs. Sweeney said cryptically and disappeared. In a few moments Theresa heard the whine of a vacuum upstairs.

She did a light wash and folding, then, as Mrs. Marty had suggested, attacked with brass polish the plates and knobs on the downstairs doors, a task, she soon saw, that would go well into the afternoon. At noon, she made herself a cup of soup and a sandwich, and saw by the look on Mrs. Sweeney's face as she passed through the kitchen with a mop that Mrs. Marty had always made the cleaning lady soup and a sandwich, too. She hurriedly corrected her error, set a place, and invited Mrs. Sweeney to sit down, wondering what they would talk about. Perhaps the surly cleaning lady could tell her something useful about Ned Kaplan.

Mrs. Sweeney drew up a chair, took a noisy, critical spoonful of soup and ostentatiously opened a large black book she had brought to the table. Theresa saw that it was a Bible.

"Have you worked for Mr. Kaplan long?" Theresa ventured conversationally. Perhaps the cleaning lady was uncomfortable with strangers.

Mrs. Sweeney stared at her with pale, red-rimmed eyes. "Longer than you'll ever do." She hunched up her shoulders and went back to the Book, charting her progress down a column with a chipped red fingernail.

A real charmer, thought Theresa.

The brass took her until past one. Polishing a last door plate in the morning room, she was startled to see through the sliding doors a short, dark man in baggy pants, an open shirt, and a safari hat standing with his hands in his pockets staring into the pool. Then she remembered: He must be the yard man. She opened the door and went out onto the patio. After the cool house, the thick, damp afternoon wrapped her like a hot towel. "Hello," she said, hoping she sounded professional. "I'm Theresa Foley, the new housekeeper. You must be Mario."

"Mario Ferraca, yes," said the little man. "So pleased to meet you." He gestured vaguely at the water. "I'm just deciding whether I drain the pool today, or leave it till next week." His forehead folded into four perplexed lines. "What do you think?"

"What did Mr. Kaplan say?"

"He don't say, that's the trouble. It's still very nice weather now, so he might like to swim when he come home. Then I get blamed if there's no water. If it turns cold and the leaves come down and the pool is still full, then I get blamed for that too." He shook his head sadly.

For the first time in three weeks, Theresa found herself laughing. "Look," she said suddenly, "do the neighbors have a pool?"

"All rich have pools."

"Is theirs drained?"

Mario shrugged. He was not at all sure what lay beyond the high brick wall surrounding the Kaplan property. He had never caught sight of a neighbor.

"Well, take that ladder and look over the wall. If the pool next door is drained, you drain this one. If it's not, you don't. That way he can't blame you because you're simply following a neighborhood precedent. And when you're through with the ladder, bring it inside, please, Mario. I want to tackle the big chandelier in the front hall."

·   She discovered that she could only half finish the chandelier because it was already going on four and time to fix dinner. Where had the day gone and what had she accomplished? Offering up a little prayer for its success, she assembled a casserole of crabmeat, angel-hair pasta, and artichoke hearts from a recipe she had cut out of Sunday's paper, sealed it with plastic wrap, and taped a note on the top, "8 minutes in microwave." She had crisped the Boston lettuce that morning; now she shook together olive oil, basil, freshly ground pepper, and a dash of white wine and refrigerated the bottle in a conspicuous place on the top shelf. She laid the tray with a linen mat, the good silver and china, and a tall thin-lipped wineglass, and set it ready on the kitchen table. She installed the bottle of Pouilly-Fuissé Mrs. Marty said he liked with his dinner in the electric wine cooler on the counter. What else? Rolls, dinner bread—she'd forgotten all about them! Did he eat bread with his meals? Of course, all men did. She foraged through the pantry, but finally located a package of croissants in the freezer in the back hall, detached two, wrapped them in plastic, and labeled them "3 minutes in microwave." She looked about her. What had she forgotten? She could think of nothing. It was already quarter of five. Even though she was used to physical work, her shoulders ached from stretching above her head to polish the glass droplets of the chandelier. But, she corrected herself, it wasn't polishing the chandelier or the brass, it was the psychological strain of simply being under the roof of Ned Kaplan's house. She realized she was tired to the bone.

"So tell all!" Holly's prominent brown eyes fringed with stiff, curled, mascared eyelashes gleamed. She seemed to have gotten over her horror of Theresa's new employment. "How did it go? What is he like? What did he say to you?"

They were sitting in Theresa's living room with its two good pieces of furniture—an Adams desk with glassed-in bookshelves from her parents' home, and an eighteenth-century "Orpheus" chair she had bought impulsively at auction when she was young and thought her marriage, like the chair, would accrue in value. Matt was doing his homework in his bedroom behind a closed door. Theoretically. Theresa knew he was probably reading comics or organizing his baseball card collection, but she was too tired to do battle this evening. She replaced her coffee cup in its saucer.

"You mean the work itself? I think it went pretty well," she said slowly. "Mrs. Marty made a list of jobs for this week, and I'm just following it. After that, I'm on my own. Mrs. Sweeney, the cleaning lady, is a mild psychotic who reads her Bible at lunch and treats me like the plague, but I can't help that. We'll just have to get used to each other. The thing I'm hanging onto for dear life is Mrs. Marty's telephone list. I'm beginning to think that the whole trick of running a big house is being able to tap the right people for the right thing. She must have a hundred numbers."

Holly bounced on her chair like a schoolgirl. "Yes, but what about *him?* Mr. Dangerous."

Theresa glanced at Matt's door with a warning finger to her lips. Of course she couldn't tell him where she was working, even though she doubted he remembered the name Kaplan in connection with Mary Jane; all he knew was that she was housekeeping for a wealthy man who lived in Georgetown. "Kaplan? Well, I'm hardly going to see him at all. We'll say good morning, I'll serve his breakfast, he'll read his newspaper, he'll leave the house. I leave at four, he comes home after six. How stupid of me not to have realized how it would be!"

"If you'll excuse me, I thought the whole thing stupid from the beginning. What did you think—he was going to fall on his knees and confess that he threw Mary Jane over the banister? Which, now that I say it, sounds absolutely nuts. A man in his position risking that? You know what I think? Excuse me again. I think just possibly you're interested in the guy yourself."

Theresa recoiled. "God, no! How can you say that!" She rose, agitated. "I don't know what I want. I want to get near him, inside him—find out his psychology, what makes him tick. Discover his weaknesses, the cracks in his armor. Because he must have them. And when I find one, I want to stick the knife in and twist. Until he shouts

out the truth because he can't stand the pain." She
laughed abruptly, amused at her vehemence. "To put it
less melodramatically, I want to trip him up in his own
plausibility. I want to expose his lies."

"If he's told any. But when does an employee ever 'get
near' the boss?"

"Mary Jane did."

"I don't want to be brutal, but Mary Jane was prime."

"I don't mean sexually! You're obsessed, Holly, you
know that? Maybe I can get him to talk."

"That won't be easy."

"No, it won't. He's just what you'd expect a millionaire banker to be like. Polite. Distant. Businesslike, I
guess you'd call it. 'I prefer coffee to quizzes in the morning,' he said. Well, that shut me up, I can tell you, and yet
he said it in a pleasant kind of way. I guess when people
have that much power, they can afford to be pleasant because they damn well know you're going to obey."

Holly shook her head. "What did Mary Jane see in
him? I wonder. Sure, he's got money, but she wasn't the
kind of kid to be overimpressed with that. Is he good-
looking? Does he have sex appeal?"

Again! Collecting coffee cups, Theresa stared at her
friend in disbelief. "The way I feel about what happened,
do you really expect me to be thinking about sex appeal?" she said with heat.

Holly made an elaborate gesture of locking her lips
and throwing away the key. "I'd better keep my mouth
shut. But you know what I mean."

Theresa was still angry, but that was Holly, all heart—
and mouth. She relented. "He's quiet. Brusque. Hardly
smiles at all. There's no warmth, no charm." Yet even as
she denied it she remembered the way the muscles around

his nose drew together when he laughed, the way his melancholy eyes crinkled. "As for sex appeal"—she turned in the kitchen doorway—"definitely not."

"I hope everything was satisfactory last night, Mr. Kaplan?" Theresa poured more coffee into the blue breakfast cup. She had resolved to try to engage him, to make him really look at her. She was determined to make contact somehow.

"Last night?" Ned Kaplan looked up, frowning.

"Dinner, I mean."

"Oh, yes. Yes." He seemed to be trying to remember whether he'd eaten dinner or not. "Some kind of casserole, was it? Perfectly satisfactory, thank you."

Theresa plunged ahead. "I was concerned because Mrs. Marty said you'd never use the microwave. She said you'd eat your dinner stone cold before you'd bother."

Ned laid down the *Wall Street Journal.* Was this new woman going to be a problem? Because if there was anything he detested, it was idle chatter from people who were there to perform simple mechanical tasks for you. That was why someone like Dorothy Swerdlow was so invaluable: all business from nine to five. He wasn't even sure whether she was married or not, though he had a vague feeling she was. He and Marty had always gotten along because they let each other alone. And now this Theresa Foley actually seemed to be trying to make conversation during breakfast. Hired help these days simply didn't know their place.

"You know," he said as pleasantly as he could, "you don't have to wait on me mornings. It's kind of you, but if you'll just leave the Thermos on the table, I can pour my own coffee."

"I'm sorry." Theresa felt her cheeks go hot at the rebuke. She set the silver jug down on the table.

"Nothing to be sorry about," he said, relenting a little. "It takes time to adjust to a new situation."

"Yes, it does." She must press on. "Somehow I got the impression, talking to Mrs. Marty, that she—well, spoiled you a little. That's why—"

"Marty liked to think I couldn't function without her," he said abruptly. "But nobody is indispensable, though she was damned good at her job." He shook open the paper noisily.

Theresa put the empty juice glass and plate on her tray. He was scowling at the paper as though he'd like to throttle it. She paused at the door. "I keep wondering," she said, her voice hoarse with tension.

He looked up in disbelief.

"I keep wondering," she said into the hostile silence, "how she could have left so soon after that awful thing, the accident at the party. I don't think I could do that to an employer myself. It seems so disloyal."

She felt, rather than saw, a change pass over his face like a dark cloud, irritation replaced by—what? Caution, perhaps, recoil at having his private affairs discussed by a domestic. He folded the *Wall Street Journal* precisely and laid it next to his coffee cup, he spread both blunt ringless hands flat on the table as though he were about to address a board meeting or lecture a recalcitrant child.

"You really mustn't keep wondering, Theresa," he said slowly, "because, believe me, it won't get you anywhere. There was an unfortunate accident at a party here. It barely made the local news. And I hardly knew the young person and neither did any of my guests. Mrs. Marty understood that. If it had been anyone important, she would have stood by. As it happened, she left by mutual agreement. So in future—if your new employer may give you some friendly advice—keep your wondering to yourself and tend to business." His voice was cold, official.

Theresa fled. In the kitchen she banged the tray on the counter and hunched over the sink, her shoulders heaving, though no tears came. "Unfortunate accident." "Hardly knew the young person." "If it had been anyone important." This from the man who had dominated Mary Jane's diary for almost a year, the man she had loved. "If it had been anyone important—" Cold, sneering bastard! Heartless monster who had not even had the grace—the *courtesy*—to utter her daughter's name! Dry sobs shook her. She yanked on the faucet and splashed cold water into her face, trying to shock herself into sense.

She had to get ahold of herself. She wanted this job. She had provoked the conversation—deliberately opened the wound. He had closed against her; still, she could not judge him yet. Even if he'd cared for Mary Jane, she forced herself to admit, how unlikely he would disclose his feelings to a housekeeper. Rich people held themselves back. Money was a fence around the emotions. The coldness might be a mask. She did not know him.

Ned piloted the Mercedes along the thick artery of morning traffic pulsing down Pennsylvania Avenue into the heart of Washington, his fingers drumming the leather seat beside him. His encounter with Theresa Foley at breakfast had shaken him. His first impulse was to fire her—get rid of the bitch right off the bat, no fooling around. The balls of her! Questioning him, badgering him. Totally oblivious to the way he'd underlined the words *nobody is indispensable*. Actually having the nerve to bring up the September thing (he'd come to call it that). She must either have a hide of steel or be a damned idiot!

But he was not often a man of impulse. By the time he had braked and idled into Washington Circle, he saw clearly the possible repercussions of two of his personal employees leaving so soon after the September thing. He was acutely aware that, although Security American was sound, sounder as a bank and stock than ever, on the social level certain people he'd counted as friends had cooled—though, ironically, since the September thing Swerdlow had laid invitations on his desk from houses he'd never entered before. Washington must be talking. The Cohn slight had hit him hard. At first he'd thought it must be a mistake: the engraved postcard that always announced their monthly Sundays had misfired. At a private dinner for a visiting Argentinian industrialist, however, Bill Wylie had bent down from his great height and, apologetically clinking the ice in his whiskey, suggested that the omission was not accidental. The next morning Ned had lifted the phone to demand an explanation of Cohn; then, remembering the suspicion in the lawyer's eyes on the night of the party, had smashed the receiver back in place. And what about his old pal, the perennial scandalmonger, Elsa Frazier? Two weeks ago, for the first time he could remember, she had not returned his call. Of course, Elsa notoriously bent with the wind, but he liked her and the wind bending his way.

Ned Kaplan was emphatically not in what one would call "society." He worked too hard for that, disappeared too often to all corners of the globe, cared too little for small talk and petty politicking. But Carol Kaplan had been rich and popular and liked to entertain, and had thoroughly tutored her husband in the importance of socializing on some kind of regular basis with people who could be useful—"You have to knit people into *your* pattern, Ned. You'll never get anywhere unless you do." "What the hell do *you* know about knitting!" Instantly he'd been on the defensive, for he could never match the cool of old money, Vassar, natural savoir faire. No, but he'd come to know who counted. Bob Cohn and his legal hotshot friends. "Jesse" James, who had pushed through Congress more legislation friendly to Security American than anyone else on the Hill. Sam Frazier, whose influence with the Senate Judiciary Committee weighed like Fort Knox gold. Elsa, whose forked tongue could make or break a reputation. And the Wylies, the wealthy, wealthy Wylies. Aboveboard. Nonpartisan. Irreproachable. Benevolent. Ned smiled a little as Nancy danced into his head. Elegant. Exclusive. Loyal. Dearest Nancy.

There was no denying that he needed to keep on connecting with people on the personal level, needed to dispel over and over the impression that the vice-president of the board and president of Security American's International Division was some kind of ruthless money lender. And the new housekeeper was a vital part of that personal life, the modern equivalent of a gentleman's devoted staff. She was there to maintain his personal circle. Why else keep running a house that bled him to the tune of a quarter million a year?

Besides, any kind of help these days came with a price tag. Maybe Foley's was a flapping mouth. But he couldn't fire her; it wouldn't look right. He'd just have to correct her behavior—firmly and fast.

And there was the definite possibility he'd overreacted, he concluded as he pressed a button and watched the door of his private garage beneath the Security American building silently fold out of sight. Her mentioning the September thing had given him a nasty jolt, all right. But on second thought, how natural for her to bring it up. Anyone he hired might have remembered the accident at his residence on Q Street, especially when they applied for a position at that same residence soon after. Theresa Foley had just been displaying natural curiosity.

He locked the Mercedes, pocketed the key, and headed briskly for his private elevator, swinging his attaché case confidently. Natural curiosity. He nodded his head decisively. Nothing to worry about. Perfectly normal.

CHAPTER NINE

Besides a conventional "Good morning," Theresa hardly spoke to her employer the rest of the week. Fear of his cold disapproval locked her tongue; but more, his apparent indifference to the death of her daughter somehow paralyzed her. It was as though only she in all the world knew or cared about what had happened to Mary Jane Jones. Even Matt seemed to have shed his sorrow as easily as his new waterproof tent shed rain. She was alone in her doubt and grief; and with no one to share it, her hope of understanding more about her daughter's relationship with Ned Kaplan took on a hallucinatory quality, even to herself. Even Holly had come to look on her job as something of a game, a stunt that maybe she'd win a prize for if she managed to pull it off.

Then on Friday, Ned Kaplan came into the kitchen where she was loading the dishwasher and said, "I'd like you here at seven on Monday if you can make it. Some things we should go over. Shouldn't take long, half an hour at most."

"Fine," said Theresa, startled. Somehow she had

imagined they would never speak again. "I can be here."

"Take Monday off early, of course. And have a good weekend."

"Thank you, Mr. Kaplan."

She spent a good deal of the weekend wondering what Ned Kaplan would have to say to her. It turned out he was planning to give a dinner party.

"On the twenty-sixth. More than a month, should be all right."

"A month?" Sitting opposite him in the study, a pencil poised over the notepad on her knees, Theresa tried to keep from looking dismayed. A dinner party already when she scarcely knew her way around! She would have to make careful notes; she would have to consult Mrs. Marty if the Martys weren't already rolling toward California in a new mobile home. "A month?" she said again, and then understood: more than a month since Mary Jane had died here in his home. Plenty of time for people to have forgotten.

He ignored the question. "Nothing elaborate, about twenty people. There's a catering service Marty gets in; they do the menu and send over a chef on the day, though Marty always helped out." He paused.

Theresa realized he was waiting for her to volunteer. "Of course," she said flatly, "I expect to help out, too."

"Good. You'll want to get someone in to help in the kitchen. One girl should be enough. Marty must have given you names."

"I think so. Yes, she did."

"And Franchot will be on duty."

Franchot? Her head whirled. Who was Franchot? Oh yes, the peripatetic butler.

He glanced at his watch. Really, this wasn't his business, but he wanted this party, for many reasons, to go well, and the Foley woman was still an unknown quantity. In fact, the dinner party was going to be crucial. If the Cohns refused, or the Fraziers . . . "And the flowers, don't try to do them yourself. Marty's told you about Claussen's?"

The premier Washington florist. "Yes, Mr. Kaplan." She hesitated. "Will I have a guest list?"

He winced slightly, anticipating refusals. "My secretary will send you a copy. She always takes care of the invitations herself. And the seating. Well!" He looked at his watch again, this time pointedly. "You've been here one whole week. How does the shoe fit?"

So this was the "discussion" he'd promised her. Clearly he expected neither questions nor complaints.

"A little snug," she said, managing a smile. "I mean, I've still got a lot to learn. But so far, no disasters."

"I don't expect disasters, I think you know your job." Ned spoke curtly, disguising the fact that from him this was high praise. Her silence after the second morning had reconciled him to her presence. He was beginning to believe that Theresa Foley had got the message; that, as under the capable hand of Mrs. Marty, the house would pretty much run itself without him.

He looked at her now, jotting notes on her lap, and approved. Short, curly dark hair. Discreet earrings. Little makeup, no other jewelry. Black skirt, plain white blouse, gray cardigan. Businesslike. Coffee better than Marty's, too. And good legs, he added, seeing nothing incongruous in the inclusion.

* * *

After he left, quiet settled over the big house. In the morning room, polishing the glass table, Theresa felt the stillness in her nerves and bones. Inside, and outside on the patio in the walled backyard, nothing moved; on the huge tree, leaves slicked gold by the night's rain hung motionless. Mrs. Sweeney would not be coming in today because, she said, she had the flu. Mario would not show up to do the hedge clipping until midafternoon. No plumbers, no carpet cleaners, no window washers, not even a delivery from Delmonico's, the exclusive grocer that the Kaplan establishment patronized. Had Mrs. Marty ever gotten lonely? wondered Theresa, shivering a little. And why, she wondered again, did Ned Kaplan keep up such a lavish establishment just for himself? It didn't make sense.

She would do it today, as she had planned. No time last week, too much going on, too many people in and out, the whole house too demanding for her to do anything but cope minute to minute. Not that she expected to find anything. No, Ned Kaplan would never keep souvenirs of "no one important." The tide of rage flooded her again, but it no longer took her by surprise as it once had: She felt its pulsing progress through her brain and lungs and heart as a cancer patient might tolerate the throbbing of a long-familiar pain. The surprising thing was that she could remain calm in Ned Kaplan's presence, speak to him as she would to any employer. That was the wonder.

Another wonder was that she would do his bedroom, like a dutiful wife, before she began to search. She smiled grimly at the irony as she entered the room where the blond madonna smiled enigmatically from the dressing table against the wall. Not the sort of work of art one would expect in Edward Kaplan's bedroom, if one would expect works of art at all; she still found it puzzling. She drew back the curtains and secured them behind brackets shaped like leaves. She hung his pajamas with the scarlet blaze EDK on the pocket in his closet. Strange to be touching something so intimate to him, feeling between her fingers the fine silk that had caressed his skin all night. How would Ned Kaplan like it if he knew his intimate wearing apparel was being handled by the mother of the young woman who had died in his house? She turned to ask the question of the blond madonna, but the blond madonna only gazed inscrutably below heavy lids at the child in her arms.

She went through every drawer, meticulously restoring objects to their original places. She turned out the closet, even sorted through the contents of the cabinet above the sink in the master bath on the chance of finding a familiar tube of Revlon lipstick or mascara pencil. Nothing. Nothing, of course. She hardly knew what she had hoped for, though she suspected Mary Jane might have written him, remembering the evening she'd come into her daughter's bedroom unannounced and Mary Jane, reddening, had quickly slipped a sheet of stationery into a drawer. Yet, she told herself again, Ned Kaplan did not seem the kind of man who kept letters.

Where else? she wondered, closing the door on the room she was forced to enter every morning. She went back down the big staircase, walked through the entrance hall into the large drawing room on the right, through a smaller room, and into Ned Kaplan's study with its French windows leading out onto the patio. They had talked there this morning; it seemed long ago.

She looked around. His big black leather chair and

hassock. Thick, dull-looking books, the kind nobody
ever read, in the built-in case along the left wall. The big
square mahogany desk where, she knew from Mrs.
Marty, he often worked evenings. Fax machine, computer, copier, telephones: Ned Kaplan, it seemed, never
stopped working, even at home. Incongruously antique,
a big globe, brown like parchment, nestled inside a
wooden stand. She spun the orb idly, watching conti-
nents flash by. They meant nothing to her: She hardly
knew that India or Greenland or Australia existed; why
should she, what did they matter? Then she noticed the
Rolodex file on the desk. She went to it, slid back the
metal lid, and found herself staring at a name. Diana
Maynard. Without thinking, she took a pen from a brass
shell case serving as a holder and jotted down the name,
address, and phone number on a pad lying on the blotter.
Diana Maynard. She had no idea who Diana Maynard
might be, but she was the last person Ned Kaplan had
called and that might mean something. Then she flipped
the Rolodex to *J.*

Herbert Jackson. Sol Jacobson. James and James of
Bond Street, Custom Tailors. Ellis and Scooter Janeway.
Gunter Jarling, Munchenbank, Germany. Jenkins, Ter-
williger, and Dunn. Serge Jentoff. Jonas Brothers.
Thomas Jonay. Stanley and Cynthia Jordan. She flipped
back through the names. No Mary Jane Jones. Never
had been. Not important enough.

Theresa stood up, hollow with the renewed realization
that her daughter hadn't mattered to Ned Kaplan, hadn't
mattered at all. Mary Jane had been here—died here—
but she was no longer here because he hadn't cared. Like
a patient in a crowded hospital, the breath stops, the
body's whisked away on a gurney, the few pathetic be-

longings are dispatched, the area is disinfected, and presto, the patient has never existed. Zero. Nada. Wiped off the slate.

At noon she made herself a tomato, mayo, and lettuce sandwich on whole wheat, ate a few bites, pushed it aside. Hour by hour the huge silent house, ponderous with its precious freight of rare carpets, burnished woods, polished silver, and fine crystal, weighed more heavily upon her. How can I go on? she asked herself. How can I get through today, tomorrow? Why am I here? Holly's right. I must be crazy. I can't touch him; I can't bring her back. There's nothing I can do.

She dug in her purse, slung over the back of a chair, and pulled out Mary Jane's diary. She read it often, partly to feel closer to Mary Jane, partly to try to solve the puzzle of her daughter's last year alive, partly to boot up her courage. But today she found no inspiration. Words that had lept damningly out of the pages now looked innocuous. *I think he could be dangerous. . . . Sometimes I'm afraid of him.* Well, a young woman *could* be afraid of a boss she was pursuing, couldn't she— afraid of his anger and scorn, afraid she might lose her job or a good reference? And Mary Jane, as Holly had reminded her, had possessed a highly developed sense of drama. She shoved the diary back in her purse. She felt drained, empty.

By one-thirty she had finished another wash. Two and a half more hours, she thought in despair, entirely forgetting that Ned Kaplan had said she could go home early. Perhaps it wasn't too soon to start working on the dinner party. Feeling distinctly nervous, she went to the kitchen wall phone and dialed Ma Cuisine.

"The twenty-sixth, for twenty?" The tenor voice on the

other end sounded young, experienced, and bored.

"That's right."

"How many courses?"

Theresa went red. She had no idea how many courses, but she couldn't let Ma Cuisine know that. "How many do you usually do?"

"Depends. Sometimes uno. Usually three. Sometimes four or five. Six if it's a real fancy do."

"Six, then." Should she be asking for prices? Some menus might be cheaper than others.

"Right." She could hear his pencil tapping. "That's hors d'oeuvres, starters, hot or cold soup, entree, salad, and dessert. What kind of entree do you have in mind?"

"Beef or lamb. Or possibly veal." Mr. Kaplan's favorites, Mrs. Marty had confided.

"We do a classic Beef Wellington that Mr. Kaplan always likes. Also a rather special roast saddle of lamb *persillade.* I can also recommend our chef's version of Veal Prince Orloff."

Happily Theresa suddenly remembered that the menu for the last dinner party had featured Beef Wellington. "The roast saddle of lamb *per*—"

"—*sillade.* For twenty. How soon do you need the menu?"

Menu? Why did she need the menu? Of course, she was responsible for some of the shopping. "Is the end of this week possible?"

"That's rather soon," drawled the bored male voice. "We can get it to you sometime next week. You say you're Mrs. Marty's replacement? Right. Then you'll be doing dessert yourself?"

Dessert for twenty! Theresa's hands went cold. "No,"

she said firmly. One had to take a stand. "I never do desserts."

"Hors d'oeuvres yourself?"

"No." Though on second thought, she certainly could handle hors d'oeuvres.

"Then that's six courses."

She hung up in a sweat, unreasonably shaken by the worldly languor of Ma Cuisine, to whom a six-course dinner seemed no more complex than a Boy Scout pancake supper. She hadn't dared to ask prices.

She flipped through her notes. Mrs. Marty had given her the names of three people who were usually available to help out at social functions. Two of them were married, one was a student at Georgetown University working her way through graduate school. She dialed Ann Moore first, but got no answer; Geneva Smithers, however, picked up the phone.

"The twenty-sixth? Yes, all right—no, wait. Oh golly, I can't. The twenty-sixth's our anniversary and my husband will kill me if I work that night. He's taking me out for dinner and dancing."

Theresa hung up bleakly. So far preparations for the dinner party were not going particularly well. She dialed the last number without much hope of getting through, supposing that Stephanie Ruso would be in class.

"Stephanie Ruso?"

"Yes."

She was in after all. "This is Theresa Foley, Mr. Kaplan's new housekeeper. Mrs. Marty gave me your name and number. I'm calling to say Mr. Kaplan is having a dinner party on the twenty-sixth of this month and I'll need someone to help in the kitchen. I hope you're available? . . . Hello? Is this Stephanie?"

"Yes." The voice was hardly more than a whisper.

"As I said, this is Mr. Kaplan's new housekeeper, and I hope you're available the evening of the twenty-sixth."

Silence again. Was the girl retarded, or what?

"I'm sorry," Stephanie said at last. "I can't come. I—I don't do that kind of work anymore. I've got a regular job."

"Oh," said Theresa, deflated. "I'm sorry to hear that. Mrs. Marty said such good things about you."

"I can't; that's all. And I've got to run."

The phone clicked in Theresa's ear.

She hung up thoughtfully. A strange conversation, though perhaps Stephanie was embarrassed about letting her down? No, embarrassment could hardly explain the whisper, the silences, the abrupt termination of conversation. Theresa frowned. The young woman had sounded afraid.

CHAPTER TEN

Ned Kaplan sat tapping the gold pen grimly as he listened to Greg Barry from the investment division trying to explain why Security American's holdings in a certain foreign petroleum company had plunged to half their value in seven months.

"All right, all right." Ned cut him short. "What I want to know is, who fucked up? This was supposed to be Union Petroleum's big year."

"That's the point, Ned." Greg ran both hands through his blond hair, destroying an expensive styling job. "It was too big. Britain got the jitters; so did Germany and France. With major elections coming up, they had to do something to pacify the environmental faction, especially after that disastrous oil spill. Finally, Union Pete had no choice but putting their drilling operations in the North Sea on hold while they see which way the political wind is going to blow."

"But this isn't the government. We're running a business here, not a bureaucracy. We have shareholders to answer to. I want an inside report on Union Pete's strategy for the next fiscal—" A buzzer sounded and he picked up the phone. "No calls. I'm busy. Who? Mrs. Wylie?" For a moment his voice lost its cutting edge. "All right, give me a minute, then put her through. Listen"— he cupped the receiver, glaring at the too sportily dressed young man edging toward the door; loafers and checked shirts, even with a tie, belonged in the Ivy League, not Security American—"put Delino onto this. I want the inside story, understand?" He stared Barry out of the room. "Hello, Nancy."

"Hello, Ned." They hadn't seen each other since the day of the funeral and her voice was tentative. "I've been thinking of you. How have you been?"

"Very well. Quite recovered, as a matter of fact—if that's the word for it. Did you get the invitation?"

"This morning."

"I hope you and Bill are free."

"We are, and looking forward to being with you. It seems like years."

"Look, Nancy." The frown that had been playing constantly between Ned's brows the past weeks darkened. "I don't quite know how to say it, but this dinner is damned important to me."

"I see," she said. He could feel her taking in the situation in her usual alert, delicate way.

"I've invited the Cohns and the Fraziers."

There was a silence. "And they *must* come, mustn't they," she finished for him.

He let his breath out in relief. She understood. "Yes, dear Nancy, they must."

"Then Bill and I will do everything short of hijacking to get them there. Don't worry, Neddy." She laughed lightly. "Leave it to me."

"You're an angel," he said, his throat tightening unaccustomedly. His voice rasped as it climbed the scale. "Truly an angel."

Three days later at a quarter of two the back doorbell rang. Theresa glanced at her watch in surprise. The cleaners had asked for an extra day with the gold silk dining room draperies, and Delmonico's didn't deliver until after three. She went down the short flight of stairs off the back hall and opened the door.

A young woman with sallow skin, a square face, and thick black hair pulled back with combs behind her ears stood there. She had heavy shoulders that made her look shorter than she was, thought Theresa, meeting her defiant eyes. She wore black leggings, a long bulky oatmeal-colored sweater, and a book bag slung over those powerful shoulders.

"I'm Stephanie Ruso. Somebody left the front gate unlatched. Can I come in?"

"Of course," said Theresa, surprised. She led the way back to the kitchen. Stephanie stood awkwardly in the middle of the room, not meeting her gaze. "I'm Mrs. Foley. I hope this means you've changed your mind about the twenty-sixth? Sit down. Can I get you something? Tea? A cup of coffee?"

"No, thanks." Stephanie pulled out a chair and sank into it, still armed with the backpack. Her large, black eyes traveled the kitchen, reluctant to meet Theresa's. "It looks just the same," she said finally.

"Yes, well, I guess kitchens don't change much." Theresa tried again. "I do hope you can help out for the dinner party. I desperately need someone who knows the ropes."

"I've been trying to get Mrs. Marty on the phone." Stephanie studied her rather dingy fingernails. "I think it must be disconnected. I thought maybe you'd know where she is."

So that was it. She hadn't come to volunteer her services after all. "I know she and her husband were thinking of buying a trailer and going west," said Theresa, disappointed and just a little hurt that Mrs. Marty had simply disappeared. "Is it something I can help with?" How little some young women care about their appearance these days, she thought, smiling encouragingly at Stephanie. No poise. Hardly clean. And no manners at all.

"No," said Stephanie. Yet she didn't move. Instead she traced a circle on the shiny painted tabletop with her little finger and carefully bisected it.

"Well, then," said Theresa, thinking of the tiled floor in the breakfast room that she had pledged herself to do this afternoon on hands and knees, the only way you could ever really get floors clean, something Mrs. Sweeney had failed or refused to grasp.

"I suppose she's left then. I wanted to talk to her."

Theresa felt irritation. "If her phone's disconnected, she probably has." She stood up. "If there's anything I can do," she said with finality.

". . . About that night. The night of the big party. When the girl died."

A shock rattled Theresa from skull to toes. She sat down again. "Why?" she asked carefully. "Why do you want to talk to Mrs. Marty about that night?"

Stephanie squirmed uncomfortably. "I don't know. It's just that I keep thinking about it—about that girl, lying there."

Theresa's mouth was dry. "You saw her?"

"Yes. The poor kid." Suddenly Stephanie was loquacious. "I can't get it out of my head, that beautiful girl, all dressed up, dead. God, I wish I hadn't come that night. I had a gut feeling about it, you know? And I always trust my feelings. Usually. I'm very intuitive. But I needed the money like you wouldn't believe and they pay well here—ten dollars an hour—and I'd really had it with the books, so I said I'd work. Besides, you get to take home incredible leftovers; you can live for a week—"

"How did you happen to see her?"

Stephanie bisected the bisection. "I was in the kitchen filling trays all night. I didn't lay eyes on any of the guests. I never do. Didn't even see Boss Kaplan. I just did my lousy job."

"Yes, but"—Theresa felt she must scream with frustration—"you did see the girl." She spoke very slowly, mouthing each word. "How did that happen? When?"

"Marty sent me out to get more trays of canapés from the freezer in the back hall. It must have been midnight or just after. She was lying there, kind of broken, like a doll, at the bottom of the stairs. Her head was wrong." Stephanie shifted uneasily in her chair, as though embarrassed by her own near-eloquence. "I saw her. There was blood."

"What did you do?"

"Screamed and dropped the trays. No, just kidding. Ran and got Marty, naturally. Then she got the butler and I told the rest of the people in the kitchen and everybody wanted to see. I didn't, though. I'd seen enough."

Theresa sat silently, watching Stephanie begin another circle on the polished table. She had been the first to find Mary Jane and had alerted the others. She had, quite naturally, suffered a shock. She'd kept on thinking about it, natural again. She'd tried to call Mrs. Marty. Why? To talk over the evening? Marty wasn't one to rehash the past. To absolve herself in some crazy way? It didn't make sense. "I still don't understand," she said, "why you wanted to talk to Mrs. Marty."

Stephanie pushed back the chair. Her square, rather handsome face had closed like a wooden door. "Nothing really," she said. "It's not important. I just thought you might know where she was." She pulled back her sleeve and grimaced at the oversized man's watch strapped to her wrist. "Got to run. G.U. prof kills anyone who's late. Just kidding."

"Wait a minute, please!" said Theresa, hurrying after her.

Stephanie flung up her arms in an exaggerated gesture of protest. "Can't! Late for seminar. Sorry." The back door banged after her.

Theresa walked slowly back to the kitchen and stood at the sink, staring out the window. A sudden shower of pale gold fluttered down, like torn leaves from an old diary. It didn't seem to make sense. Stephanie's strange behavior on the telephone, then her coming here. Wanting to talk to Mrs. Marty about that night. Then rushing off with some excuse about a class. Stephanie's brutal description—she felt it brutal because it had come from a stranger—had shaken her. She felt uneasy, profoundly dissatisfied.

The doorbell shrilled again. This time through the small window to the left of the door she saw the brown shirt and cap of Delmonico's delivery man. She received and unpacked four sacks of groceries automatically, wondering about Stephanie Ruso.

* * *

For as long as anyone could remember, even though the hotel had declined in prestige since its heyday in the Truman-Eisenhower era, a certain suite at the Mayflower had been reserved for the Thursday night poker game. Different players revolved around a core of regulars— Bill Wylie, Bob Cohn, Jesse James, and Lee Tyler among them. Ned Kaplan did not play poker. "Why should I?" he'd say when pressed. "My whole life's a gamble."

Tonight Bill Wylie and Bob Cohn arrived before the others, dropped their briefcases, hung up their Burberrys, threw off their jackets, and unknotted their ties. Bob stretched and groaned, massaging his ribs until his shirt crawled out of his pants. That accomplished, he headed for the always-bursting refrigerator.

"What's the matter, Bobbie? Too much Senate investigating?"

"You know, Bill, you're a genius. Always manage to stick your finger right in the open wound. Beer? Catch." He flipped the lid of his own Miller's, courtesy of a Wisconsin lawmaker privy to the Thursday nights. "You bet too much SI. Actually, too much ADT. Can you believe a congressman who not only defrauds the government but keeps all his receipts for it? Suitable for framing. Corruption in Washington ain't what it used to be."

"No," said Bill thoughtfully. "I suppose it isn't." Unlike Bob Cohn, he measured his beer carefully into a tilted glass. He folded his long frame under the poker table and let Cohn finish off his brew. "I'll tell you one particular way it's not like it used to be, Robert. Friends used to stand by friends."

Bob Cohn shrugged, splayed the waiting poker deck

into an arc, drew a card, held up the ace of clubs and grinned. "Hot tonight."

"Maybe so." Bill leaned forward earnestly. "But you're playing a game Ned doesn't play." Aware of interruption at any moment, he pressed on. "Tell me you're not going to let him down, Bob. I'm talking specifically about the twenty-sixth."

Bob screwed his small eyes shut, drew another card, opened his eyes, and grinned as he snapped down the jack of clubs next to the ace. "Straightening. Let him down, is that the pitch? Poor Neddy, as the fair sex seem to call him. And here I thought he let *us* down. Way down."

"You don't seriously think—"

"Let's call it 'shadow of a doubt.'" Bob triumphantly flipped over the queen of spades.

"Look, Bob." Bill hitched his chair closer, knotted his huge, freckled hands. "You've known Ned long enough to be sure of one thing. The man's straight. You can't succeed in his business and not be. He can be ruthless, but he plays honest. And it's the same in his personal life. Nancy and I know things—well, I won't go into them. Let's just say he stuck by Carol longer than you or I ever would in his situation. You've got to go by the record, and Ned's record is clean."

Bob made exaggerated passing motions over the deck, nipped a card with a flourish, and flung away the seven of hearts in disgust.

"Bill of the pure in heart," he said ironically. "Ned stayed with Carol because she was his golden charm. Everybody knows that but you. How a guy can be rolling in dough, like you, and still have the mentality of an Eagle Scout, I'll never know."

"We're not talking about me; we're talking about Ned," said Bill patiently, "We're talking about him needing us maybe for the first time in his life—"

"All right, what're we waiting for? Deal the suckers!" boomed a familiar voice. Milo "Jesse" James suddenly filled the room, followed by Lee Tyler, already looking oppressed, and House Speaker Corbin Wright.

"What's the hurry, Jesse?" said Bob Cohn. "Draw up a beer and relax."

"Jesse's afraid if Initiative 553 passes, this'll be his last game." Wright laughed, then flung down his briefcase and followed it with his coat.

"You're damn right it'll be my last! Where's that beer?"

"Come on, Corby. Texas will re-elect Jesse James as long as he wants to run." Bob winked at Tyler. "That right, Lee?"

"That's right," said Tyler, without enthusiasm. He pulled up a chair to the table and loosened his tie fractionally. For a prim man, he played a deadly game of poker and was eager to begin. "Cut for the deal, gentlemen?"

They played for long hours and high stakes. It was past one when Bill Wylie and Bob Cohn found themselves in a face-off across the table. Wright had dealt and folded immediately.

"Five and raise you five."

Jesse whistled. "Too rich for my blood. I'm bailing out."

Tyler laid his cards facedown in a precise stack. "I'm out."

Bill Wylie pushed five chips into the middle. "Five and see you."

With the air of a conjuror pulling rabbits, Bob laid down his cards. "Three cowboys."

Jesse banged the table. "Why the hell don't I get pictures like that!"

"Wait a minute," said Wright, "let's see what Bill's got."

Bill Wylie gave Bob Cohn a look, then shrugged and folded his cards. "Got me beat," he said pleasantly.

Jesse belched and clapped him on the back. "I gotta hand it to you, Bill. I've never seen a man drop five thousand with less sweat."

"He's got it to drop," said Tyler with grudging admiration.

As they were leaving, Bill drew Bob aside. "See you at Ned's?"

Cohn looked sullen. "Obviously you think I'm corruptible."

"Pardon me, I don't. I'm the Boy Scout, remember? But you tell me that everybody is. That's not the point, though. I do you a small favor, you do me a big one."

Cohn shrugged. He didn't look at Wylie because he hated craning his neck. All his life, from his five-foot-eight, he'd had to look up to his colleagues. "I admire your loyalty, misplaced as it is. All right, Bill. You win this round."

Nancy sighed and turned over as Bill lifted the covers and eased his six-foot-four inches into bed. "Mmmm, home at last. Good game?"

"Not particularly." He bent over and kissed her warm ear half buried in comforter. "But you'll be glad to hear the Cohns will be at Ned's dinner."

"Lovely, darling." She yawned and burrowed deeper

into the covers. "So will the Fraziers."

"How did you manage that?"

"I had nothing to do with it," said Nancy with another, terminal yawn. "Elsa's changed her mind about Ned. 'After all, darling,' she had the nerve to tell me, 'be reasonable. You know how we all loved Claus von Bülow.' "

Theresa let herself into 3001 Q Street the next morning as usual. Somewhere upstairs Ned Kaplan was shaving, or exercising, or knotting his tie. She turned the TV next to the sink on low to catch the morning news, as she always did, measured coffee into the Krups, and went to lay the table in the morning room. She unlocked and pushed back the sliding-glass doors, because if the weather was at all fine, Ned Kaplan preferred to breakfast demi-alfresco. Catching her reflection, she paused, wondering whether he would look into her face this morning and know she had passed a sleepless night. *I think he might be dangerous*—Mary Jane's words had tormented the long wakeful hours. What if she said to him over the toast rack, "A young woman who has worked for you came here yesterday because she wanted to talk about the night the girl died." Unthinkable, of course. But could she prevent the spark of suspicion leaping from her brain to his?

"Good morning, Mr. Kaplan."

"Good morning, Theresa." His hair was still wet from the shower and she smelled the clean tang of an expensive aftershave. "You're looking well this morning." Since discovering that she was not going to talk through breakfast, he ventured such phrases from time to time.

She smiled and poured his coffee. If he could not read fatigue in her face, he probably could read little else.

"Thank you. I must say, though, Mr. Kaplan, you look as though you didn't pass the best of nights."

He frowned. He'd had a hell of a night, but he hated to be told he looked tired. "You're very observant," he said briefly, shaking out his paper with purpose. "That will be all, thanks."

Satisfied, she retreated to the kitchen.

Because Ned Kaplan unaccountably lingered over breakfast, Theresa did not get to the mail until after ten. A quick glance told her there were only the usual bills to be paid out of the household checking account. The balance in that account—$168,000—had stunned her when she'd first opened the checkbook; she couldn't remember ever seeing a figure over $1,000 in her own. Yet, though paying bills with someone else's money amused her, the mail was seldom interesting even to speculate about. Ned Kaplan got few personal letters.

Now as she sat at the kitchen table finishing off his flask of coffee, she discovered among the bills a letter addressed to Theresa Foley with the initials *DAS* over the Security American logo in the upper-left-hand corner. She stared at the vaguely Teutonic initials blankly, then slit the envelope with a fruit knife, pulled out two sheets, and smiled at her obtuseness.

DAS was, of course, Dorothy Swerdlow, who was sending her the guest list and the seating plan for the dinner on the twenty-sixth. She leaned back, drinking her steaming coffee in small gulps and scanning the list: William and Nancy Wylie, Robert and Sally Cohn, the Hon. Milo James, Mrs. Santos (Elena) Rivera, Adam and Christine Burkett-Franklin, the Hon. George and Myra Schier, the Hon. Samuel and Elsa Frazier—

Coffee slopped in her saucer. Elsa Frazier. Elsa Frazier

and Ned Kaplan friends . . . Theresa seized the table plan. She saw that Dorothy Swerdlow had seated her supposed former employer on Ned Kaplan's left.

Her first impulse had been to quit immediately. Because she surely could not escape unmasking on the night of October twenty-sixth. What more natural when she came in with the soup than for Ned Kaplan to lean over to Elsa Frazier and say with a nod in her, Theresa's, direction, "Your former housekeeper is working out quite well." "*My* former housekeeper?" Mrs. Frazier would reply, swiveling in her chair. "Why, I've never laid eyes on the woman in my life!" And then the game would be up.

Her second thought was to call Ma Cuisine. "I have an out-of-town funeral I've *got* to go to on the twenty-sixth," she would explain. "Immediate family. Could one of your staff possibly fill in for me just the one night?" But she was informed that Ma Cuisine was not in the business of coping with household emergencies.

"I don't see it as a crisis," said Holly, who was not paying much attention. They were sitting in P.J. Rubicon's, where Holly, divorced just over a year, liked to go on Friday nights to scout for men, though she'd been discouragingly unsuccessful thus far. Her wide brown eyes roved expectantly around the bar area that was so murky, however, that Theresa wondered, as she had before, how anyone could make eye contact. "The very *last* thing people like that are going to talk about at a big dinner party is the household help." She swigged her beer and reached up to pat a bleached, blow-dried lock into place, smirking into the gloom. "I mean, how boring."

Theresa was drinking the quite-awful house white wine. She would have been horrified to realize that her employer's nightly glass of Pouilly-Fuissé, some of which she'd sampled one afternoon, had influenced her, but it had: She'd always ordered a bourbon old-fashioned before. "I don't agree," she said stubbornly. "Good help is hard to get these days. I bet that's exactly the kind of thing they do talk about. Especially when the person's right in the room to remind them. Which I realize I simply can't be. I'll have to find someone else to help Franchot serve and clear. I'm praying that Ann Moore has a friend."

"Actually, you don't know that old Kaplan ever saw your references. Didn't you tell me his secretary handled the whole thing while he was in South America?"

Theresa's jaw relaxed a little. "That's true," she said reluctantly. She coughed as a cloud of cigarette smoke drifted south of the bar. "I suppose it's possible he never looked at my file."

"Probable, I'd say. A big guy like him would delegate." Holly automatically dimpled at a balding man with a big belly who was squeezing past their table holding aloft two dripping beers, then slammed down her mug in disgust. "If that's the talent in this place tonight, I can do my drinking at home!" she said loudly.

"Shh, Holly, you're awful!" Theresa spun the wineglass stem between her fingers. "All right, maybe he did delegate. But if I want to keep this job, I can't take the chance. I've got to stay out of their way. Elsa Frazier can't see me—it's too much of a risk."

"But how much does the job really matter? Don't tell me you're still on that 'dangerous' kick."

Theresa thought of nervous, frightened Stephanie Ruso. She ought to tell Holly about Stephanie; she realized she was holding back. She shrugged. "Perhaps," she said, "I went a little overboard."

Her friend relented. Privately Holly had bet that Theresa would not last two weeks at Q Street, had prayed that she would not because she still thought working for Kaplan a morbid obsession. But she had to admit that so far Theresa was handling it all very well. "I've got it," she said brightly. "You can call in sick."

Theresa shook her head. "I'd be fired. For some reason, this dinner party is important to him."

Holly pushed back her chair. "Go figure. You've got eight days. You'll think of something, you always do. I'm ready to give up Desert Patrol. Let's go home."

CHAPTER ELEVEN

The day before the dinner party, John Franchot came to go over preparations with the new housekeeper. Wearing an ordinary blue flannel shirt and wash pants, Franchot, as he was always called—middle height, lean jawed, with thinning, precisely parted sandy hair—looked more like a garage mechanic than a butler (not, Theresa reminded herself, that she knew what a butler looked like) except for his wooden expression and exquisitely manicured nails. She stared at them, fascinated: pinkish, spade shaped, cleanly trimmed, with perfect white half-moons and cuticles. Her own were unkempt by comparison, and she self-consciously knotted her hands behind her back as Franchot stood in the pantry lecturing her about the silver, linens, and crystal. They had taken out the silver from two large teak chests, each piece in its separate royal blue monogrammed flannel bag tied with a silk drawstring. Franchot held up a large serving fork critically.

"Of course, this isn't the good silver," he said with a doleful shake of his head. His voice was deep, yet curiously funneled, perhaps with the effort of maintaining an almost impeccable British accent. "Mrs. Kaplan took that with her to the shore. It gives me the shudders to think how the Gorham is tarnishing next to that saltwater!"

He *is* a butler, thought Theresa, smiling despite her nervousness. Only a butler could get the shudders over tarnished silver.

"I'll do up a few pieces myself before I leave," said Franchot when they'd unveiled the last of the humbler silver, though to Theresa it all looked imposing. "Might as well start the table now; you'll need help with the extra leaves. Now if you'll just give me a hand with these pads." He loaded her arms and she followed him into the Chinese gold dining room.

They fitted in five extra leaves. Theresa had never seen such a gleaming expanse before. She touched the surface reverently. "It seems a shame to cover all this beautiful wood. Walnut, isn't it?"

But Franchot was already unfolding the felt-bottomed pads. "Cherry. Mr. Kaplan likes a cloth. So did Mrs. Marty. What linen are you using?"

"I thought the pale yellow."

Franchot cocked his head critically; though he had been born in the Bronx, never had he seemed more Empire. "I believe I should have chosen white. Yellow seems to me more suitable for spring or summer. However, I don't mean to teach you your business. By the way"—he nailed her suddenly with a cold blue eye—"where did you say you'd worked before Mr. Kaplan's?"

Theresa blinked. She hadn't said; she'd hoped he'd never ask, but of course how predictable that he should.

"The Cummingses," she said bravely, "and the Fraziers."

"Ah," said Franchot, as though measuring her credentials with his precise social calipers. "There, that's finished, ready for the cloth. Do you want to lay now, or tomorrow?"

"Now, I think. Yes, now. It's best to get everything done beforehand that you can." She hoped she sounded like an old pro.

Franchot nodded approval. "Then I'll start getting down the china for you. Some of it's stored so high that Mrs. Marty could never reach it, even with a ladder. Of course, you're a good deal taller than Mrs. Marty, but I'd better do it all the same."

"Thank you," said Theresa. Suddenly she felt more optimistic. Franchot had not reacted to the names of her "former employers." The books she'd purchased with her first weeks' salary—*Formal Dining, The Well-Dressed Table, Elegant Entertaining, Miss Manners Says,* Julia Child's *The French Chef Cookbook*—had proved extremely useful. Julia she found particularly comforting, grinning on the dust jacket as she brandished aloft a meat hammer in triumphant celebration of the massacres demanded by haute cuisine. Moreover, she had not only found an extra woman to help Franchot and Ann Moore with the serving and clearing, but had hit upon the idea of removing Elsa Frazier from the danger zone at her host's left by switching her placecard. She was beginning to feel she might get through the evening after all.

"What candlesticks will you be using?" said Franchot behind her.

"What?" Still, after all, that little thrill of dread. "Oh, I haven't decided. Any suggestions?"

"You don't have to have candles at all, of course; there's the chandelier and the wall lights. But Mr. Kaplan prefers candles, always has. So I'd suggest the branching silver candelabra, three pairs—they're always elegant. Or the Tiffany hurricanes, though they're not as formal. Or the six pairs of Romans, I call them—very nice, a trifle austere. Then there's the crystal—"

"The branching candelabra," said Theresa hastily. "You certainly know your way around here."

Franchot arranged the muscles around his mouth in what could almost be called a smile. "After all, I've been with Mr. Kaplan for many years. Ever since Mrs. Frazier lured me away from the Belgian Embassy back in 1972, I've worked for her and the Kaplans and the Judds. But now that I think of it, Theresa—if I may call you that? You never could have been a housekeeper for the Fraziers as you said you were. Because if you had been, we'd have been rubbing elbows at Number 15 Benton Place all these years, wouldn't we? As it is, I've never laid eyes on you before in my life."

Theresa heard the dreaded words through a roaring as though a Concorde were taking off inside her head. She stood there paralyzed, staring into Franchot's small pale eyes, clutching the counter behind her.

Franchot unswathed one of the candelabra from its flannel sweater and inspected it critically. "Needs a touch or two, might's well get at it now." He rolled up his sleeves. "Didn't work for the Cummingses either, did you?" he continued conversationally, slipping a polishing mitt over his hand. No toothbrushes, Theresa noted automatically, for John Franchot. "Because I'd have known if you had. We're a pretty cosy little club, you know, us old D.C. regulars—except for Marty; she kept to herself. You pulled the wool over her eyes, all right. But I'd say if anybody asked me—*which* they haven't—that you're new to the game. Oh, you're pretty good, I'll admit. You've got the kitchen organized just like downtown. But an old pro wouldn't be asking a butler's advice about laying the silver, would she? Or have forgotten to get in candles for tomorrow night?" He jerked open a drawer with his left hand and held up a box. "You've got exactly three left, and you're going to need at least two dozen. Glad I reminded you?"

"I needed this job," said Theresa, finding her voice. "Badly."

"It's none of my business," said Franchot loftily, "and I don't intend to go blabbing to anybody. It's your funeral. I just wanted you to know that you're not fooling *me.*" Holding the gleaming candelabra aloft, he made a regal exit.

By seven the next evening, the large drawing room was humming. Franchot opened the tall door to the Fraziers, the last to arrive because Elsa liked to make an entrance.

"Darling, how lovely!" She took quick little steps toward Ned, all she could manage in her extraordinarily tight midnight blue sequined gown. Her sunset hair had been blow-dried into startling proportions by the most fashionable coiffeur in Washington. "I've told Sam he can talk about anything tonight except the Senate confirmation. I'm sick of it! If I hear one more word about it, I'm going to throw up!" Laughter greeted her remark, as she had intended.

"That will never do," said Ned, kissing her firm white cheek. "I will certainly avoid the topic." He clapped her husband on the back. "Good to see you, Sam."

"Good to be here," said Sam, leaning forward automatically to catch a reply. "Good lord, what a crowd! Looks like you've raided the whole chicken coop."

"Not at all. Just a few valued friends."

At the words, he felt a glow as though he'd swallowed the sunshine of a rare old brandy. This party—these nineteen people sipping his Veuve-Cliquot, nibbling the caviar and smoked salmon canapés, laughing and chattering—had dispelled the black cloud that had hung over the house ever since . . . the September thing. Hung over not only the house but also over him, for there was no denying that during these long weeks he had walked in deep shadow. No appetite. Sleeping badly. No energy. The Foley woman had noticed it. Damn her observancy.

But tonight the dark cloud had miraculously lifted. They had all come; they had all kissed his cheek or pumped his hand; they were all just the same as before the September thing. So that actually—improbable as it seemed—it was as though nothing had happened at all. Listening to Sam, who had launched immediately and loudly into the topic of the Senate confirmation, the happy thought struck him so hard he raised his hand to his lips to hide his smile. Just as though nothing had happened at all. It hadn't, had it? That's what they were telling him, these familiar, warm, wonderful, colluding, ruthless, politic people sharing for a few hours his hearth and home. He lifted his head and surveyed the softly firelit room throbbing with perfume and laughter. He felt light as air.

The placecards, inscribed with gold ink by Dorothy Swerdlow's precise hand, fitted into crystal holders shaped like lyres. Theresa had distributed them around the table late that afternoon, the final touch except for three arrangements of lilies, fern, and freesia from Claussen's. Nancy Wylie sat at Ned Kaplan's right, Elena Rivera presided opposite him at the far end of the table, flanked by Robert Cohn and William Wylie. Isolating Elsa Frazier, then, had meant seating her at the far end next to either Cohn or Wylie. She had hesitated, then set Myra Schier's card at Ned's left and Elsa's next to Robert Cohn. At seven-forty-five she was supervising the assembly of another iced bowl of caviar in the kitchen when she realized with the impact of a hammer to the skull the consequences of seating Elsa Frazier anywhere but at her host's elbow. Seizing the guest list, she hurried into the dining room.

Franchot stood there, formidable in black cutaway coat and dazzling shirt front. He was holding Elsa Frazier's placecard in his hand.

"I know why you did it," he hissed, "but it won't fly!"

"I don't know what you're talking about," said Theresa briskly. She boldly snatched the square from his fingers. "I should know better than to trust the help with anything more complicated than chopping an onion, but then I always give the table a last inspection myself. There!" She flounced past him and reestablished Myra Schier in her proper place.

Franchot was not pacified. "Switching placecards! Any idea what would have happened if Frazier had found herself next to Cohn? No, of course you don't because you don't know the circuit. She detests the man!"

He followed her ruthlessly into the kitchen, which the chef from Ma Cuisine, though he looked a mere baby, completely dominated with his big flashing knife. In the butler's pantry, Franchot caught her arm.

"If you value your job, those cards better stay that way."

She shook herself free. "I consider the matter closed, Mr. Franchot," she said coldly. "Now please let me pass. I have work to do."

She went through the rest of the evening mechanically. Bursts of laughter exploded into the kitchen every time the dining room door swung inward; the dinner party evidently was going well. She was intensely aware of Franchot's ironic eye upon her, intensely aware that he knew the reason for the extra serving woman. Intensely aware that out in the dining room at any moment either Elsa Frazier or Ned Kaplan might launch the subject of housekeepers into the stream of conversation. But finally such acute apprehension numbed her; she discovered that she had lost interest in both her employer and the guest seated at his left. Let them find me out, she thought defiantly. I don't give a damn!

She let Ann Moore and the other helper go at eleven-thirty. The party was slowly breaking up. Franchot had canvassed the drawing room with a trayful of Courvoisier in big bubble glasses, had returned to the pantry with his tray only three glasses lighter, and had hurriedly gone to assist with coats and fur wraps. Calm was gradually moving into the house again like clear air after a thunderstorm. At midnight Theresa ventured out of the kitchen to collect glasses and plates from the drawing room, but stopped in the doorway.

Ned Kaplan was standing before the glowing remains of the birch-log fire with a slender blond woman dressed in black who looked somehow familiar. They were alone in the room, but even had the room been crowded, Theresa felt, they would have been alone in their absorp-

tion. They were not looking at each other—Ned Kaplan
seemed engrossed in trying to nip a stray bit of birch bark
with the fire tongs; the woman's head was bent contemplatively, a faint smile touching her lips. Yet they seemed
connected, as though invisible wires of sympathy criss-
crossed between them, binding them close. The woman
sighed, then turned her head in Theresa's direction, still
with that abstracted smile. Theresa retreated, but not
before she realized why the woman looked familiar. The
bent head, the stillness, the near smile—this was the
blond madonna in the triptych in the master bedroom
before whose image she suspected Ned Kaplan burned
votive candles at night.

"I believe your housekeeper wants me to leave," said
Nancy Wylie.

"Who?" Ned frowned; his thoughts were elsewhere.
"What are you talking about?"

"That rather attractive woman with a tray hovering—
at least, she *was* hovering—in the next room."

"You mean Foley?" said Ned irritably. "She'd better
back off. It's none of her business when my guests leave.
You may stay," he said with a slight, ironic bow, "until
the dawn comes up like thunder if you like. Is that Kip-
ling, by the way?"

"Must be. He was always thundering away." Nancy
covered a delicate yawn. "We must go, but it's been a
wonderful evening. You know, I've often wondered why
you've kept on living here in this palazzo all alone when
you could have a comfy condo right in our building if
you liked. But I'm not wondering anymore. This was entertainment on the grand scale tonight, Neddy. Bill and I
can't manage anything like it in our humble digs. All that

silver and crystal—I felt like Alice Keppel dining with the king!"

Ned had finally managed to trap the bit of birch bark between the tongs. He tossed it on the fire and watched the tongue curl; then he turned to her, "I'm glad you enjoyed the evening," he said soberly, "but believe it or not, I don't run this house just so I can throw two or three parties a year for my friends. Two years ago, in fact, I put this place on the market. But I took it off again."

"Really!" Nancy looked at him with interest. "You never told us that. Why did you decide not to sell?"

"Do you really want to know?"

"What a question! Of course I want to know."

"All right." It was Ned's turn now to stare into the distance, that convenient horizon resorted to by the shy, embarrassed, or guileful. He spoke rapidly. "Two years ago, when Bill had his near-fatal heart attack, I took the house off the market five minutes after you called in tears from Bethesda Hospital to say he was in intensive care. I pictured Bill dying, Nancy. And that was just the beginning. I pictured you turning from the grave and leaning on my arm. I pictured you marrying me and coming here to live. I pictured a twenty-foot Christmas tree in the foyer and your children coming home here for the holidays. I thought of us spending long lazy Sundays by the pool. I thought of you on evenings like this facing me down the table, being gracious to our guests as only you know how to be. I thought of making love to you in my admittedly humble bed. I thought of us finally finishing what we started so long ago. And then Bill sat up and recovered and came home to you, and you did not come here to me." His voice rasped as it rose with emotion.

Nancy touched the sleeve of his black dinner jacket.

"You wanted him to die?" she said fearfully.

"I wanted you, and his death might have given you to me." He looked at her for the first time.

"Oh, Ned, for God's sake." Nancy tossed her head impatiently. "You really, *really* don't understand, do you. I *hate* this ache of the past, this eternal conjuring up of the days when we were all so young, and knew and expected so little, and nothing mattered—"

"And now we are old," said Ned. His mouth clenched bitterly. "And expect even less."

"No, you're wrong. We expect a great deal. Bill does of me, you know. And I do of—" She broke off, overwhelmed by a new thought. "And so all those years with Carol, all those twenty-five years . . ." She bit her lip and turned her head away as her husband and Bob Cohn came into the room. Bob Cohn's hand rested fraternally on Bill Wylie's tall shoulder, which he could just reach; Bill cradled a brandy snifter in a cautiously celebratory way.

"Nothing like a little business to cap pleasure," said Bob. "I think Bill and I finally have solved a particularly bitter financial argument."

Ned raised his eyebrows, but Bill was looking at his wife, who had snatched up a black beaded evening bag from a chair and seemed intensely absorbed in its contents.

The Wylies were the last to leave. Though he'd been on his feet for seven hours, Franchot stood at the door, ramrod straight. They were not aware of him; he was used to that. It meant that he was doing his job. Ned took Bill's hand.

"I don't know how to say this, but I think you know what this evening has meant to me," he said, his voice rasping again with emotion, "and how grateful I am for your part in it. Both your parts—"

Bill cut him off kindly. "It's morning, man—spare us the rhetoric. Nancy and I enjoyed ourselves tremendously, didn't we, sweetheart? Hell, everybody enjoyed themselves. You're the host with the most. And so to bed."

Ned watched them walk side by side through the misty arcs of the outdoor lamps to the gate where Morrison was waiting with the car. How probable, how right they looked together. He lifted his face to the invisible sky. The air was thick with autumn damp and rot. Nancy had not even said good-bye.

"Well, Franchot, you've done it again."

Franchot knew he had, but he said, "Hardly, sir, but it appeared to be a very successful evening."

"Thanks to you and Foley. She still here, by the way?"

"She is still doing the Spode by hand. I hate to say it, but if I hadn't stepped in, I think she might have put it in the dishwasher." Franchot's tone expressed disbelief.

Ned laughed. "Have to ride shotgun on Foley, do you?" Franchot was indeed a gem.

He found Theresa in the pantry drying dessert plates. He could not compliment her now on looking well, certainly; she was pale, haggard. She had laid aside her glasses on the counter, and there were dark shadows beneath her eyes.

"You've worked long enough, Theresa. Marty always left some of the cleaning up for the next day—damned sensible. It's very late. Why don't you stay the night? You could use Marty's old room, right at the top of the . . . stairs."

Theresa stared at him, fascinated. He had tripped just the fraction of a beat on the last word. It might mean simply fatigue, or it might mean that he had cared about Mary Jane a little after all. At the thought, the tense lines about her mouth and eyes relaxed a little.

"Thank you, Mr. Kaplan. That's very kind, but I'd rather go home. I'm almost finished up here and I'll just call a cab." She had not brought her car because she hated driving at night; besides, parking in Georgetown was impossible.

"You don't have a car? That settles it. I'll take you home myself. Least I can do. Wait here while I get the car."

"No!" she said quickly. "I couldn't possibly let you." Quite apart from the fact that she did not at this, her lowest ebb, want to be closeted in a car with Ned Kaplan, he could *not* take her home; he would certainly recognize Knox Circle or the house. On her application Theresa had given a false address, one within the 301 telephone area code but far enough away that if Ned Kaplan saw it, he would not connect her address with Mary Jane's. "No, please!" she said again too vehemently and immediately thought she saw a flicker of recognition in his eyes. He knows who I am, she cried silently; he's playing with me; he knows exactly why I don't want him to drive me home.

"That won't be necessary, sir." Franchot broke in smoothly. "I'm going Mrs. Foley's way. No trouble at all."

Theresa looked at him in astonishment. Franchot could have no idea where she lived. "No, please," she said. "I want to take a cab." Emphatically, she did not want either of them driving her home.

Franchot shook his head. "Cabs these days aren't necessarily safe late at night," he said with authority. "Woman abducted into Virginia in a cab and molested just the other day."

"Raped and strangled, I think you mean." Ned Kaplan looked at Theresa ironically as he spoke as though to say, "You're one of these modern women: you can take it."

"I'll drive you home," said Franchot again. He flashed a ring of keys to end the argument.

"No, really—"

"Excellent," said Ned Kaplan. His was the final word after all. "That's settled then, and I'll say good night." Yet Theresa was sure she heard disappointment in his voice, the disappointment of a man denied his moment of power. For that is certainly what he would have enjoyed when he'd pulled into the Circle and turned to her and smiled and said, "I think I've been here before. Come to think of it, you look rather like her. Why didn't you tell me you were the girl's mother?" Power—tremendous power.

Instead, he was holding out his hand. "Thank you both for making this evening such a success. I knew I could rely on you. Don't bother locking up. I'll see to it myself."

No farewell could have been more correct.

Franchot drove a low, sporty new red Camaro, the last kind of car Theresa would have associated with the rigid butler.

"All right, Theresa," he said, gunning the motor with a roar, "what *is* your way?"

"I thought you knew."

"Not really. I just wanted to save Mr. Kaplan the trouble. No matter how hard we work, the pressure is on the host."

"How considerate you are!" Her tone was barbed. "And it would have been trouble for him, too. I live out in Silver Spring."

"Know it well." Franchot made an U-turn at the corner, the motor roaring in frustration under his brake. "Old stomping ground." He sounded like a swinger gone cautious. She wondered tiredly if Franchot was his real name.

They drove in silence, navigating an almost 360-degree turn around Sheridan Circle into Massachusetts, then Florida Avenue. He sat stiffly upright in the sporty bucket seat; she could build a house between his back and the leather. She was exhausted, still angry about her gaff with the placecards, still shaken by Kaplan's and Franchot's overbearing insistence that they drive her home. But she wanted to sound out Franchot, take his measure. She didn't trust him for a moment not to run to Ned Kaplan with the news that she had lied about working for the Fraziers and the Cummingses. That would be, she judged, right in his line. On the other hand, like an acrophobic who can't resist looking over the precipice, she wanted to ask him about that night. And that she couldn't do directly; she would have to placate him first, get him on her side. The man was formidably competent, she had decided, but also very vain. Perhaps she could appeal to both qualities.

"You know," she said, deliberately crossing a leg since he'd admired them. "I really thought you wanted to do me in tonight. When you found Frazier's placecard down where Schier was supposed to be. Maybe you did." In the

unreal yellow fog of the arc lights, she could not read his
expression.

She had flicked him; he snorted like a horse. "Do you
in? Use your head! I was trying to save your pathetic
skin. What would have happened if old Elsa *hadn't* sat
next to the boss? I can tell you what. Bloody mayhem!
And who'd of been blamed? I can tell you that, too—
Mrs. Theresa Foley! 'Well, she was *your* housekeeper,' I
can hear him saying, 'why didn't you teach her better?'
'*My* housekeeper?' says Elsa—and the game's up for
sure. I was trying to save your bloody neck tonight,
Foley. Not that you'll ever thank me for it."

"Why did you bother?" Surprise made Theresa blunt.

She sensed his shrug. "Arter all," he said, dropping
into a nasty pseudo-Cockney whine, "us workin' clarsis
arta stick t'gither. By that I mean, Foley, you've gotta
hell of a lot to learn. For instance, what kind of wine did I
serve after nine o'clock?"

Theresa racked her brains to remember the wine order.
"Chateau Margaux."

"You're an innocent, you know that? A genuine innocent. Touching, in a way. No, not Chateau Margaux, Innocent, but a wine from Chile that tastes almost like the
real thing. I get it from my special wholesaler for $4.99 a
bottle compared to $24.99 for the real Margaux. By nine
o'clock the guests don't know the difference, and neither
does the Boss. That's a twenty-three-dollar profit per
bottle for old Franchot, which—since Kaplan ordered
three cases of Margaux, one of which he got—amounts
to a nice take for the evening of five hundred and seventy-
six smackers." Franchot's British speech, Theresa noted
ironically, even while listening with fascination, had
taken a Bronx holiday. "My wholesaler gets a nice cut; I

get a *very* nice cut, and you, Foley, if you knew your business, could also be turning a tidy little profit."

"What do you mean, if I knew my business?"

"I mean, Innocent, turnabout is fair play. Marty didn't train you all that good, did she! Ma Cuisine charges eighteen hundred plus for the six courses we served tonight—three hundred bucks a course. Kaplan's secretary goes over the bills and wants to see Ma Cuisine on the list. But Marty knows a place that'll put on the same feed for a third of the price. Hell, her sister-in-law runs it! So you order a course from Ma Cuisine, just to be legit, then you fill in the bill for eighteen hundred when you've only paid Sis-in-law six hundred bucks out of your own pocket. And somehow—just somehow!—you pocket the difference at the end of the month. And then you pass a bit on to old Franchot, seeing as how I did you a favor with the wine. See?" He stretched his thin lips almost to a grin.

"That's dishonest," said Theresa, genuinely shocked.

"So it is," he said contemptuously. "And they expect it of us, let me tell you. We wouldn't want to let them down."

She reminded herself that she was trying to win him to her side. "I suppose you know best, a man with your expertise. You must think I'm terribly naive."

"Well," said Franchot, relenting, "you're new at the game. I dare say you'll catch on fast."

Theresa took advantage of the friendlier tone. "By the way, something odd happened the other day. One of the extra help showed up at the back door looking for Mrs. Marty. Stephanie Ruso. She'd been trying to get her on the phone."

Franchot shrugged, bored. "I have nothing to do with the hired help. Anyway, what's so odd? Except for the fact that Marty can't be got because she's on her way to sunny Cal. Sunny Cal! Quakes, firestorms, mud slides, race riots, and smog. You couldn't pay me to live there."

"What's odd," pursued Theresa, "is that Stephanie wanted to talk about Mr. Kaplan's big party. In September." She glanced at him and knew by the closing of his hands on the wheel that he vividly remembered the night. "The night the girl fell down the stairs and died. She claims she was the first to find her."

Franchot did not take his eyes off the road, but she felt a stillness settle over him. He didn't like or trust her. He had been flirting with her, she realized; no more.

"What party?" he asked coldly. Damned women! The night replayed itself in his head like a bad black-and-white film. But it had not been the body at the foot of the stairs that had shaken him. Rather, it was the phone call the next morning—Robert Cohn wanting to know whether he, Franchot, had advised Kaplan to check on a guest who was ill in the library. No, certainly he had not: He knew nothing of a sick guest and, ignorant, obviously could not have advised Mr. Kaplan. "Ah," Cohn had breathed, as though satisfied. Something was up then, but, though he padded wine bills, it was not his business to speculate about his employers' personal affairs.

Now he said with the hauteur for which he knew he was famous, "What girl who died? Why do you listen to the kitchen?" He spat out the words like garbage.

"She wouldn't tell me; she ran off with some excuse. But she seemed upset—afraid. I thought it strange."

"Hysterical," said Franchot more coldly. "Women are. I wouldn't give it a second thought."

"No, I suppose not," she said, biting back the retort he deserved. "I must say, though, that I've sometimes wondered whether Mrs. Marty's leaving had anything to do with what happened that night." Theresa realized this was landmine territory. "From one or two things she said—"

"So that's what's buzzing in your brain! I might have known. First place, I don't believe for a minute Marty *said* anything, because there was nothing to say. Husband's been at her for years about heading for Tucson or San Diego. Bad asthma, can't stand the humidity here, never could. Besides, Marty's not the type to go to pieces because some chippie breaks her neck on the stairs. Accidents happen. So that's the answer to your wondering! What's the address?"

"Four Knox Circle. Along Highview Avenue a few blocks, then right." "Chippie" was a new one; from the tone of his voice, it meant "cheap." Just what Ned Kaplan had said: "nobody important." She clenched her fists.

He slowed the Camaro to a crawl along the deserted street, pulled cautiously into the Circle and around to No. 4, geared to park in front of the small brick house, and turned to her. Under the streetlight his face was green and sharp.

"Learned something tonight, have you, Innocent?" He sneered, not unpleasantly. "Trust old Franchot."

Theresa jumped out of the car and slammed the door. Patronizing her—a butler! Then she yanked the car door open and thrust in her head. "I've learned to cheat, lie, and not to ask questions," she said pleasantly through her teeth. "Is that what you mean?"

"You're bright," said Franchot. He nodded approvingly. "We'll get along."

The Camaro padded off in a circumspect way.

CHAPTER TWELVE

She woke sweating and blinking at the bald strips of sunlight framing the window shades. She struggled up, tugging at the nightgown that wound her like a bandage. She hadn't dreamed of him for years. She could remember her father decked out handsomely in black tuxedo and red carnation for an evening in the good days when she'd had velvet dresses with lace collars for Sundays and her parents had come back tanned and laughing from Caribbean holidays. The good days—the years before Theresa's tenth birthday, before he'd lost the franchise because he'd speculated with the profits, hoping to buy still another dealership, but instead bankrupting the first and himself. He ended up an employee for the business he had once owned, that is, until he started to drink and could no longer be relied upon to deal with customers, after which—following still more lurches down the ladder—he ended as a night janitor, wandering with bucket and pail through showrooms like those he'd once owned. The physical abuse had intensified then, especially after supper when he'd had four or five under his belt and was sitting at the kitchen table unshaven, marking time before leaving for the night. After Theresa had missed ten or eleven days during the semester because her eye was closed or her lips swollen shut, the principal himself came around one afternoon after school. Theresa hid in a closet with her fingers in her ears, which failed to deaden her father's roar and the principal's increasingly high-pitched indignation. But the upshot had been that she and her mother had moved out. And that had been the end of Daddy, who moved away and bumped farther down the ladder till he hit bottom and a letter came from Florida saying he was dead.

Yet he'd given her some kind of vision that had not quite faded when he vanished, a yearning for a world lost when she lost him.

In the living room Matt was on his stomach on the rug reading the Sunday comics just the way he'd done when he was a kid, chin propped on fists, big feet wagging in space. The elbows of his sweatshirt were smudged with newsprint. He glared up at her accusingly. "You said we'd go out for breakfast, and it's afternoon."

She'd forgotten all about going out for breakfast. What a stupid promise after a grueling evening. "It's not afternoon," she said, squinting at her wrist, "it's only half past ten. We can still go."

He rolled over and held up a skinny arm weighted with a baseball-sized watch. "Yours stopped," he said scornfully. "Yours always stops. It's ten past twelve."

"Then we'll call it brunch," said Theresa with a briskness she did not feel. "And you'd better get a move on. You're not dressed yourself."

He refused to go to the cemetery with her after they'd

eaten; or more precisely, he put up such a clamor about watching the ballgame with Todd that she gave in. She dropped him in front of the house and sped away, feeling again the bleeding of old wounds. He'd acted as though he didn't care at all, even though she would never forget the way he'd held her hand, manfully, at the burial service. Oh, let it go, Terry! she told herself angrily, drumming her fingers as she waited for a light. The young don't care about death. Care! They know nothing about it. Her agonized decision to bury Mary Jane without embalming so she would go quickly to earth (she couldn't shake off her old Catholic prejudice against cremation) had been met with indifference by Matt. "Why not?" he'd said on his way out the door. "Anyway, everybody knows cemeteries are an environmental disaster."

The drive down Georgia Avenue seemed endless. She made a quick turn off the avenue to the blare of a crowding horn and drove through white gates standing open in inevitable welcome. Right or left? She turned left and immediately felt disoriented in the flat green expanse blooming here and there with bright knots of flowers. She had not visited the gravesite more than twice, though she had the number and row of Mary Jane's grave on a slip of paper next to her. As she crawled down the white alleys at five miles per hour, nothing looked familiar. Finally she pulled over and got out of the car. She was sweating in the close damp air, still struggling among cobwebs of dreams, wide awake but lost in the still landscape of death.

In the farthest reaches of the cemetery there were monuments and obelisks instead of flat stones. Her eye caught a blooming mound of pink, and she walked toward it, eager for any point of reference. When she came

upon the grave, she saw it was no simple monument but a
Hollywood production. The dead girl's photograph in
living 3D technicolor under convex glass bulged out of
sparkling pink marble like half a fishbowl; wide-set
brown eyes, water-smooth hair, peony cheeks, and a pet-
ulant mouth. Two trophy cups also embedded in the
stone commemorated second and third place at the Bethesda Junior Horse Trials; a riding crop, embalmed in
Plexiglas, rested below. Marble cherubs playing pipes
flanked the headstone, straining pearly ears toward the
photograph for a word of approval from those dissatisfied lips. At the foot of the blanket of pink carnations
flung like a prom cape over the shoulders of the tomb,
humbler plastic flowers of red, white, and blue bloomed
scentlessly under domes of glass. Two silver heart-shaped
helium balloons floating chin-high in the still air announced, DEBI SUE, WE LOVE YOU. In the stone above
Debi's photograph were carved—unnecessarily—the
words NEVER FORGOTTEN.

Theresa turned away in disgust at the perverse ostentation, wondering whether her parents had actually loved
spoiled Debi Sue. But at last she'd got a clue to Mary
Jane: down this road to the first crossing, then right.
When she'd parked the car and got out and laid the trite
sidewalk-bought sheaf of flowers in its bright green
waxed paper on the plain stone, her tears came. They
jumped between her fingers, wetting throat, hands, and
the front of her jacket; they defied handkerchiefs, Kleenex, and her sleeve. Through the storm of weeping, she
sobbed over and over, "I'll make him pay, I'll make him
pay!" Yet it was not until she later opened her own front
door to the roar of whatever fans cheering whatever Sun-

day game that she realized what she meant. She knew that she must find and talk to Stephanie Ruso.

Since Georgetown University did not give out students' addresses over the phone, Theresa with great trouble had to get ahold of a directory at the Graduate Office. She stood on the porch of an old three-story house with peeling lime green paint, hanging shutters, and a slumping porch and wondered whether the ancient doorbell she'd been pressing still functioned. Stephanie's name decorated a rusting mailbox with half a dozen others. It must be a sort of boarding house or commune, thought Theresa with an irrational shudder, reminded of the Sixties, which, as a Catholic school teenager, still impressed her as a psychedelic devil's dance. She hammered on the door. When this effort brought no response, she tried the door itself and found herself in a dark hallway heavy with rancid cooking oil and the dullingly sweet smell of what she suspected was marijuana. Four doors gave off the hall; she chose the first one and knocked.

"Mel's out," said a soft voice above her, and she looked up to see looking down at her a young man with a new beard stippling his chin and long black hair falling into his eyes.

"Actually, I'm looking for Stephanie," said Theresa. "Stephanie Ruso."

"Steph's on third."

Theresa hesitated. "Shall I go up? Is she there?"

The young man smiled sleepily, shrugged, and disappeared. Feeling very much the intruder, Theresa began to climb. The chipped brown steps revealed a green undercoat and beneath that blotchy yellow. She shuddered, sensing phalanxes of cockroaches fleeing like a dark

cloud across the peeling walls. On the third floor she
found a door with the initials *S.D.R.* typed on a dirty
card inserted in a bent brass frame. She knocked again.
Stephanie, looking as if she'd been missing a lot of beauty
sleep, answered the door.

"Theresa Foley," Theresa reminded her. "Mr. Kaplan's new housekeeper. Mind if I come in?"

"What do you want?" said Stephanie, not budging.

"Just to talk. I won't stay long. I know you're busy."

Stephanie opened the door just wide enough for
Theresa to squeeze in and stood eying her warily in the
midst of chaos—books and papers everywhere, sweat-
shirts and underwear festooning chairs. The bed was
populated by a menagerie of stuffed animals who apparently accompanied Stephanie each night into dreamland.
Eying a bowl of hardening cereal remains on the floor
next to the bed, Theresa stopped being sorry that Stephanie no longer did kitchen work. She looked around for a
place to sit and did not find one. "I'd still like to know
why you couldn't help out on the twenty-sixth."

Stephanie folded short arms across a bosomy sweatshirt. "I told you, I've got another kind of job now. I
thought I made that clear."

"Yes, that's what you said. But I got the idea the other
day that there's more to it than that. You seemed awfully
upset about what happened the last time you worked at
Mr. Kaplan's, upset enough to want to talk to Mrs.
Marty about it. Is that why you won't work for me now,
because of the girl dying on the stairs?"

"That's crazy. I told you, I've got another job."

"What if I said I don't believe you?"

Stephanie was very busy propping assorted cats and
rabbits against the bulky bed pillows. A large rusty teddy

bear missing an eye did a one and a half gainer onto the floor, but she was too distraught to notice. She picked up the cereal bowl and disappeared with it into an alcove; she came out armed with the oatmeal sweater and the bookbag. The door slammed behind her before Theresa realized she was gone.

She stood there, mortified, in the middle of the room staring at posters of U2, Jimmy Buffett, and Santa Fe stuck up with strips of dirty tape; smelling overripe athletic shoes; feeling the thud of New Age drumbeats kicking the floor. Thank God Mary Jane had not had to live like this, she thought: thank God she'd stayed at home and gone to a perfectly good business school nearby. But then she remembered that Mary Jane had left home and was dead and that Stephanie Ruso, who certainly knew something, was alive and putting distance between them. Theresa ran, forgetting to shut the door behind her.

She stood on the pavement looking up and down the street. Rain had washed the muggy air clean; amber light suffused the sky; arcs of pale streetlights glimmered wanly in the dusk. To the left, a blank line of houses; to the right, a cluster of neon signs beginning to pulse as though waking up for the night. She turned right. She passed a laundromat where a lone man in combat fatigues sat reading with his boots up on one of the machines, an Italian deli, a video rental, a pub called The Sportsman's Bar, a soft custard stand. At the corner she stopped and went back to The Sportsman's Bar. Thick red curtains masked the windows. The handle was a baseball bat bolted to the door. She pushed the heavy slab open with both hands and walked in.

Five people, none of them Stephanie Ruso, hunched on stools at the bar watching TV. Theresa found her

squeezed into the far corner of the last of the old-
fashioned wooden booths that lined the wall. Stephanie
stared at her incredulously. A line of foam frosted her
upper lip; she was drinking a beer.

She wiped her mouth with the back of her hand.
"You're persecuting me," she said. Her face was hostile.
"I can take legal action."

"Crap! Don't pass off your phobias on me! You
started all this by coming to the house the other day.
When I asked you in a perfectly reasonable way what was
on your mind, you bolted like a stung horse. Just now in
your room when I tried to talk to you—you bolted again.
What's coming off?"

"Nothing," said Stephanie sullenly.

Theresa signaled the bartender for two beers. She
leaned back against the hard plastic padding of the
booth. Funny how she'd thought booths cozy when she
was young.

"I'm Mary Jane Jones's mother."

Stephanie took a long time with this piece of information. Finally she said carefully, as though trying each
word on for size, "You mean the girl's. The girl that
night."

"Yes."

"I don't get it. Why are you working for that guy?"

"Kaplan?"

"Yes."

"That doesn't matter. I want you to tell me about the
party. I want you to tell me what was so urgent about
seeing Mrs. Marty. What happened?"

"I don't want another beer," said Stephanie. "I've got
to go." She humped toward the end of the booth, shoving
her backpack along the table in front of her.

Theresa caught her arm. "No, you don't! Not again. *Please!* Have a little common humanity! Don't you understand? My daughter's dead. I've got to know."

For a moment they remained locked, Stephanie twisted, half on her feet, Theresa gripping her arm. Then Stephanie sank down and shook off Theresa's hand. "Shit!" She threw the backpack into the corner. "Well, just remember you asked for it." She pushed up her sweater sleeves and leaned across the table, shoulders hunched, her square face working with the effort. "I know he killed her."

Theresa sank back against the booth. Suddenly she was aware of high-pitched laughter at the bar, the pounding of the jukebox, the chinking of glass. The bartender placed two coasters on the table and set their beers on top of them.

"Running a tab?" he asked cheerfully. When neither woman answered, he walked back to the bar, whistling.

Stephanie gulped her beer. The floodgates had burst. "I haven't slept a wink since it happened. Just kidding, but no—no kidding—it's been absolute hell. Last week I flunked an *exam* because I couldn't concentrate. I've lost seven pounds. And I haven't even started my paper. I can't believe that anything could get to me this way. Even my dad's death—and I found him—didn't hit me like this. Was it really your daughter?"

"Yes. What makes you think he killed her?"

"I don't think. I know! That's why I wanted to talk to Marty, somebody who knows Kaplan, to ask her what I should do. You see, I saw him."

Theresa's head was pounding in rhythm to the jukebox. She made a path with her thumb down the side of the glass of beer she wasn't drinking. "Tell me about it, Stephanie."

"Like I said, Marty sent me out to get another tray of appetizers from the freezer in the back hall. I was going to get them when I heard people talking at the top of the stairs and I recognized his voice, Kaplan's."

"How did you know it was him?"

"I've talked with him a couple times, once at least, and I've heard him talking to Marty and the butler. It's a funny voice, with a kind of scrape in it, you know what I mean? And I heard a woman's voice too."

"Well?"

"Well, I thought it was *weird*, you know? I mean, what's Kaplan and some woman doing up there when his big party's going on downstairs? I thought I must be hallucinating, so I go, Why not just take a look? Aren't you drinking that beer? Thanks. So I did. And there they are. At the top of the stairs. It was pretty dark, but I could see that she was blond. She had on a glittery dress, pink maybe or white. And I heard what she said. She said, 'You can't do this to me. I know too much'—or something totally unreal, you know, the kind of thing people say on the tube."

"Then what did you do?"

"Nothing! I was feeling definitely out of place. The last thing I wanted was them finding me listening. I went and got the trays out of the freezer, and then—God, it was awful—I heard this sound of falling, like something broken bouncing off the walls all the way down. And then I saw her lying there. I knew she was dead."

Theresa gripped the table. "But you did not see Kaplan push her."

"I didn't have to! One minute they're up there together, the next minute she's lying there with her neck broken."

"Conceivably," Theresa spoke slowly through the tunnel of a violent headache, "conceivably he left her at the top of the stairs and went away and she started down and fell. The stairs are very steep and badly lighted. I know because I occasionally use them myself."

"Then why did he lie and say the last time he saw her was in the library? That's what he told Marty and Marty told me. Come on, he didn't leave her! Not the way they were talking. It was heavy weather up there, I can tell you, real heavy."

"Oh, God," said Theresa, closing her eyes.

"You see? I didn't want to tell you, but you made me." Stephanie sighed deeply and drained the last of the beer. "Actually I feel better now that I have. It's been one big nightmare. I can't get it out of my head—that murdering bastard! What are you going to do?"

Theresa opened her eyes slowly. Stephanie was looking almost cheerful. Catharsis, what a fine old thing it was. She had told her tale, shifted the burden.

"I have to think about this," said Theresa. Red bolts of pain volleyed back and forth behind her eyeballs.

"You don't believe me?" Stephanie was clearly offended.

"I believe you saw what you said you saw. And heard. That's all I can say now."

"Then you're not going to the police?"

"Would the police believe your story? Would it put Kaplan behind bars? But I can't talk about it now."

"I definitely think you should see a lawyer."

Theresa prayed for calm. "Look, I've got your number and here's where you can reach me." She pulled her checkbook out of her purse, tore off a deposit slip, and wrote down the Kaplan number and her home phone. "We'll be in touch. And thank you, Stephanie, for telling me. I know it wasn't easy."

Unexpectedly, Stephanie squeezed her shoulder. "I'm real sorry about your daughter."

Theresa realized that she owed for three beers and was going to be violently sick.

CHAPTER THIRTEEN

Theresa did not run to Holly Bauer in triumph with Stephanie's story. Why she did not she hardly understood herself. It was as though now that she had proof of the truth of Mary Jane's *I think he could be dangerous,* she had lost the need to convince Holly that her suspicions had been right. Partly it was because her nervous system still reverberated from the shock of Stephanie's revelation. She was too shaken to act. Contacting the only lawyer she knew occurred to her, but he had been on Dan's side in the divorce and she could not imagine him treating her seriously or fairly. Of course there were other lawyers. . . . And the police.

Two days later, she knew she must somehow act on Stephanie's information. She consulted the Yellow Pages and discovered that there was a Precinct Seven not far away, on Wisconsin Avenue and Volta Place. She knew nothing about contacting the police beyond dialing 911, but it seemed to make sense that a Georgetown police station would be concerned about something that had happened in Georgetown. She decided to call Stephanie after Ned Kaplan left and ask her to meet her there.

She had thought she could not face Ned Kaplan again, but she had been wrong. She had gone through the motions impeccably. He couldn't see her heart, clenched like a fist of hatred against him. This morning, unaccountably, he lingered after breakfast, tapping his fingers on the glass table, gazing abstractedly out onto the patio. "It was a mistake, that pool," he said to her without turning his head when she came to remove the remains. "No one should try to turn Georgetown into the suburbs."

She was so surprised at this, the first unbusinesslike remark he'd ever made in her presence, that she had nothing to say. Instead she looked at her watch. "Won't you be late, Mr. Kaplan?"

He took time consulting his own watch. "Do you know what is the occupational hazard of housekeepers, Theresa?" he asked, raising an eyebrow.

"No, I don't."

He brought his fist down on the glass table with a crash. "I'll tell you then. They get overconfident. They get smug. They begin to think they know their employer's business better than their employer. Recognize the syndrome? Good morning!"

The Mercedes roared out of the drive.

Loading the dishwasher, she smiled, delighted to have angered him. "The occupational hazard of housekeepers"—it was good, that language. Classy. She liked it. Too bad it came from the mouth of a murderer.

She reached Stephanie at quarter to nine.

"I'm just on my way to class." Stephanie sounded remote, as though she were talking from the moon.

"But you'll meet me today, won't you? I've been thinking of nothing else since our talk, and I know we've got to go to the police with your evidence."

"Listen, Theresa, you don't understand. I'm flunking out because of this damned thing! If I miss another class, I'm dead in the water."

"But you can't have classes all day. Come on, Stephanie, don't let me down now. I'll meet you at the Seventh Precinct at Wisconsin and Volta Place. You name the time."

"Well, okay," said Stephanie finally, just as Theresa was wondering whether she was still on the line. "Two o'clock. But I don't like it. I'd much rather talk to a lawyer. It's not that I'm not concerned; it's just that—"

"I know," said Theresa decisively. "I'll see you there. And Stephanie, *thanks.*"

Theresa locked the door behind her at one-thirty, and saw Mario at the gate.

"I am doing the pruning today," he said as she let him in. As usual his large brown eyes looked perplexed. "Mr. Kaplan say the backyard looks like a jungle. But then if I do the pruning, what about all the raking needs done?" He waved his hand at the rich red tapestry of leaves woven by a maple.

"I wouldn't worry, Mario; it will all get done." Oh, to have only the problem of whether to prune or rake to solve. "I'm running an errand," she said, not at all certain that she needed to explain her movements to the yardman, but she liked him and wanted to be friendly. "I'll be back before you leave."

"That's all right." He grinned suddenly. "Maybe you go to the movies, maybe you put a little something on the horse! Take your time. I don't care!"

If it were only that, thought Theresa grimly, letting

herself out through the black wrought-iron gate. Dread
was settling heavily on her stomach. She had not decided
whether to admit or not that she was Mary Jane's mother
or how to explain her presence in Ned Kaplan's house if
she did. And she was not at all sure that the police would
credit Stephanie Ruso's word against the word of one of
Washington's most prominent bankers and citizens.

But when she arrived at the corner of Wisconsin and
Volta, she found only an old brick building newly
painted olive-gray with coral trim. Surely this was no police station! Through a window with bars, she saw one
woman working at a computer under fluorescent lights;
the other windows were dark and, when she peered inside, she saw that the rooms were empty. Iron bars suggested a jail, but there was no other sign that the building
was connected with the law. Should she ask the woman at
the computer whether this was Precinct Seven? All her
courage seemed to have evaporated. She already felt like
a fool. She glanced at her watch. Only one forty-five; she
must have flown. Fifteen minutes until Stephanie would
arrive to find that she had come on a useless errand.

She looked up and down Wisconsin Avenue, a street of
trendy businesses largely catering to Georgetown and
Georgetown University students. She must wait, of
course. A bus going up Wisconsin pulled over to the opposite curb with a gasp of brakes. She scanned the decanted passengers, but Stephanie was not among them.
She waited three more minutes, then caught sight of a
heavy, dark-haired person in jeans waiting across the
street for traffic. The girl started across briskly. Stephanie
isn't brisk, thought Theresa, waving again even as she
realized that the young woman approaching looked
nothing like Stephanie Ruso.

She waited until two-fifteen, then decided to call from a public telephone.

"Steph's out." She connected the soft voice with the young man she'd met on the stairs.

"Do you know where?" She pressed her hand against her right ear, trying to block out traffic. "She's supposed to be meeting me. We had an appointment at two."

"Is this Theresa Foley?"

"Yes."

"Just a minute. I've got a message here for you." The receiver clunked, then was picked up again. "Ready? It says, 'Theresa, I just can't get involved. I'm flunking out, no kidding, and I've got to get away by myself for awhile and think and study. Please let me alone. I'm sorry.' "

"Is that all?"

"That's all."

"Look, I've got to talk to her. Can't you call her to the phone?"

"Steph's gone."

"What do you mean?"

"Split," said the soft voice patiently, "out of here, history."

"I don't believe you!"

"Sorry," said the voice even more gently. The receiver clicked in her ear.

How could she! she raged, storming blindly through the warm, still October afternoon back to Q Street, skidding on leaves that slicked the old brick pavement, butting into an elderly man carrying a curly white dog. How could she have betrayed me! But by the time she let herself back in the silent house, she had got her anger under control. She had been deceived to think that Stephanie

Ruso would ever go to the police with her story. And deceived to have thought for a minute that the police would
believe it—wherever their location. She could hear the
hard skepticism in their voices, the finality with which
they would dismiss her. I've been a fool she told herself
again bitterly. As though she could ever touch somebody
as powerful as Ned Kaplan. She could not even get
within striking distance.

She went into the butler's pantry to prepare the tray
for his supper. At that moment she thought of the night
of the party and Ned Kaplan discovering her after the
guests had left, exhausted in the butler's pantry. Marty
always left some of the cleaning up for the next morning.
Damned sensible idea. It's very late. Why don't you stay
the night? You could use Marty's old room, right at the
top of the stairs. Striking distance. She hadn't meant it in
the physical sense, of course. And yet . . .

Ned Kaplan was bound to give more parties: He
seemed, incongruously, that kind of man. Inevitably he
would ask her to stay the night again. If not, she could
suggest staying herself.

She laid the tray with the good china and pulled a linen
napkin through his silver napkin ring. Then she went into
the kitchen, sat down at the table, pulled her notepad toward her, and automatically began jotting down the
week's grocery list: lamb chops, cooking sherry, green
beans if fresh, shiitake mushrooms, cucumbers, shallots.
She laid down her pen.

Striking distance.

But all November and early December passed without
Ned Kaplan entertaining again or even suggesting entertainment. On the contrary, from the number of times she

was obliged to send his black-tie evening wear to the cleaners, she knew he was being entertained handsomely elsewhere. Then on the morning of December 12, he announced he was leaving the next day for an international banking conference in Tokyo, and going on from there to Thailand for the first real vacation he'd allowed himself in three years.

Theresa, who was sitting at the little Sheraton secretary in one of the lesser drawing rooms with the checkbook open before her and a stack of bills at her elbow, went very still. "When do you expect to be back, Mr. Kaplan?" she asked deferentially.

"Not until after the holidays. It won't be a real vacation, of course—I'll be in touch with Washington every day." He belted his trenchcoat with a scowl of dissatisfaction at the lack of slack and picked up his black leather attaché case with EDK stamped in gold. "Goodbye, Theresa."

"But Mr. Kaplan!" Theresa caught him in the next room. "What am *I* supposed to do?"

He looked surprised. "I'd forgotten. You're still new, aren't you." He jiggled the attaché case impatiently against his knee. "It's a compliment to you that I keep forgetting it. I don't see any reason to keep the house open while I'm gone. The Agency will keep tabs on the place; the security system will be on full lock. Dorothy Swerdlow will alert you a few days before I'm due back. Then"—he smiled with deprecating charm—"business as usual."

Theresa thought of Christmas, the inevitable expenses. "So I won't get paid the rest of December?"

He laughed indulgently at her distress. "Why should I punish *you* for *my* vacation. You'll be paid as usual. Take a holiday; you look like you could use one." He enjoyed saying that. "Where do you live, by the way?"

"Silver—" Too late she remembered that he must not connect her with Mary Jane, yet the word had been said. "Silver Spring," she said lamely, and thought she saw consciousness flicker briefly in his dark eyes.

"Well, enjoy yourself anyway, Theresa," he said, apparently oblivious to the insult. "See you next year."

Theresa and Matt spent Christmas day, as they had since Theresa's divorce from Dan Jones, in Baltimore with her mother, Coral Foley. Theresa had to force herself to make the forty-mile drive this year, not only because she dreaded the first Christmas without Mary Jane but because her mother seemed to be drifting a little farther from the shores of reality each time she saw her. She had begun writing letters to world leaders urging peace, commendable in itself, but disturbing because every time the powers held a summit, she was sure that she had inspired it. Theresa had tried arguing her into sense, but it was useless: much simpler just to agree that Mrs. Coral Foley was masterminding foreign policy. Matt loved her because she spoiled him, but if he preferred being anywhere at Christmas, Theresa knew he would choose to spend it with Dan.

Mary Jane, her blond head haloed in studio lights, smiled radiantly from her high-school graduation photograph in its blue leatherette frame on the spinet piano just as though nothing had changed. They did not talk about her, but she was present in the awkward pauses, the avoidance of certain topics, the extra attention paid to Matt, in Coral's distressing propensity to hurry tearfully from the room. Unwisely, Theresa had packed Mary

Jane's diary in her suitcase—unwisely because she could not prevent herself from reading it again.

Sunday August 25: At Rehoboth with Chris and Keith and Mark. Burning hot, and blue. It's strange to be with someone my own age. Somehow Mark makes EDK seem unreal. There's not that aching distance; he's there whether I want him to be or not! We fight sometimes, but it's o.k. because we just blow up and then it's over. I feel light with him, whereas just thinking about EDK weights me down. I'm beginning to realize he's all in my mind. I feel as though I've been under an evil spell, and Mark is waking me up, like the Prince in a fairy tale. Which he is definitely not, thank heaven.

On an abnormally warm Christmas morning, they gathered self-consciously around an overdressed plastic tree clutching mugs of Tom and Jerrys, one for Matt because this was a holiday. Matt tore Santa paper from an oblong box. A plaid flannel shirt. "For chilly winter days, darling," said Coral. "Gee, thanks," said Matt. Theresa opened a package and pulled out a frothy white negligee trimmed with lace and blue satin ribbon.

"For me?" she said incredulously. Her mother usually gave her gloves and scarves, or some gadget for the kitchen. Then, sickeningly, she understood.

Coral Foley's faded blue eyes were misty. "I thought you might— Would you ever wear it, Terry? I bought it last summer and it seems too pretty to go out of the family."

She could not have made a scene, Theresa told herself bitterly that night, lying on the narrow bed, her cheek pressed against the lavender-scented pillow. Yet Coral had been cruel. She would never wear the innocently seductive negligee. It was Mary Jane who had been too pretty to go out of the family.

CHAPTER FOURTEEN

N ed Kaplan returned shortly after the first of the
year. A few weeks later, Dorothy Swerdlow rang
Theresa. "Just giving you warning," she said in her brisk
yet cordial way. "Mr. Kaplan will be entertaining seven
bankers next Thursday at dinner. *Chez lui* or *vous* or
whatever." Dorothy, who never relaxed with her boss,
had begun fractionally to relax with Theresa. "I'm having a terrible time with the seating. Don't know whether
to put the Israeli next to the German, the Russian, or the
Iranian. What do *you* think?"

Theresa laughed. "Aren't there any other choices?"

"Yes," sighed Dorothy. "The Saudi. Well, never mind.
I'll solve it somehow. You'll have Franchot, of course.
Get anybody else you want. Mr. Kaplan likes entertaining international clients at home because he thinks it in-
spires confidence in America and in Security American.
So I think the menu should be very, um—*solid*, if you
know what I mean. But that's your business."

"I'll do my best," said Theresa. "Thanks."

She hung up and stood there in the middle of the

kitchen, hands knotted at her mouth, thoughts racing. A dinner party. Next Thursday. Matt could sleep at Holly's or overnight with a friend. She would stay the night in Marty's room. And then, and then—

The taunting question danced in her head, unanswered. Yet as she filled the big enamel watering can for the plants in the morning room, she felt that somehow the answer would come.

Theresa was wiping down sixteen dusty bottles Franchot had brought up in a wooden crate from the cellar. "This wine certainly isn't from Chile," she said ironically over her shoulder to Franchot, who was inspecting a goblet against the light. "Surely eight people can't drink sixteen bottles before nine o clock."

Franchot gave no sign that he understood. "If they are not all required, I shall take them to the cellar again," he said in his superior way. "Stop! The Riesling does *not* go into the refrigerator. It goes outside on the back steps where it is thirty-nine degrees, until it's ready to be decanted. Semi-dry white wine should *not* be served cold, only lightly chilled. It kills the bouquet."

He cocked an eyebrow at Theresa. She was looking very well tonight, he thought: the pink blouse put some color in her cheeks, and for once she had laid aside the discouraging horn-rimmed glasses. Good long legs, he noted, and nice dark hair. He preferred brunettes to blondes: blondes seemed cold, diluted somehow. He did not regret their conversation the night of Ned Kaplan's last social evening. His little secrets would be safe with Theresa Foley because she was forced to depend on his keeping hers. And he had no intention of betraying her, yet. In fact he was decidedly enjoying his own magnaminity. If she satisfied Mr. Kaplan, he had told his reflection in the mirror that night as he knotted his black bow tie, that's good enough, John old boy, for you.

I do believe he's after me, thought Theresa as she climbed the portable stairs and got down the big Meissen platter for the stuffed tenderloin that she and Antonio from Ma Cuisine had decided would suit tonight's occasion. Feeling the heat of his gaze on the backs of her calves, she got down quickly. Ogled by the butler, she thought, and nothing I can do about it. "Excuse me," she said coldly, twisting past him with the platter held high, deliberately ignoring him.

She had more important things to think about.

Her overnight case was sitting upstairs on the bed in Mrs. Marty's old room. Ned Kaplan had shown no surprise when she'd told him that she preferred, this time, to stay the night and finish things up the next morning. "Sensible girl," he'd said. "It could be a late evening." She was committed now.

The arrival in the kitchen of young Antonio from Ma Cuisine accompanied by two slaves lugging his equipment sent Franchot, stiff backed, into the butler's pantry. Antonio (his name, thought Theresa, was probably Joe or Mike) wore a three-day beard and tawny blond hair caught back in a short ponytail twisted with a rubber band. His cat-green eyes were fringed with long black lashes, his full lips were red, and the tail of a dragon tattoo showed beneath a rolled white shirt cuff. He looked more like a rock star than a chef.

"Just want you to understand that I'm out of here at eight," he said, arranging cutlery and various pots and pans on the counter. "Big Embassy show, two hundred dudes."

"Oh, no!" Theresa had chosen not to get extra help for the evening, sure that she, Franchot, and Antonio could handle eight. "You're not leaving?"

"Relax," he said as though she were a patient on the operating table. "It's under control." He unveiled a heavy shallow pan in which rested a six-pound cylindrical work of raw tenderloin art. He checked his watch and nodded at one of the serfs, who hurried to open the preheated oven door. Antonio slid his creation in. "Now, these are the artichoke bottoms. The minute the meat's on the heated platter at nine o'clock, you're going to set 'em around artistically, like in this picture I've drawn. Sid, where's the *béarnaise* sauce? All you have to do is warm it, very gently, *no* boiling, then you spoon it into the artichoke bottoms on the platter. Don't overdo it, just a tablespoon each. Then you stack the *pont-neuf* potatoes crisscross like in the picture. Then cress for decoration, between the artichokes and the *pont-neufs*. Get the idea?"

"I think so."

"It's a masterpiece if you get it right," said Antonio comfortlessly.

At seven-fifty he checked his Rolodex, yanked his apron over his head, and signaled his slaves. Franchot watched them go. "Even though we employed it in a limited capacity, Ma Cuisine *used* to be an establishment of some distinction," he said sourly in his highest British style. He consulted his own watch. "I shall announce that dinner is served."

Theresa only saw the gleaming wedge of knife half buried under spinach leaves when the van, flashing yellow warning lights, was backing out of the drive. She seized the heavy implement, ran out of the kitchen, and down the back stairs. The van had gone.

She hesitated there in the back hall, the knife in her hand, then without thinking walked to and looked up the dimly lit staircase with the torturous turn halfway to the top. She ran quickly up those stairs, entered Mrs. Marty's room, and thrust the knife under a bed pillow.

Franchot bore the steaming tureen into the dining room, Theresa following. It would be the first time she had ever waited at formal table; she prayed that the instructions in still another text, *The Well-Served Guest,* would see her through. Her hands shook slightly as she leveled the plate of soup toward the guest on Ned Kaplan's right, who, the book had instructed, was to be served first. How different this gathering was—even in her nervousness she couldn't help noticing—than the mixed party for twenty. Two men had lit cigarettes between the starter and soup courses, an act that would have been considered a breach on the night of October 29. The pitch of talk had sunk an octave: Conversation was more forceful, strident, abrupt. Then, too, as palpable and clinging as cigarette smoke, were the gazes of the men. Good God, thought Theresa, are things so desperate in foreign ports that they have to examine *me?* She felt their eyes exploring her breasts and buttocks as she moved around the table setting plates of soup before each guest. Most disconcerting of all, she realized that Ned Kaplan had joined the expedition.

Disconcerting because she was coming to the conclusion that sex was the only way to get close enough to harm him. Because harm him she must. That she had decided. Since she had come to believe in the truth of Stephanie's witnessing, the most fantastic schemes had come and gone like bad dreams—poison in his wine, a bomb in the Mercedes tailpipe, carbon monoxide in that private Security American elevator, which she would somehow succeed in jamming between floors. Yet what did she know about poisons, bombs, jamming an elevator! She realized she was hoping for a miracle, some kind of message whispered in her ear by who knows what good genie, who would show her the way. But no miracles were happening.

Sex. The thought filled her with dread and loathing even as she told herself it was impossible. She didn't have a chance with a man who could either attract or buy any desirable woman he chose. And yet she could feel his eyes on her. Soup sloshed almost over the rim of the plate she set down before the Saudi banker. "So sorry," she murmured into his burnous.

The pink blouse was seriously annoying Ned. Marty had always worn black to wait on table, and though Theresa's skirt was indeed black, she had tied a fluty white apron around her waist. But it was the pink silk that every time she bent forward gaped a little between buttons, that was the offender. Naturally, he continued to converse with the Bundesbanker on his right. Terms like prime, Fed, single monetary policy, Eurodollars, indicators, short-term, and Group of Seven traded back and forth—for although the bankers struggled from time to time to turn the conversation into more general avenues like Bosnia, Hollywood, the Redskins, or graft on the Hill—they returned with the inevitability of the tide to dollars, pounds, marks, and yen.

Franchot's after her, thought Ned, following the butler with his eyes as he moved around the table in

Theresa's wake filling the second of the glasses in the gleaming crystal phalanx before each guest. The thought annoyed him more, if possible, than the pink blouse.

But no, it was Foley herself who really got under his skin, he decided, pulling a small notebook from his breast pocket to jot down a few figures confided by the Berlin banker. It was nothing criminal, nothing for which he could definitely fault her. Little things, needling things. Like the way she walked into the morning room with her chin exploring the air. The way a certain quality in her husky voice made him know her "Good morning, Mr. Kaplan" was a duty, not a pleasure. The way she left him terse little notes thrust under the potted geranium on the kitchen table. The way she pared down the dinner portions she left him as though subtly suggesting that he should watch his waistline. And he hadn't called her on any of it. Damn the woman, said Ned behind his teeth as Theresa disappeared again through the swinging doors. Anger burned him, and something else. He reached for his glass of water and drank quickly, as if to put out a flame.

From the set of his horsey jaw when she told him she did not need a ride home, Theresa knew that Franchot disapproved of her staying the night.

"But it's simplest. I came down on the Metro at three this afternoon. It's nearly one and I'm dead." Why am I explaining to this man? she rebuked herself. What business is it of his! But there was something about Franchot's straight back that seemed to demand explanations.

"It's nothing to me," he said loftily, unknotting his black tie. She stared again at those immaculate pinkish nails, fascinated. "If you think it looks right."

"But how Victorian! Mrs. Marty lived in."

"Not quite the same thing, is it," said Franchot, folding the tie neatly and slipping it into his pocket. "Well, I'll be on my way. Nice to have seen you again, Theresa. Good night."

Her employer told her curtly that he would lock up. She stood there in the kitchen feeling light-headed with fatigue and dread. She switched off the overhead light, and shadows sprang at her; she turned off the lights over the stove and sink and pushed quickly through the swinging door into the back hall. There were the stairs, with Mrs. Marty's room at the top. It must have been just about this time of night. . . .

Monday September 2. Back at SA. I feel like a fly caught in the web again. But I did some serious thinking over vacation, and yesterday I acted on it. I wrote EDK at his home address requesting an appointment with him. I had to. I hardly ever see him here. I said I wanted to talk seriously about a matter that was important—at least to me. I intend to be totally dignified. But I have to settle this. Last week I realized that I have been involved with this man since December. I can't go on.

Oh, Mary Jane, if only you had not gone on. Suddenly she envisioned him, Ned Kaplan, the spider who had spun the deadly web, hunched at the top of the stairs, his hands gripping the banister, leaning over, waiting for her, smiling, as he almost never did, because he knew that she knew. He was thick and dark and his hands were strong, and she was afraid.

Nothing waited at the top of the stairs except deeper shadow, yet she discovered that her knees were rubbery as she stood outside Mrs. Marty's door, looking down the long expanse of hall lit at intervals by wall lamps glowing in parchment shades. The library was at the other end; next to it, Ned Kaplan's bedroom. In terms of physical—and psychological—distance, it seemed miles away.

Mrs. Marty had inhabited a plain, four-square room. A maple double bed covered by a white cotton chenille spread; a faded rag rug on the floor; a tall, old-fashioned bureau; a high-backed rocking chair; a small television on a stand; and a stack of ancient *National Enquirer*s on the bedside table. Nothing could seem less sinister. Theresa almost smiled imagining the stout housekeeper in a flannel nightgown nodding off over the scandal sheet.

She opened her overnight case and pulled out her own nightgown. It was white and frothy and had been meant for Mary Jane. She did not know why she had chosen it, nor did she wish to know. Shivering, she pulled it over her head, shrugged on her blue robe, and went to use the bathroom next door. The hall was silent, empty.

She did not take off her robe, but slid into bed and drew the quilt up over her knees, shivering more violently. Her hand, exploring under the pillow next to her, touched cold steel. She hugged her knees hard, swaying back and forth, her eyes closed as if in prayer.

"You're not a good general," she heard Dan Jones telling her. "You don't plan. You just rely on some last-minute inspiration to pull you through. Every once in a while you get lucky; but baby, I'd hate to be a soldier in your army."

It's true, she thought, I have no plan. That's why I grabbed the knife—a bit of last-minute inspiration because I thought Antonio's accidentally leaving it behind might be a sign. So make a plan for once, she told herself roughly.

> *Friday September 6. EDK told me to meet him at seven at his elevator. I called Melissa and canceled our tennis date at the club. I've decided I'm going to be totally dignified. The trouble is, I still love him. I knew that the moment I saw him again. I love him and I want him—far more than he wants me, I know. So what happens to dignity when you're in the arms of a man who, for the first time in your life, makes you know you're a woman?*

Her daughter had pursued a man she found sexually desirable. Theresa threw off the quilt, burning. Admit it, she told herself fiercely: You, too, feel desire—against your will, with shame, in every muscle and vein. And he had looked at her that way, hadn't he? But that was not the reason she would try to tempt Ned Kaplan into bed.

There was no place to secret a knife on her person; she would have to carry it in her purse. Ridiculous, carrying a purse to a seduction. She studied her still-slender silhouette in the mirror, wondering at this strange, feverish woman she hardly knew, and slung her purse over her shoulder. She had forgotten to bring slippers; her feet were naked. She left Marty's bedroom door wide open as though it were a pair of arms to welcome her if she was lucky enough to return. The corridor was dead still. She willed her feet to walk it.

His door was ajar, the room dark. She slipped through the door and cried out.

In the dark, Ned Kaplan swore, fumbled, flipped a switch. He looked at her incredulously in the hard overhead light, his grip tightening on her arm. "What the hell!" His voice rasped; a nerve skipped in his cheek.

"Let me go!" said Theresa, shocked by pain. "Stop it!"

He released her. He stepped back, rebelting his dressing gown; she saw that he was naked underneath. He ran his hands through his dark hair. "That's good, Foley, that's very good, considering that you're just slightly out of line."

But he was recovering the equilibrium he'd lost at the dinner table. How obliging of Foley to come to him, to allow him to reject her. For he intensely distrusted this spasm of desire for a woman who, he sensed, was somehow braced against him. Now he could chastise her for his own folly. "I think you owe me an explanation," he said coldly.

"I had to see you."

"I find that hard to believe."

"You don't understand." If only she could coax him off guard.

"You're dead right about that."

"I—" She willed herself to say it. "I'm attracted to you. And at dinner you— It's cruel to make me say it this way."

He folded his arms, his face relaxing into a grin. "How flattering. And to think I've been oblivious. You must think me a real brute."

Her fingers gripped her purse. She could feel the hard ridge of knife inside.

"You know I could fire you for this."

"Damn you!"

"A lover's quarrel just when we're getting acquainted? Look," he said harshly, "I think you value my good will."

She turned her face away.

"Do you? Value it?"

"Yes," she said tightly.

"Then this will go no further if you want to remain in my employment. Do you understand?"

"Apparently I have no choice—"

But he was no longer listening. Theresa smelled a heavy floral scent before hearing a voice husked by a Spanish accent say, "Have I got the wrong night, Ned? Or are we playing different games?"

The woman in the doorway had a cloud of black hair and a small but perfectly proportioned body balanced on improbably high heels. Her nose was aquiline, her brows black wings. Her red mouth was sharply curved and clever. She looked amused. A name Theresa had copied down long ago from Ned Kaplan's Rolodex flew into her head. Diana Maynard.

She advanced with a slender dance of hips. "Aren't you going to introduce me?"

He had completely forgotten about Diana. "Mrs. Foley is the housekeeper," he said furiously. "She's just leaving."

"Too bad," said Diana Maynard. She winked at Theresa. "He is very old-fashioned, this guy."

Theresa fled. Back in Marty's room she flung the shoulder bag with its deadly contents onto the bed and laughed. A woman had saved him.

CHAPTER FIFTEEN

The bedside clock said ten to nine when Theresa opened her eyes the next morning. Matt, she thought; then she realized that today was not Sunday but Friday; he would be in school. She closed her eyes again. *He* will have gone long ago, she told herself; he will certainly be gone. Then she got out of bed, reached for her robe, and opened the door.

Mrs. Sweeney, in a blue denim coverall, stood three feet away making vague passes with an ostrich feather duster at a picture frame. Both women froze. Mrs. Sweeney was the first to recover.

"I didn't think anybody was about," she said in a righteous sort of way, "so I just got on with my work. I suppose you remember I switched days this week to Friday." She looked Theresa up and down, and her hunting-dog nostrils quivered. "I didn't think you stayed *nights.*"

Theresa flushed as she yanked the robe across her chest. "How did you get in? You don't have a key."

"Oh, yes I do." Mrs. Sweeney dipped into an apron pocket and held up the proof. "I have my own now, and a good thing, too. I could have rung the front gate off its hinges this morning and not raised a soul."

Theresa stared into her hard, white face, hating her. Mrs. Sweeney must have helped herself to the extra key hanging on the hook behind the kitchen door. This was the most arrogant kind of insubordination; she could fire her on the spot. She wanted to. But she felt somehow, standing there in his house in her bathrobe at nine in the morning, that her authority was decidedly in question.

"We'll discuss this later," she said. She slammed shut the door of the bathroom and turned on the shower.

The kitchen when she finally went downstairs was sunny, empty. The dishes she'd been too tired to finish seemed to have multiplied overnight. The Krups, she saw, had not been used. He had gone out, then, without breakfast. And the woman, when had she slipped away on her little stilty heels? *She* hadn't left by the back staircase. She must have her own key, to have appeared so suddenly in the dead of night.

She opened her purse and laid the knife on the counter, feeling foolish and angry. She made herself a cup of coffee; she needed it badly. The knife winked cheerfully in the sun.

She was drinking her coffee when she noticed something white under the geranium pot. She set down her cup, pulled out the paper, and unfolded it: *You will expect the day off, I suppose, after your labors last night, but please remember that Mario is coming at one-thirty to work in the basement. You will need to let him in as he has no key, and I'd appreciate your staying until he leaves at four, EDK.*

She had not thought of taking the day off, but suddenly the idea was irresistible. Upstairs Mrs. Sweeney,

the vacuum, and the feather duster had progressed halfway down the long hall. Brushing past her, she pulled
down clean sheets and pillowcases from the linen closet
and hurried them into the master bedroom, where she
yanked apart the mulberry drapes and attacked the bed,
noting their condition as she ripped off the used sheets. In
Mrs. Marty's room, she thrust the futile white nightgown
along with the rest of her things into the overnight bag
and hastily made up the bed. Downstairs she bundled the
sheets and pillowcases into the washing machine. They'd
have to wait for Monday for the dryer. Back in the
kitchen she tore a leaf from the notepad next to the telephone. *Dear Mr. Kaplan,* she wrote, toppling the letters
together in her haste. *You are right, I do expect the day off
after working past one last night. Mario will have to come
an extra day next week. Mrs. Sweeney will lock up today. I
hope you understand. TJF.* She wrote another hurried
note to Mrs. Sweeney, instructing her to include the
dishes in her cleaning, picked up her bag, and fled, feeling
she was leaving chaos in her wake.

To where? Suddenly she saw her house clearly: Matt's
unwashed breakfast dishes in the sink, the beige carpet
with its worn path between the front door and the
kitchen, the wingback chair she'd bought for a week's
salary that now needed recovering. She had tried her best
to make a home, and it was pinched and frayed, and she
was sick to death of it.

She'd been divorced almost five years, since she'd discovered that Dan Jones, who had demonstrated nothing
but devotion before their vows, was screwing his twenty-
year-old redhaired secretary. Five years. She must have
sleepwalked through them, because on a witness stand
she could not have sworn where they had gone: five days

a week cooking and cleaning for other people before the real estate job, supper for Mary Jane and Matt, TV or a book in the evenings, Friday nights at the bar, trying to think of "family" things to do with Mary Jane and Matt on the weekends, her sexuality on hold.

One spring, in a burst of hope, she had gone to a meeting of a singles' club in a church basement on Sligo Avenue and danced with two or three men. One of them had asked her out the next weekend, but it turned out he smoked and lived with his mother. After that catastrophe, it took courage to venture one night to P.J. Rubicon's with Holly, and there—miraculously—she had connected. Not in any kind of *spiritual* way, of course; that was too much to hope. He was tall and skinny with hair that curled to his broad shoulders, and she was so excited by him after rubbing knees under the table for an hour that she'd let him go all the way with her, like a teenager, outside the house that night in his car because Mary Jane and Matt were inside and he didn't seem to have a place of his own. The next night she'd gone back to P.J.'s, head over heels in love. She'd gone back many nights, but he'd never come again, and finally she'd stopped thinking about him and went to P.J. Rubicon's indifferently with Holly to kill an evening, because nothing was going to happen if she stayed home.

She passed a row of mellow, rosy brick Federal houses standing shoulder to shoulder like Washington's troops, passed the tall black iron gates of Oak Hill Cemetery, protecting the wealthy dead as they had been protected in life, and found herself in Montrose Park. A few roses still miraculously survived in a round bed surrounded by a clipped hedge of holly, and from the courts came the *puck-puck* of an improbable tennis game in progress. She

had never been in the park before: Georgetown was still
unfamiliar to her; if it came to that, she knew little about
the rest of the city. Incredibly, she had never toured the
Capitol or attended an event at the Kennedy Center.
She'd accidentally seen Ronald Reagan's inaugural pa-
rade, and she'd taken Mary Jane and Matt to the Lincoln
Memorial and the Smithsonian and to see the Yoshino
cherry trees in blossom one April around the Tidal Basin.
Apart from that, she might as well have been living in
Detroit or Atlanta.

Children were running and squealing in the bright Jan-
uary air. Their black nannies sat on benches, thin ankles
crossed below dark coats, talking to each other, breaths
smoking, eyes automatically following the movements of
their white charges. She sat down on a vacant bench, set
the overnight bag beside her, tugged her navy blue wool
coat around her knees.

I have to think about it, she told herself, but her mind
dodged skittishly about the perimeter of the ring, unable
to come in close and land a blow. What had Holly said?
"Murderers are attractive." Because that was the real
shame of last night, she thought, quitting the bench and
starting down a gravel path, her mind suddenly closing
on the enemy with quick jabs. Not that she had started
for his room with intent to kill, but that she had started
with desire. She hated him, but she wanted him herself.
What had drawn her to his house, after all? she asked
herself fiercely, her heels spitting gravel. Mary Jane?
Mother love? Righteous anger? Or the seduction of the
words *I think he may be dangerous.* Luring bait in the
tepid waters that were drowning her by inches. Danger
was sexual.

She found herself home at four, scarcely aware of having spent the rest of the afternoon walking aimlessly with one stop at a deli for a cup of coffee. Matt charged in fifteen minutes later, demanding early supper so he could get to the game.

"Game?" Theresa was blank.

"You know, Friday night j.v. And it's your turn to drive. Gee, you look *weird,* Mom."

"Rather a bad day," said Theresa, staring into the refrigerator.

She deposited Matt and three friends at the school, confirmed that another parent would restore him to her by eleven, retraced her route, and knocked at Holly's door. Holly greeted her with a curling iron in one hand.

"I'm early," said Theresa, "but let's go anyway. I've got the jitters, can't face my four walls."

Holly looked guilty. "Yeah, but Terry, I'm going out tonight. Actually out. With a guy. You know the fellow that sat down for awhile at our table last week? Well, he called a couple of hours ago and asked if I wanted to go to a movie. Short notice, but I thought, What the heck? I was just going to call you," she added unconvincingly.

"Oh," said Theresa dully. She saw now that Holly was wearing her good leather miniskirt and new high-heeled suede boots. She stood in the doorway, not knowing what else to do. "What movie?"

"I want to see the Jessica Lange like you do, but he wants to see something with De Niro. Who do you think'll win? Listen, come on in, for heaven's sake. You look terrible. Is something wrong?"

"Sort of," said Theresa. She dropped onto the loveseat and huddled there against the hard unhelpful arm, unable to say another word.

"Not with Matt?"

Theresa shook her head.

"Kaplan, then! I knew something was up because you don't talk about him anymore. Look, whatever it is, believe me, Terry, he's not worth it. You've got to give up this crazy idea of yours once and for all. Quit tomorrow. Just hand in your notice. All you're doing is punishing yourself. You'll never be able to touch him; you said so yourself. It's all wrong—like that awful dyed hair of yours. It's just not you." She stood there helplessly, hands on leather hips, then plumped down next to Theresa and patted her awkwardly.

"I've got a great idea. Come with us tonight. That'll make two of us who want to see the Lange flick. No, really. This is no big deal to begin with—two retreads taking in a movie. We'll make it a trio."

"I couldn't" said Theresa. Tonight she had wanted to tell Holly at last about Stephanie Ruso, explain that she now knew she was working for her daughter's murderer, perhaps confess what she hoped to do.

"Don't be a spoilsport. Sheridan won't mind."

"*Sheridan?*" Theresa smiled in spite of herself.

"Sheridan Pope—don't blame me, I'm not his mother. Come on, Terry, please. I can't leave you alone like this."

"Yes, you can." Theresa stood up. "I'm all right now."

"I'll feel a lot better if you're along." She circled Theresa's shoulders with her arm.

For a moment Theresa let her head rest in the warm curve of Holly's shoulder. "I know you mean it, but I'm not coming. You can tell me all about *Sheridan* tomorrow."

She poured herself a glass of the white wine that she had come to prefer and sat down, in the armchair that needed recovering, in front of the silent television set. "It's all wrong," Holly had said. Little did she know just how wrong it was. Theresa watched the woman reflected in the blank screen lift the glass to her lips, take a sip, set the glass down, move restlessly in her chair.

She had not thought at all about Monday, but when she finally tried to imagine letting herself in the rear door of 3001 Q, she doubted that she could go back. Since the talk with Stephanie—since the *knowledge*—the strain of working for Ned Kaplan had become almost unendurable. The failure of her attempt (she could hardly even call it that) last night utterly depressed her. Now she would hate entering the morning room with his coffee, hate meeting his eyes, hate saying his name. Hate entering his bedroom, touching his belongings.

Then she laughed aloud. How naive to think she actually had a choice. What had she said in her note? *Yes . . . I do expect the day off.* You didn't say things like that to Edward Devereaux Kaplan. Then there was the good china still unwashed on the counter—Mrs. Sweeney would not have touched it. And that same Mrs. Sweeney rampaging around with a stolen key. And Mario locked out.

Ah, yes, Theresa, she told herself, your phone's going to ring before Monday, but it won't be Ned Kaplan on the line. It will be Dorothy Swerdlow telling you in that nice, efficient voice never to darken the door of Mr. Kaplan's residence again. You're history, as that young man said on the phone. Your problems are solved.

Feeling lightheaded, she got herself another glass of wine and turned on the tube. She hated Friday-night TV, but there must be something, she thought rather desperately, running through the channels. She went through them twice, then clicked back to an old black-and-white film with—who was that blond movie star—yes, Lana Turner. She didn't recognize the male lead, but after a while it became clear that Lana, in her white turban, and the boyfriend wanted to do away with Lana's silly fat old Greek husband, Nick, though they didn't quite know how to go about it. Of course it had to look like an accident; that was the whole point. She poured more wine, scrunched deeper into her chair. Eventually Lana and the boyfriend cooked up a scheme about holding Nick under in the bathtub; but then, confusingly, a cat outside the bathroom got electrocuted instead and a policeman saw the ladder they had propped against the house, so they had to scuttle that plan.

She considered the second ploy far inferior because wrecking the car with old Nick drunk in it was such a public thing, and anything could go wrong. After all, she'd read somewhere that most fatal accidents happen at home right in the bathtub. And, in fact, pushing the car over the cliff did go wrong, and though old Nick got his, so did Lana, accidentally, and then her boyfriend got the chair for killing her. Depressing, like so many of those old black and whites; yet in its way, she decided, quite a compelling film.

She waited all day Saturday for the call, but no one rang at all. Saturday night she went with Holly to an early show and discovered, eerily, that it was about a woman who invaded a home as a housekeeper and seduced the husband. Everything seemed to have coincidental significance these days. In the car coming home, Holly asked again what was wrong, but she couldn't tell her; she found it unspeakable. She asked instead about Sheridan Pope.

Holly shrugged. "We're getting along fine, then after the show he goes, 'Why did you laugh?' 'Laugh?' I says. 'What do you mean?' He says, 'You know, when De Niro hitches a ride under the Cherokee, you laughed. And when he cuts the anchor and stuff, and crawls back into the boat after the kid sets him on fire, and at the end when he's going under talking in tongues—you laughed.' So I says, 'Well, I guess if I laughed I must have thought it was pretty funny.' After that, he just clammed up, and when he dropped me, all he said was, 'I don't get you. So long.' " Holly made a rude noise. "I told you you should have come along!"

That night Theresa slept fitfully. Sunday morning a friend from the real estate office rang wanting to meet for a matinee and an early bite of dinner. Theresa explained that she'd seen a movie the night before, and made a tentative date for the following Sunday. Then Coral called from Baltimore complaining in her "I really don't want to bother you" way that she hadn't heard from her since Christmas. Theresa hung up, feeling guilty as hell; she had not been much of a daughter since September. Coral's call reminded her of the white nightgown still in the bag thrust into the back of her closet, and she went around the rest of the morning with the cold stone in her stomach heavier than before. The phone rang three times for Matt between twelve and two; the fourth time it shrilled, she snatched it off the hook with a thrill of irritation and dread.

"Theresa? Dan here. If you're going to be home this afternoon, I'd like to drop by for a minute. I want to talk to you about something."

"What is it?"

"I'd rather not discuss it over the phone."

"Matt won't be here. He's gone off with friends."

"It's you I want to see."

Half an hour later he knocked at the door. She'd hardly looked at him at Mary Jane's funeral. Now she saw he hadn't changed in five years; in fact, he looked younger. Not a hint of gray in his thick wheat-brown hair, so like Matt's, his boyishly round face unlined. But he stepped back to look at her critically.

"Your hair! Since when have you been a brunette? I could pass you in the street without recognizing you."

"Good."

"Look, I'm terribly sorry we didn't get together when Mary Jane—I tried calling a couple of times, but you were out, so I wrote instead. I wasn't sure . . . The signals I intercepted at the funeral were all negative."

"That's all right." she said briefly. "Let me have your coat."

He followed her out to the kitchen, where she put water on for coffee. He leaned an elbow against the refrigerator, discovered the magnets, and pulled out a chair from the round painted table instead. His beautifully tailored navy wool sport coat and designer loafers didn't fit the surroundings, and she realized how well he'd done and how poorly she'd fared since they'd parted.

"Well?" said Theresa at the stove. She was glad he hadn't brought an expensive present for Matt—easy blackmail for the absent parent; but she wasn't glad to see him and wanted to get it over with.

"Well, Terry, I've decided to get married again."

Even after five years, it stung. "Why tell me?"

He grinned Matt's grin. "Still a tad bitter, are we?"

"Bitter? Why should I be bitter. Just because you and your lawyer saw to it that after the divorce my standard of living declined seventy-five percent." She'd read that statistic somewhere and it had hit home. She concentrated on the teakettle. "Who's the unlucky woman? The redhead from the office?"

"Oh, for God's sake, Terry, grow up. That's been over for years—not that it was anything to begin with—"

"So you dumped her too. Figures."

"Look, Terry, I didn't drive all the way out here to take a lot of shit about my character." He smoothed his hair, hunched his chair toward her earnestly. "What I want to say is I've been lucky enough to meet this great gal. Lawyer with a big insurance firm, divorced herself with two kids, boy twelve and a girl ten. Justin and Monica. Great kids, amazingly unspoiled. Has a place in Virginia, a farm with stables and horses—the real thing. We'll be living in the country, commuting in." He was trying hard not to look smug, and failing. "We plan to tie the knot this spring."

"Congratulations. I still don't see what this has got to do with me."

"I've been thinking about Matt, what a great thing it would be for him to live in the country, have a brother and sister, horses to ride."

Theresa stopped pouring water into the coffee filter and set the kettle down. "So you're sorry about Mary Jane, are you," she said tightly, "and in the same breath you're planning to take Matt away from me?"

He squirmed a little on his chair. "I wouldn't put it that way, Terry. I wasn't thinking of *taking* Matt away. I was thinking of *giving* him something he hasn't got now." He couldn't help glancing around the small kitchen.

"Matt thinks what he's got is okay," said Theresa stiffly.

Dan saw he had made a tactical error and changed appeals. "After all, Terry, he's my kid, too."

"Do you have any idea how attached Matt is to his friends and his school? I can understand your disregarding my feelings, but what about his?" She banged a full coffee cup down in front of him.

"But that's it," Dan persisted, ignoring her hostility and the slopped coffee. "This is his last year at Forest anyway. Surprised that I remember, aren't you? You never did give me any credit. This fall he'll be transferring to a big high school where everything's going to be new and pretty overwhelming. And rough: I've heard bad things about that school. I've also heard that you're pretty busy these days, Terry. Why the hell did you take a job in Georgetown, anyway?"

"Who told you about Georgetown?"

"I have my sources."

"You're accusing me of neglecting Matt?"

Dan modified quickly. "My point is, you've got a job that seems to demand a lot of your time. What I really want to say, Terry, is that if you'd ever consider letting him live with Tippy and me, this is in every way the ideal time."

First Terry, now Tippy—how cute. She closed her eyes. Dan Jones had begun as a salesman. The salesman's cant, including the over-employment of first names and the ability to believe his own spiel, had never deserted him. She found she was too exhausted to argue with him.

Dan took a hasty sip of coffee and put down the cup.

"Look, nobody's talking instant decisions here." He stood up to go. "Just promise me you'll think about it, that's all I'm asking. After all, we both want what's best for Matt. Will you? Think about it?"

"I doubt it."

"You haven't changed a bit, have you?" he said with sudden, honest bitterness. "Fucking pig-headed as ever." Then, because he was an incorrigible optimist, he grinned appealingly, not wanting to end the session on a sour note. "Consider it, Terry. For *his* sake."

When he had been gone about an hour, she suddenly realized that neither Dorothy Swerdlow nor Ned Kaplan had called to fire her. So even her sassy, openly insubordinate note had no effect on that iron man. Powerless, she was. Never could touch him.

Yet the idea of the note clung to her mind as she chopped green peppers, garlic, and onion for spaghetti sauce. Not the note she had written, but *a* note—a note that would hurt him.

After she had washed and Matt had put away the dishes, she took a piece of cheap, anonymous typing paper from a drawer and cranked it into the antediluvian Smith Corona on her desk. She hesitated, her fingers poised over the keys. Something that really would hurt him. A message that would bring him crashing down onto his knees.

Regarding the night of September 21, she typed slowly with two fingers, *there is a witness who saw you with Ma—* She stopped, tore the paper out of the machine, crumpled it, and inserted another. Better to say *the young woman* because after all this time who but someone damningly close to her would remember the name Mary Jane Jones? *Regarding the night of September 21,* she sang under her breath, punching keys, *there is a witness who saw you with the young woman at the top of the back stairs and knows you are a murderer.* She studied the message for a long time and decided that it said what she wanted to say. She went into her son's room, where, to her surprise, she actually found him doing math homework.

"I'm going out for a little while to mail something. Back soon. You'll be all right?"

"Naturally," said Matt with elaborate scorn. "But you hate to drive at night."

"I know, but this is important."

She felt it urgent to make the morning pickup, but did not want to risk a Silver Spring postmark, so in her small tan Honda she retraced the route Franchot had taken from the city. She finally spotted a mailbox on the corner of Florida Avenue and W Street—safe territory, she judged—pulled over, got out, and dropped the business envelope addressed to *Edward Kaplan. Personal and Private,* at Security American into the box.

That night, sitting on the edge of her bed in a cotton nightgown, brushing her hair, she felt again that fine net of steel settle over her soul like armor, and knew that she could face him tomorrow and the next day and the next.

As long as it took until she found a way to kill him.

CHAPTER SIXTEEN

She let herself into Ned Kaplan's residence at six-thirty on Monday morning, spurred by unpleasant visions of unwashed dishes. And there they were: Mrs. Sweeney, as she had predicted, had ignored them, and obviously so had her employer. She quickly ran hot water and detergent into the sink; by seven-fifteen she had succeeded in transferring the now pristine set of good china into the butler's pantry for future storage. She began breakfast, feeding oranges into the Juicemaster, activating the Krups. She felt braced for anything.

He came into the kitchen tucking a silk handkerchief into his breast pocket. He smelled discreetly of tangy aftershave, and his tie was so perfectly knotted, she wanted to throttle him with it. He actually smiled. "Good morning, Theresa Joan."

A spoon clattered to the floor. She knelt to retrieve it.

"Good morning, Mr. Kaplan," she said, shouting above her pounding heart. What had he called her? Theresa *Jones*? In her panic, she couldn't tell. She followed his well-tailored back into the morning room with the tray and set it down.

"Excuse me, but what did you say?" she asked, her hand trembling a little as she set the blue coffee cup in front of him.

"Say?" He was already deep into the stockmarket.

"Yes, just now. You called me something."

"I suppose I called you Theresa Joan." He jerked his head at a note lying on the glass table and she recognized it. "You signed your little billet-doux *TJF,* remember? But then, it might be Theresa Jean or Theresa Jane."

Theresa Jones Foley. Stupid!—she'd never written her name like that before. In her haste, she'd thought only of mocking his *EDK.*

"Theresa Jane," she said faintly.

"Very good. But I trust that is the last time I'll ever receive such a communication from you." He crumpled the note in his fist and tossed it contemptuously onto her tray.

She met his hard, dark eyes. "Yes, Mr. Kaplan. I'm sorry about last Friday."

"You should be, Foley. But enough said. By the way, the shower in the master bath is on the fritz again. Call Merchant's, will you? Tell them to get over here this morning if not sooner. And tell them this time they'd better get it right. That will be all."

"Yes, Mr. Kaplan," said Theresa, retreating.

He would not, she thought with satisfaction, receive such a communication from her again. But if the postal system of the capital of the United States did its job, he would receive a communication by tomorrow that would shake him far more than an innocuous little note from a housekeeper taking the day off. She smiled grimly.

* * *

As usual, Dorothy Swerdlow went through the mail in the morning, and promptly at ten-thirty took five letters marked *personal* into her employer's office and laid them precisely in the middle of the black blotter on his desk. Two bore embassy crests, and he slit open the invitations with little interest, conversing at the same time into the phone cradled under his chin with the OSI of the Banque Nationale in Brussels. The third letter, he saw, came from his mother's lawyers; he surmised it had to do with the power of attorney business she had called him about from her apartment in New York last week. He set it aside with respect. The fourth envelope, he saw as he hung up the phone, contained an invitation to a surprise black-tie birthday party for Myra Schier. He winced. The fifth envelope he had deliberately left for last because it was so incredibly . . . crude. He was not accustomed to receiving dime-store envelopes with no return address and *Private and Personal* printed in tacky blue ballpoint. He fingered it for a moment, an amused smile on his lips, trying to imagine its sender and contents. A disgruntled Security American stockholder of senile years? A chain letter (he had received one once) from some True Believer in South Dakota? More likely one of millions of shirt-tail organizations asking for a contribution. Then he slit the envelope and pulled out the few lines of typing on the single page. His smile froze.

Coming in a few minutes later with a sheaf of papers for signing, Dorothy Swerdlow was shocked out of her usual impassivity. "Why, Mr. Kaplan! Is anything wrong?"

He made an effort. "Nothing is wrong."

"You're sure? Excuse me, but you don't look well."

"A touch of indigestion. Evidently I've got to cut down on the morning coffee. Moderation in all things. Here, give me those to sign."

She saw that his hand shook. "You're sure you don't want me to cancel your eleven o'clock appointment?" She hovered over him anxiously, then recalled herself and stepped back a pace.

"Quite sure," he said dismissively.

His first reaction had been that it was damned unfair, after all this time, to bring up the September thing. He actually felt abused. *He'd* forgotten it; why couldn't everybody else?

His second reaction was, What does the bastard want? He thought immediately in terms of hundreds of thousands if not millions; yet there was no signature, no return address, no instructions to drop a suitcase stuffed with greenbacks somewhere out of town.

His third reaction was, Who had it in for him? Pool balls, propelled by a cue of fear, spun in a dozen directions. Ironically, his own lawyer, Bob Cohn, sprang first to mind. Then Franchot, that damned cool butler who owed loyalty to no one. Marty he dismissed with a shake of his head. No reason, no motive. Not the type. The pool balls collided, spun across green baize, failed to drop. Cohn, Cohn. Elsa? Someone at Security American? Possibly. Dr. Brian Phillips! Yes. No.

He felt his shirt, as on that evening, clinging damply to his back as he realized with certainty that this was just the first of many notes, until he paid.

Serving him the next morning, Theresa saw that the message had done its work. Ned Kaplan looked older, ill— much as she had looked in the weeks following Mary

Jane's death. His lids were heavy from sleeplessness; the
muscles about his mouth taut. The *Wall Street Journal*
lay open next to his plate, but she did not think he was
reading it; he was meditating on something else.

"Fine morning, Mr. Kaplan." She nodded at the winter sunshine pouring into the breakfast room and, above
the walled enclosure, the blue sky.

"Yes." His voice was toneless. "That will be all."

"Yes, Mr. Kaplan," she said cheerfully, whisking
away the tray.

Yet when on her way upstairs she passed him, walking
with bowed head, his raincoat over his arm, she felt an
unaccountable spasm of pity. He was suffering now as
she had intended him to do, yet for a moment she saw
him merely as a fellow human being, and regretted what
she had done and was going to do.

In his room, she drew the curtains and saw his tormented night confirmed by the disarray of the bed. The
room smelled faintly of smoke and wax, and her eyes
went to the handsome dressing table that seemed to function only as an altar for the triptych of the madonna and
child. He had referred to it once the very first week of her
employment; he had said, "Ignore the dressing table in
my bedroom, if you don't mind. Marty never touched
it." She had never touched it either, only watched pale
wax accumulate before the portrait of the woman whose
dreaming half smile seemed to float her so enviably above
the troubles of the world.

Without thinking, Theresa crossed the room, fell to
her knees before the triptych, and clasped her hands. She
wasn't religious anymore, but Catholic reflexes died
hard. Please, she prayed silently, please grant me the
strength to do what I must. But if I do not have that

strength, please grant me the strength to leave this place
and put the past behind me. Before I destroy myself completely.

Midmorning, as Theresa was polishing the glass lamp-
shades in the dining room, Dorothy Swerdlow telephoned. "Hello, Theresa. Just to say that Mr. Kaplan
has left for Tokyo for three days. You can expect him
back on Friday."

"Tokyo?" said Theresa, bewildered. "He didn't tell
me."

For some reason, Dorothy took offense. "I don't think
Mr. Kaplan feels obliged to inform you every time he
leaves the country on business," she said coldly. "That's
what I'm here for."

"Yes, of course," said Theresa. She hung up quickly.

Three days. Three days to make her plans. To tighten
the screws of her determination.

She went upstairs into the big master bath and turned
on the shower. Water spurted with a rattle of pipe, then
collapsed into a trickle. She hadn't yet called Merchant's,
who had said last time that the pipes were old and filled
with roots, that the whole upstairs east-wing system
should be rehauled and connected with the new pipes
they'd installed for the Jacuzzi. She turned the heavy,
wedge-shaped brass taps of the tub and water gushed
out.

So if she didn't call Merchant's and the shower were
still not working, he would have to use the tub. He had
the last time; she knew because she'd had to clean it. And
if he used the tub . . . accidents happened in the tub.
Lana's boyfriend in the movie that had impressed her
had said so.

She looked around the big tiled bath. On the marble

lavatory lay his electric razor; he must have another for travel. If she could manage to drop that electric razor, live, into the Jacuzzi when he was bathing, would the charge be enough to kill him? She had no idea. Lana and her boyfriend had planned cruder methods, like bashing old Nick on the head, then holding him under until he drowned. She did not think she could bear to hold anybody under water. Besides, Ned Kaplan was fit and not old.

That night she read about electricity in Matt's encyclopedia—about ions, conducting solutions, electrolytes and cathode rays. She was no wiser. With more interest, she read the short article about electrocution invented in America for infliction of the death penalty on criminals by passing through the body of the condemned a current of electricity sufficient to cause death. But then, she had no access to an electric chair. She located her First Aid book at the back of a kitchen drawer and learned that in an emergency like electrocution, one gave artificial respiration. But, she thought, closing the book again hopelessly, my purpose is not to save him by artificial respiration.

The next day, under the pretext that she was concerned about electrical outlets in her bathroom, she called three firms listed in the Yellow Pages under Electric Systems— Service and Repair. She didn't really know the right questions to ask. "Frankly." she said. "I'm worried that my husband might electrocute himself. Sometimes he shaves in the shower. Couldn't something dangerous happen? I mean, the outlet shouldn't even be near the tub, should it?"

When the woman answering the phone at the first business said incredulously, *"Pardon me?"* she hung up in a panic. She was told emphatically by the other two firms that she should have the bathroom rewired, particularly since her husband appeared to be an imbecile. She thanked them and hung up quickly.

Because Ned Kaplan's flight from Tokyo set down at the National Airport three hours late, he decided to go straight home instead of putting in a couple of hours at his desk in the penthouse at Security American. If another *Private and Personal* letter waited for him there, it could wait, he had decided after a certain amount of agony, until tomorrow or even Monday. He felt tired, dragged out, and his head throbbed. This is more than jet lag, he thought irritably; I must be coming down with something. He seldom came down with anything—*down,* in fact, was hardly a word in his vocabulary. Today he preferred it, however, to admitting the real cause of his malaise.

He gave the taxi driver the Georgetown address; halfway there, realizing that Theresa Foley would be on the premises, he opened his mouth to direct the cabbie instead to the Security American Building on Pennsylvania Avenue, then changed his mind. He leaned back against the seat and closed his eyes.

He had decided with the assistance of several Chivas Regals somewhere over the Pacific that the Judas, the viper who had sent the anonymous message, must be one of the hired help. It was the only thing that made sense—unless, of course, the letter was simply a hoax, a wild shot fired by someone who had it in for him. None of his guests the night of September 21 had reason to be anywhere in his house but on the patio or in the rooms adjacent. Only the help had any possible business in the back hall, though even then it was doubtful what it could be. And that meant Marty or Franchot or any one of the girls she had hired that night to help in the kitchen. He didn't know their names, but he could find out.

He had called Dorothy Swerdlow from Tokyo with orders to discover Marty's whereabouts and get him the names and addresses of the three (he vividly remembered three women, two of them black, huddled against the sink that night as he went through the kitchen) who had worked the night of September 21. "Yes, Mr. Kaplan," she had said, masking the surprise in her voice. She had rung him back with the information that the Martys had left for California last October and still had no address or telephone number.

"What do you mean, no address? Everybody's got an address."

"Not in this case, Mr. Kaplan. According to their former neighbors, they're taking their time on the road, putting up in trailer camps on the way, seeing America. The neighbors get postcards from time to time. But I do have the names of the people who worked that night from Mrs. Foley. Mrs. Marty gave them to her for future reference."

He had taken down the phone numbers, addresses, and names of Ann Moore, Geneva Smithers, and Stephanie Ruso. "By the way," he added casually, "any personal mail that you think I should know about?"

"No personal mail today or yesterday, Mr. Kaplan."

He did not exactly know what he would do about the three names, or about Marty and Franchot. Very risky, getting a detective on the trace. He might talk to Phillips who, he was sure now, had been suspicious, or worse, to Bob Cohn. No. Best, he decided, to wait for further developments. He was sure there would be another letter, this time naming a price. The thing stank of money.

He shoved three five-dollar bills into the turbaned driver's hand and lifted his suitcase out of the back seat. Early March, a day like spring—soft, bright, promising. The beeches offered their tight red buds to be admired; certain spring flowers—he'd never known their names—had sprung up seemingly overnight in patches on the front lawn. He scowled and fit a key into the hidden lock in the pillar of the heavy iron gate. It was going on four. She wouldn't be expecting him, and he prayed that she would make no fuss.

He let himself in the front door and stopped short with the key in his hand. Theresa Foley was standing before him in the foyer with a boy of about fourteen. Their hands were joined and the sunlight pouring into the rotunda through the fanlight gave the illusion that her dark hair was blond. They turned to stare at him.

"Oh, Mr. Kaplan," cried Theresa, her hand flying to her heart melodramatically, "you scared me to death! I wasn't expecting you."

"I know."

"This is my son, Matt." She was breathless, her eyelids fluttering rapidly. "His friends suddenly decided to go camping in the mountains this weekend and he wants to go along, so he stopped by to get some money from me."

The boy shoved the bills she'd given him into his jeans pocket and held out his hand. "Pleased to meet you," he said with surprisingly good manners.

Ned shook hands silently.

The boy appealed to his mother. Was she going to make him *converse* with this guy? "I gotta go," he said, "they're waiting in the van."

"Are you taking something warm?" Theresa planted half a kiss near his ear.

"Gee, Mom!" He twisted away in embarrassment and was gone.

Theresa laughed. Her normally pleasant contralto was high and nervous. "I'm just making your supper, Mr. Kaplan. Now that I don't have to get home for Matt— my son—I could stay and serve it to you hot. I'm sure you're dead tired after your long trip."

"That's very kind, but I prefer to manage the usual way."

He mounted the broad stairway, crossed the hall, and went into his room, throwing his pigskin bag onto the bed. He stood in the middle of the room, head bent, contemplating, then went to the window, tore back the curtains, and stood staring down into the walled garden where the daffodils and tulips planted last fall by Mario were making an annoyingly bright display. He frowned.

Foley and that boy just now . . . Reminding him of something familiar, something trying to struggle up out of the past into his present consciousness. Their hands joined, the light from above . . . blond . . . Suddenly he stiffened.

He saw again the open grave and bright green grass and a tall blond woman in a navy coat walking toward the Mercedes clinging to a boy's hand. Her face had been stormy with grief, and she had paused just as he was about to get out and fixed him with unseeing wet eyes, Mary Jane Jones's mother. He had felt she must be Mary Jane's mother at the time, but Nancy had preempted him with her own surmise, and he'd denied having noticed her. But he had noticed her, all right. And now the tall, ash-blond woman in the cemetery and his own dark-

haired housekeeper merged before his eyes. The two
women were one. T.J.F. Theresa *Jones* Foley. The dead
girl's mother.

He took a deep breath to steady himself. Why was she
here? His dark brows knotted; he swore. This was not coincidence; he scorned coincidence. She was here in his
house for a reason. What the hell did she want?

He glanced at his watch, picked up the telephone next
to his bed, and dialed the Fraziers' number. Remarkably,
it was answered by the Hon. Mrs. Sam herself.

"Elsa, darling? Ned. A quick question. How long did
Theresa Foley work for you? Theresa Foley. F-o-l-e-y
. . . You've never had a housekeeper by that name? Absolutely sure? All right, that's all I wanted to know. No, I'm
not being mysterious—I'm in conference." He rang off.
He wouldn't bother calling the Cummingses; he knew
what Sybil would say.

No wonder—it came to him now—no wonder Foley
hadn't shown herself the night the Fraziers came to dinner. She'd hired an extra to serve, whereas Marty had always helped wait on table herself. He'd thought it
extravagant at the time, especially since she was new to
his employ, but he had not questioned her decision. It
was her business, after all. Or so he'd thought. Now it
seemed it had been very much his business all the time.

There was a light rap at the door. He hesitated, then
went to open it, walking with purpose.

"I just wanted to say I'm leaving for the day." Theresa
Foley stood in the doorway. There was something in her
tone he could not decode. Challenge? Fear? "Unless
there's something else."

"No," he said. "Nothing. Theresa *Jones.*"

Her intake of breath was audible, though she recovered quickly. She smiled. "Then I'll see you Monday, Mr. Kaplan."

From the top of the stairs, though the thick eighteenth-century glass of the fanlight, he watched her go.

She had not been in his employment the night of September 21, therefore she could not have witnessed anything and could not have written the anonymous note. But she was here now, and for a reason.

He would have to do something about Theresa Foley.

CHAPTER SEVENTEEN

Theresa got off the Metro. The late afternoon was still mild, and in huge complexes of apartment and business buildings that had not existed when she was a child attending St. Michael's school in downtown Silver Spring, horizontal bands of windows blazed in the low sun. She had walked that morning to the station and was glad to walk now. She wanted desperately to think.

He had recognized her. In the foyer, into which he had exploded with the suddenness of the Devil, she had not been sure. His face when he saw them had been expressionless; she had noticed no particular reaction when he shook Matt's hand. But the man upstairs knew. Not "Theresa Joan" this time but "Theresa *Jones*." And he knew that she shared his knowledge.

So that it had to be soon, this weekend. Her thoughts, trapped, scurried like mice in and out of the mazes of her mind, nibbling at the words *Most accidents in the home happen right in the bathtub*. She had not called Merchant's. The shower in the master bath—she had tested it that afternoon—still did not work. There was nothing he could do about having it fixed until Monday. He would not use the showers in the two other second-floor bathrooms; he would use his own tub. Stupidly, she couldn't seem to think of anything else; yet she had discovered nothing practical about electrocuting a man in his Jacuzzi. Perhaps Lana's method would have to do. At least she, Theresa, would not prop a ladder against the side of the house for a policeman to stumble over. She had never understood why that ladder was there in the first place; she considered it a flaw in the film.

A car squealed rudely around the corner of Sligo Creek Parkway just as she was stepping off the curb, and she leapt back onto the sidewalk. At precisely that moment the heavy green malachite block on the long table in Ned Kaplan's library leapt into her mind.

Sometimes she went into the library because she wanted to feel Mary Jane there. Sometimes she just sat in Carol Kaplan's white leather chair next to the fireplace to see how it felt to be idle and rich; other times she walked about the room, looking at the gilt titles of leather-bound books, studying the prints of horses and hunters pursuing the desperate red fox, fingering the objects on the library table. She had held the arrogant malachite block in her palm, studied the inscription on the brass plaque: "With grateful thanks to Edward D. Kaplan from the Officers of the Banco do Brasil, 1989." She thought it must weigh five pounds.

Tuesday September 17. EDK was serious about the party after all. I ran into him totally unexpectedly near the elevators. Unfortunately the first thing I said when he invited me again was, "Oh, I couldn't, I have nothing to wear." As if I was hinting. And he said, "I think

*that can be taken care of." Of course I said I couldn't
possibly let him buy me a dress. "Yes, you can, my
dear," he said in such a kind, plain way. I refused again
and finally he shrugged and said "Have it your way,
just as long as you'll come." Needless to say my concentration was destroyed for the rest of the day.*

Kind. Plain. She looked left and started across the
street. A split skull was too good for Ned Kaplan. Both
the sexual desire she had felt for him and the pity were
dead, killed by her lasting rage. She could even feel glad
that the recognition had taken place because it spurred
her to action. And with that happy thought, she began to
know she was hungry. She undertook a quick, unpromis-
ing mental survey of the fridge and decided on the spot to
turn back and have an early supper at a good little restaurant with small marble tables and deft waiters called Bot-
ticelli's, where the saltimbocca and the melanzane were
choice. She breathed deeply, satisfied with her decision,
and smelled spring in the air. Suddenly, fiercely, she felt
in a festive mood.

"What did Bill think, my borrowing you for the day?"
They were the only customers at the oilcloth-covered
wooden tables in Joe's Fishing Shack on the Bay, a humble establishment dating from the 1940s that rented sun-
fish and catamarans in season and served steamed clams
and Maryland crab cakes whenever Joe, a World War II
vet with one arm, decided the restaurant was open. It had
long been one of Ned Kaplan's favorite spots, and sometimes he could gaze out through the shamelessly smeary
windows at the dancing whitecaps or the tranquil bay
and almost believe that the world hadn't changed.

But not today. His eyes above the coffee mug cradled in his hands were old with fatigue.

"I don't think he thought a thing about it. You know Bill. Imagination's not the darling's long suit."

Nancy Wylie sat opposite, chin on hands, studying him. To Ned she looked as impeccably beautiful as ever: white cashmere under a navy pea jacket, checked slacks, loafers, thick blond hair caught back with a navy scarf, clear skin with just a trace of makeup. Yet somehow today the perfection left him untouched. He couldn't warm his hands over it or take it into his hollow stomach. It had nothing to do with him. It was too far away. He could only stare at it between the bars of a cage.

"And you, what did you think?"

"I don't know. We've been driving two hours and you haven't said a word. Granted, I'm used to your whims and I've been rather enjoying the scenery, though March is not the most aesthetic month of the year, but you must have another reason for hijacking me. I wish you'd let me in on it, Neddy."

Ned shook vinegar from a crusted bottle onto clams he wasn't eating. "Do you know," he said conversationally, though there was an edge to his voice, "you're the only person in the world who calls me Neddy? Not even my mother dares. I wonder why I've put up with it all these years." He shoved his plate aside, thrust his hands into his pockets, and set his face toward the bay. "All right, I'll get it over with. I'm firing the housekeeper and selling the house."

"Is that all?" she exclaimed, but stopped at the look of pain that tightened his face. She reached across the table and laid two fingers on his brown hand. "I'm sorry. I shouldn't have said that. After our talk by the fire."

"No, you shouldn't have," he said ironically. "After all, it's the end of a dream."

"You mean you finally believe in Bill's good health?" she said, equally ironic, hurt by his sudden aloofness.

"Not only believe in it, but devoutly wish it. Come on." He stood up and flung bills onto the red-and-white checked oilcloth. "No use pretending we're eating."

Outside the wind whipped the silky ends of her scarf into her eyes. In an unfamiliar gesture, as though to atone for the less-than-successful lunch, he put his arm around her shoulders as they walked toward the end of the pier. An old catamaran with flaking paint plunged at anchor; boats were stacked prow-down along the side of the fish shack; tarps snapped in the wind; a fleet of gulls bounced on choppy green waves. Slapped by water, the dock itself sagged landward, weak in old knees, slats missing here and there.

"Taught Carol to sail here, many moons ago." His voice was flat. "Many many moons. Place is going to hell these days."

"Really? Then you were a good teacher. She certainly can handle a boat."

He faced her, suddenly furious; he seized her and held her at arm's length as though studying something monstrous.

" 'She certainly can handle a boat'! Is that all you can say? Don't you care? Haven't you ever cared? My God, you're a heartless bitch, Nancy Wylie!"

"You're hurting me," she said patiently. "Let me go."

When he released her, she made the effort due an old friend and smiled.

"It wasn't Carol's fault, Ned. Why can't you understand that after all these years?" She turned and began to walk back along the dock, head bent, gloved hands tucked beneath her arms. The wind swept her words and the long tail of her scarf back to him. "What's the old story? Once upon a time, little Ned and Nancy were engaged to be married and very, very happy. Then someone named Carol got pregnant. Ned married Carol, Carol miscarried, and Carol couldn't have more children. Then Nancy married Bill, and Ned, the knight very errant, stayed with Carol. Isn't that the way the old story goes?"

"Yes," he said sullenly. "You married Bill. I stayed with Carol."

"Exactly. Except that there's something missing, isn't there? One little twist of the plot? No, wait, I can supply it—the silly little old missing link. Once upon a time, during the three months little Neddy and Nancy were engaged and so very, very happy, little Neddy took Carol out in a boat and screwed her."

She faced him. The tip of her nose was raw, and he saw clearly for the first time the fine lines about the pretty mouth, the wide-set eyes. The pretty gray eyes were very bright. "I want to go home," she said, turning up the collar of the pea jacket around her pink ears. "Take me home."

He waited until she had settled back and composed herself and they were on the main highway again. No use talking to a woman in that state. He reached out and covered her small hand.

"I explained about that, remember?" he said gently. "And you said you forgave me."

Nancy sat up and pulled her hand away. Her profile was sharp as a knife. "Yes, I forgave you. But what good did that do? You still married Carol. I still married Bill." She turned to him, and he felt a force, a presence in her he had never sensed before. "You've never seemed to understand that actions have *consequences,* Ned. At least you haven't understood it on the personal level. It's a kind of—moral lapse in you. No, I'm wrong, it's much more than that . . ."

"Really," he said heavily after a silence.

"Yes, really." She ignored the sarcasm, unable to stop the truths she felt she had never been able to say. "Like the Jones girl. Admit it, Ned; she'd be alive today if you hadn't decided to relieve your boredom or your sexual itch or whatever it was by a little fooling around. She meant nothing to you, just as you've always said Carol meant nothing—yet look what happened! The *consequences.* The terrible consequences! No, I've got to say it, Ned. For your own good. Oh, God, that sounds so terribly pompous—I mean for both our goods. Please, now you say something. Let's talk about it, for heaven's sake."

But Ned drove in silence until the seemingly endless urban sprawl had solidified into suburbs. Finally he said, "What is there to talk about? You've got it all figured out. Perfectly."

"Oh, *don't* be so predictable!" she said, anguished. "There's everything to talk about, and you know it."

"I disagree. What was it you said at the party?—something about hating the ache of the past. Well, suddenly I hate the damned aching past more than you do. I think we should both forget the old story, all the old stories. They're dead. Let them rot."

They were silent until he pulled up in front of the tall block of exclusive condominiums overlooking the wooded ravine of Rock Creek Park. She got out of the Mercedes quickly, but he was there. "Give my regards to

Bill." he said. He took her small gloved hand and kissed it with irony. "Tell him I appreciate the loan."

"Ned . . ."

He took the Rock Creek Parkway at high speed, his hands gripping the wheel. He had intended to tell Nancy about Theresa Foley, maybe even about the anonymous letter. He had wanted to lay open the whole bizarre situation to her, bare his troubles and misgivings to the one person in the world he had felt he could trust. But she hadn't understood a word he'd said; she hadn't even let him talk. Instead she'd taken it upon herself to deliver a sermon on his morals—or lack of them! Lovely Nancy Wylie was not so attractive in the pulpit.

Suddenly he saw something as clearly as if he'd opened the pages of the photograph album she'd kept when they were first in love. Nancy Painter, his young fiancée of nineteen. Rather plump, starry eyed, pretty in an ordinary way, gauche, naive. Nothing to do with the elegant Nancy Wylie he had worshipped these many years. That Nancy was the creation—he suddenly understood—of William Wylie's millions, of William Wylie's infinite care and sophistication and connections. No wonder, then, that he himself had been able to marry Carol, though resenting her even as they walked down the aisle. Carol was smart, hardheaded, and rich. Poor compensation, he had thought her; he had wondered how he could go through with the marriage, the years, though he had to admit that everything that had financially prospered in his life had started with Carol. But the Nancy then wasn't the Nancy she had become. Perhaps she had become perfection simply to torment him.

He swore, braked, swung off the Parkway at P Street, and headed west. One thing was certain. This was the last weekend he would spend under that damned roof. Sunday he would move to the Club until he found an apartment. Monday morning he would congratulate Swerdlow for having so carefully checked out Theresa Foley's references before hiring her. No, he wouldn't fire Swerdlow—though she deserved it; he would only order her to terminate Foley immediately with no severance pay. He felt sure now that she had some connection with the anonymous message, and that the message had been no hoax. If she tried stalking him again—if he ever caught her in his vicinity—he would get Bob Cohn to issue a restraining order. If that didn't work, he would take matters into his own hands. He was through with the goddamned women. They had put him through hell, all of them.

The garage door rolled back silently and he piloted the Mercedes into its berth. He locked the car and, as the door closed behind him, passed along the privet hedge between the drive and the pool. He let himself through the low gate into the patio and stood there, shoulders hunched, hands thrust into the pockets of his windbreaker, hardly needed at four in the afternoon in this sheltered backyard. High overhead, fat-budded branches rocked in the March east wind, but here in the walled enclosure the accumulated warmth of the afternoon sun seemed already tropical, a forecast of the steaming Washington summer to come. Carol would already have been stretched on her lounge chair, face glistening with oil, eyes hidden behind enormous black glasses. He had marveled how she could lie there motionless for hours, when he could not sit down in a chair without reaching for a file or pulling out a notebook.

But their differences hadn't mattered for a long time

now. Soon Mario would rake the borders, free the white
patio furniture from its plastic shrouds, clean and fill the
pool. He smiled grimly. But not for me, he thought, not
for me.

He let himself in the back door and felt the weight of
the dark empty house fall upon him. Cavernous, it was,
and dead as Roman catacombs. The freezer droned in
the back hall; in the kitchen the refrigerator hummed, a
clock ticked, a faucet dripped. He turned it off automatically, ignoring the dishes in the sink. It was his habit to
leave them until Monday for Foley. She would arrive at
seven-thirty as usual, make his coffee as usual.

But this Monday would be different. Eventually she
would wonder what was delaying him upstairs. He could
imagine her climbing the broad front staircase, hips moving beneath the tight black skirt, trailing two fingers
along the banister as he'd watched her do. Tapping at his
door, putting in her head, discovering that his bed had
not been slept in. She'd want to call Swerdlow immediately, but would have to wait until nine for the startling
news that Mr. Kaplan was living at his Club and she was
terminated. Or should he have Swerdlow call her tomorrow, Sunday? No: He preferred the first scenario.

Strange that for three years he had not noticed the silence, the chill geometry of these useless rooms, the cold
ostentation of their ornaments. He shook his head, as if
trying to clear the fog, passing through the morning
room into the dining room, then into a small reception
room, then into his study. Perhaps he had been oblivious
because late Saturday afternoons usually found him either finishing a half day's work at Security American,
jogging in the park, or dressing for a cocktail party that

would last until it was time to call a taxi and go on somewhere else for dinner.

In his study he pulled off his windbreaker and went to the telephone. Eventually Diana Maynard's answering service clicked in.

"Diana, Ned Kaplan," he said smoothly. "Sorry I can't make it this evening, sorry for myself, that is. I've brought home some kind of Japanese bug and it's the last thing I'd want to pass on to you. Call you next week, Dia mia."

He hung up with a feeling of satisfaction. Diana sometimes stood up her exclusive clientele, but no one canceled Diana Maynard. He would still have to pay, of course—"Dia mia"! But nothing could have induced him to visit Diana's townhouse tonight.

Neither, he decided, would he look in at the Schiers' party tonight as he'd planned. He poured himself a scotch, flung himself into a chair, and stared out the tall windows at the fingers of shadows creeping along the ivied garden wall. Strange how long it had taken him to feel the futility of playing lord of the manor. Lord of the manor! Lord of the goddamn blood-sucking ring— Foley, Franchot, Mario, Sweeney, Washington Power and Light, the District of Columbia, the IRS, and a host of other sustainers and retainers all with their hands deep in his pockets. Because he and Carol had lived and entertained lavishly, he'd thought all along that he'd have to go on playing the game twice as hard, while she escaped with a personal maid to the shore and clambakes on the beach. And Nancy had laughed at him.

Nancy. He groaned. Even now he was trying to kid himself. He hadn't kept up the place because he was locked into a role, he had kept it up in hopes of Nancy.

That hope, he had realized only today, was dead. What
had she said?—"a kind of moral lapse in you . . . no . . .
much more than that." The words had stunned him. He
was used to judging, not being judged. And yet it was
true, these moral lapses. He could admit them at last.
Odd for someone so straight in business—he was
straight, as business goes—to slip privately. For Mary
Jane Jones had been a lapse, no mistake. And today, finally, he had understood that there was no intimate place
in Nancy Wylie's ordered world for someone who stumbled morally.

To hell with it.

He poured himself another scotch, eased himself into
the contours his shoulders had molded in the black
leather over the years, and flicked on the news. Washington murders—two, three a week. Only last night a
middle-class white woman, driving home with her husband, shot through the head by a random gunman in the
next car because, his friends later testified, "He wanted to
kill someone that night." She had been a young woman,
the earnest, young male newscaster with the fashionably
long hair informed Ned, at the threshold of a promising
career. He jabbed a button and the screen went dark.

Work waited on his desk. He propped his glass against
a pile of folders, pulled up a chair, and turned on the
green-shaded lamp because dusk was settling over
Georgetown. He opened the first file, leafing through the
Third Vice President's report, scrubbing his nose with the
edge of his thumb, brows working. Amazing that he
could work, all things considered; but then work, for
him, was the great healer. An hour passed; he studied
more reports, reading faster. Suddenly he thrust them
away and flicked the switch of his computer. Finally he

could see how the acquisition of Bank United and Uni-bank International, which had been Security American's top priority the past two years, was to be managed. It was a comparatively simple matter of liquidating certain holdings no one had dared to think liquidatable while borrowing long and lending short. He hit the keys clumsily at first—damn it, this was Swerdlow's job; then more swiftly as the logistics of the takeover took shape on the electronic blue screen. He worked with intense concentration, completely absorbed.

CHAPTER EIGHTEEN

At eight thirty-five Theresa Foley rode the escalator up out of the enormous depths of the Metro into Dupont Circle. Clustered about the exit were the usual hawkers selling fruit, flowers, and T-shirts; the usual petitioners shaking their plastic cups. Tonight a black woman knelt on a quilt, holding a 7 YEARS HOMELESS sign and yelling, "I'm fifty, send me a birthday card. I'm havin' a party right here on this-here quilt." Someone threw down a bill—"You look eighty." Blacks jostled each other in loud horseplay. Apart from them stood a girl playing the violin. She was slender, with fine blond hair, and her face, bent over the instrument on her shoulder, looked so young and vulnerable that Theresa involuntarily paused. She shouldn't be here at night; it wasn't safe; she should be home, cherished. Tears sprang to her eyes; self-consciously she fumbled in her purse, stooped, and thrust a five-dollar bill into the beret at the girl's feet. The girl did not notice: Her eyes were closed, her right foot beat time, she seemed completely lost in the music.

It was close and humid, like so many Washington nights, with high, curdled clouds like a rumpled quilt stretched above the white glare of Connecticut Avenue. Theresa set off swiftly west down P Street. She wore a black raincoat over black slacks, and black running shoes with thick, silent, pliable soles. She tried to ignore the hard knot of dread in her stomach. It was the kind of hard knot she used to get in grade school on poetry-recitation day when she had to go up to the front of the class and recite "The Highwayman" or "The Raven" for Sister Justina, who believed in old-fashioned verse and old-fashioned tortures—a sinking, dizzying dread that she would fail.

Then on the heels of this vision—herself lagging with lowered eyes down the aisle toward the front of the class—she saw herself instead in the choir loft of St. Michael's, far above the pews that were never very full, except at Christmas and Easter. No dread there, just the joy of lifting her pure alto (Sister Angelica had called it "pure") until it merged with the keening organ notes in an exalted hymn of praise. But that was long ago. She didn't believe it anymore. Neither did he. He believed only in money. She had smelled that right away. It didn't matter about the Virgin and Child in his bedroom. People who believed only in money always had those kinds of things around.

There was a bad moment when a drunk loomed out of the small park just before the bridge over Rock Creek Parkway and started to follow her; but she strode faster, and when she turned around again, no one was following her. When she reached 30th Street, she slowed her pace. She did not think Ned Kaplan would be at home on a Saturday night; it was her impression that fashionable

Washington seldom was at home. She also did not fear meeting anyone on Georgetown's dark residential streets. She would let herself in the back door, get the malachite block from the library, then secret herself among the machines in the workout room, or in the closet of that room if necessary, though she wondered whether she would be able to hear the sounds of bathing from inside the closet, as she must. First, of course, she would make sure the connecting door between the workout room and the master bath was just slightly ajar so that its opening would not alert him. The Jacuzzi faced his bedroom; his back would be turned.

She saw herself waiting in the dark room for hours because he was sure to be late; she was prepared for that. She saw herself steal across the room, weapon in hand, saw herself silently push the door. She tried to think further than that, but her mind kept blanking.

She passed along the thick yew hedge and stopped at the gate. Except for a fan of light under the front portico and the discreet glow of carriage lamps at the end of the walk, the front of the big house was dark. She glanced up and down the street before inserting the small key into the lock concealed in the pillar. The gate clicked open, and she passed swiftly inside, up the walk and along the left flank of the house. Turning the corner, she stopped short. She had expected only a light over the back door; she had not expected, halfway along the rear of the house, a broad shaft of light slanting across the patio and falling into the empty pool. She counted: kitchen windows, the sliding glass doors of the morning room, the tall trio of dining room windows, the French windows of his study. His study.

Ned Kaplan was at home. He was not a careless man, would not leave a light burning.

Yet, she corrected herself, a burning light means nothing to a millionaire. She had to be sure.

She moved carefully beneath the kitchen windows, hugging the wall, past the glass doors of the morning room. At the dining room windows, she stumbled against an uneven patio flag and caught a handful of ivy to steady herself. The bright windows were only five or six feet ahead, but she had reached a stand of holly so thick and prickly that she could no longer press the wall but had to walk around the bed and directly into the range of anyone sitting in the study. She could not risk it.

She retraced her way along the house to the back door, breathing in quick shallow pants. She could *not* give up her mission; yet carrying it through now meant letting herself in the back door unheard, moving silently up the back stairs, negotiating the entire length of the upper hall to the library, then doubling back and slipping into the gym which, she calculated with sinking heart, was directly over the study.

Impossible.

But perhaps Ned Kaplan was not home at all.

The locked, windowless garage gave her no clue.

She shivered in the heavy damp night, hovering between the privet hedge and the back door, which, she now remembered with horror, had caught on the sill yesterday, grating harshly when she pulled it behind her.

She would have to chance it.

She inserted the key into the lock and turned the handle cautiously, urging the door gently with her left shoulder. She had remembered correctly: the door caught on the sill. Sweating now, she shoved harder with her shoul-

der, grinding the door inward until—with a jerk that sent
her stumbling—it swung free. She caught the knob and
stood there listening for a response to the thunder.

The house was still.

The hall was dimly lit by a single ceiling fixture. She
went swiftly to the foot of the backstairs and looked up
the dark well. The via dolorósa. Seventeen uncarpeted
steps: She had counted them the first day. Not one without its creaks and groans.

She took them one at a time, pausing to listen after
each advance. At the top she paused again, straining to
catch any sound below. The long hall was in darkness;
instinctively making her way, she kept to the edge of the
carpet running down the middle: The pile there was
thicker. She paused at the library door, panting as
though she'd run a hundred-yard dash, then went
straight down the room to the big table and seized the
heavy malachite block. She was about to retreat when
light from the study probing the darkness attracted her.
She moved to the tall window and looked askance below.

Ned Kaplan paced back and forth along the patio,
head bent, hands clasped behind his back, moving in and
out of the splash of light like a large night bird of prey.
She drew back, heart banging against her ribs. He was
here.

Now was the time to hide herself in the work-out room
over his head. She sprinted on tiptoe, let herself quickly
into the room, turned the doorknob noiselessly behind
her, and looked for a place to hide. If he decided on machine calesthenics tonight, she might be trapped before
she could slip into the closet. On the other hand, she
wanted to be as close to the bathroom door as possible.
She hesitated, then crouched behind a tall contraption

with a platform and a kind of dashboard set on a column
between handles. In the dim light the silent, hulking,
black machines reminded her, unpleasantly, that Ned
Kaplan was a man in grappling trim.

In less than a minute, the calf muscle in her left leg
cramped sharply. Cautiously she shifted her weight to
her other haunch, bracing herself with palms flat on the
floor. This would never do. After a few painful minutes,
she struggled to her feet and sat down gingerly on the
platform. With a loud hiss, it sank beneath her weight.
She swore under her breath and strained forward to listen, but could hear nothing. If she could not, then perhaps he could not, either. By the tiny beam of her pocket
flash, she saw that it was quarter past nine. Hours, then,
before he might go to bed. She weighed the malachite
block in her palm.

Three weeks ago—before, curiously enough, she
thought of the pen stand—she had found Matt's Grip-
Master in his unmade bed and, experimentally flexing it,
was appalled to find that she could move the handles only
fractionally. That day she had begun hand exercises,
building up from five to fifty on each hand. She knew her
grip was stronger. She raised her arm in the dark, aiming
at an imaginary head. If she could strike with the lethally
sharp corner of the block, daggerlike.

The house was so still she might have been its only oc-
cupant. She checked her watch again. Nine thirty-five.
She began to feel the need of a toilet. Forget it, she told
herself. She closed her eyes.

Perhaps this was a dream from which she would suddenly awake in her own bed at home to hear Mary Jane
teasing Matt in the kitchen, neighbor kids shouting outside. She would rise, dress, and drive off down Franklin

Avenue to the Murrays, where included in her duties were feeding and bathing Mrs. Murray's ninety-five-year-old mother, then drive home again at five. Ned Kaplan did not exist. Mary Jane was alive.

> Saturday September 21: I bought new silver sandals to go with the dress—$175 at Sable's, but I love it. But I'm beginning to feel uneasy because I haven't seen him for days and don't really know if he's expecting me tonight. Chris says of course he is, dummy, he asked you twice. I'm still trying to talk her into going with me, but she says "Not without an invitation." I suppose I'll take a cab. The party starts at nine. That's five hours from now and I have to live through each one of them. Will I really get up courage to go? Right now I honestly don't know.

By ten o'clock Ned Kaplan realized he was famished. He had strategized in four hours what a committee of two vice-presidents, three systems analysts, and (admittedly) he himself had not been able to accomplish in two years. He stood up, flexing cramped muscles. He deserved a hearty nosh.

Damn Foley! He glared at the refrigerator shelves. Marty had always seen that a plate of cold roast beef or a big dish of the small boiled red potatoes he loved were waiting for him. Not this woman. He slammed the door, went to the phone, flailed irritably among the Yellow Pages, and finally dialed a Chinese take-out on Wisconsin Avenue. By the time the front doorbell rang, hunger and impatience had cooled the satisfaction ignited by his evening's work. He carried the steaming bag to his study, tore impatiently at the plastic-sealed cutlery, and ate out of white cardboard buckets in front of the television, still pondering the intricacies of takeover, oblivious to the animated screen.

It was going on eleven when he went up. He undressed abstractedly, pulled on his black silk monogrammed robe, sucking in his stomach automatically as he knotted the tie around his waist. He went to turn down the bed, something in the old days Marty had always done for him. He picked up the quartz bedside clock and, as was his custom on weekends, carefully advanced the setting of the alarm from 6:30 A.M. to 7:45. Then he crossed the room and stood looking expressionlessly at the pale madonna of the triptych.

The magic had vanished. After years of feeling, he felt nothing. Those days were over; she could not help him now. He clapped to the heavy gilt panels, carried the triptych to the bureau, and thrust the precious object among cashmere sweaters in the bottom drawer. He knew an old fairy antiques dealer in Georgetown who had coveted the fifteenth-century Florentine piece for years. He'd give him a ring Monday and make him happy.

He brushed his teeth carefully, as he always did, rinsed his mouth with a medicinal solution of herbs recommended once by a Swiss doctor he had met at a conference in London. Then he threw off the robe and turned on the shower. A head of water gushed out, then, with a rumble of pipes, collapsed into a trickle. He swore long and loudly and turned on the taps of the Jacuzzi.

Forty or fifty people jammed the Schiers' penthouse apartment on Connecticut Avenue that evening for Myra's surprise birthday party. She went about the room loudly admitting that she was fifty, pretending not to mind.

"What a crowd! I think it's because everybody wants to talk about Russia," she said modestly, surveying the crush at the buffet, which was particularly lavish with beluga caviar, smoked salmon, and iced vodka and champagne to toast not only Myra but the dying of the old Red Star.

"Of course Russia will get the USSR's seat on the U.N. Security Counsel. No question about it." Jesse James spoke with the authority of an amateur Russia watcher and two large vodkas. "But I don't trust Yeltsin. Loose canon. Demagogue under the skin."

"Hardly an original opinion," said a senior State Department official, sipping tonic and eyeing the glass in Jesse's hand critically. "Why not give the fellow a chance?"

"*We'll* give him a chance," said Bob Cohn drily. "Will the Russians?"

"Darling," fluted Elsa Frazier, drawing Bob aside. He noted that she was wearing the three-strand pearl choker she trotted out for semi-important occasions. "I'm terribly curious. Now that Ned's back on everybody's top ten, why isn't he here tonight? I got the most mysterious call from him the other day, positively bizarre. I want to talk to him about housekeepers."

"Not a subject I associate with your scintillating line of repartee, Elsa," said Cohn, flattering her automatically. He did not trust Elsa Frazier—not because she once double-crossed him by passing confidential information to a legal opponent, but because she had hated him for her betrayal ever since. But then he did not trust anyone except his wife. He scanned the crowd. "To tell the truth,

I thought he was here, though I don't see him at the moment. Ask Myra. She can even tell you who's in the can."

Nancy Wylie felt Ned's absence.

"Bill," she said in the back seat of the Lincoln, "I'm worried about Ned."

Bill yawned widely, covered his mouth after the fact, and patted his wife's hand. "Just because he gave the Schiers' little extravaganza a miss? Lord, I'm tuckered. Should have given it a miss myself."

"Not just that. We had such a strange afternoon together. Don't you think it's odd the way he called up suddenly and insisted I go driving?" She sighed like a diplomat who has failed a delicate negotiation. "I think we might have quarreled."

"You don't know?" Bill smiled at his wife quizzically.

"Not with Ned you don't. I don't, at least. No, it was just the way he spoke—autumnly, as though it wasn't just a case of selling the house, but of giving us up, too. Oh, I know it sounds incredible—we've been friends for thirty years and more—but I'm afraid I said some pretty harsh things." She wrinkled her small nose in distaste. "I actually preached at him about his morals."

"And now you think he's sulking?"

Nancy frowned. "Not sulking exactly. Oh, I don't know! He hasn't been the same since that girl— Kindly do not waggle your eyebrows at me, Bill Wylie! You've said it yourself."

Bill leaned forward. "We're going to make a detour to Mr. Kaplan's house, Morrison, if you don't mind. That's what you want, isn't it, Nancy?" He tucked her arm through his. "It's all right. I don't mind looking in for a minute and a half."

The Kaplan house was dark.

"Not at home," said Bill, craning to peer out the car window. "Might be out of town."

"I doubt it," said Nancy. "Go ring, will you, Morrison?"

The big chauffeur climbed out and pressed the gate buzzer. He waited, rocking back and forth on his heels, then returned and stuck his head into the car. "I don't see no signs of life, Mrs. Wylie. You want me to try again?"

She thought of the key Ned had given her after the divorce. "Not exactly the key to the city, Nancy, but you know you'd be making an old admirer very happy if you ever chose to use it." It had hung on her key ring since that day; but she had never used it, and could not now.

"Never mind, Morrison," said Bill. "We'll go along on home." He turned to Nancy, trying to read her face in the dark. It had occasionally occurred to him that he should be jealous of Ned Kaplan; but whenever he considered the possibility seriously, it seemed absurd. Bygones were damned well bygones. Nancy's behavior had always been impeccable. It was her greatest charm.

CHAPTER NINETEEN

Theresa heard the doorbell shrill and froze. Who could be ringing at this time of night? Had he heard, and if so, would he answer? She waited, tense, the malachite block heavy and cold in her cold hand. He either had not heard or chose to ignore the bell. The intruder would have gone away. She must act now.

She did not think she could move, yet she did, around the machines toward the door that was still slightly ajar. In a few moments he would get into the tub. She stared at the door sightlessly, her mouth open and dry. She heard the toilet flush, then the slosh of water as he lowered himself into the Jacuzzi. She tried to swallow but failed. She drew a long, jagged breath, seized the knob in her left hand, and inched the door forward. She could see his feet—the toes black tufted and prehensile—braced against the bronzed edge of the tub. He must be lying on his back then, his head just out of water. She must move now.

She eased the door forward until she could see his dark wet head and a pale mound of half-submerged shoulder.

A ridiculously large sponge bobbed above his stomach like an island; he was flicking water with his left hand, like a child. She closed her eyes in swift prayer, then opened them and hurled herself at the tub. His head jerked in surprise. She raised her right hand and with all her strength drove the block straight down at the dark, wet head.

The malachite block squirted from her fist and plunged into the tub. At the same time a deep well, which quickly filled with bright red blood, appeared across the front of Ned Kaplan's head just above the hairline. He raised a dripping hand to his head, lowered it, and looked at the bright stain in disbelief. His head swiveled. He saw her and his eyes grew black with fury.

"Bitch!"

He grabbed the sides of the tub and heaved himself up, water streaming from his flanks, blood running into his eyes, down his face, into the black hair that matted his chest like seaweed. "Bitch! Whore!" He stood upright, groping in air for support. She felt a crazy instinct to run to him, to give him her shoulder, but before she could move, he slipped, going down hard on one knee. Very slowly he pulled himself upright again. "God . . ." he groaned, scrabbling at the blood in his eyes. He stood swaying, then lunged, slipped, and plunged forward, his head crashing into the lethally heavy solid-brass faucet. The water turned a rusty red. She watched him sink face down.

She stepped backward, gripping the door to keep from falling, but her knees gave out beneath her and she sank to the floor. It was streaming from the tidal wave that had washed out of the tub when he hit the water, and she scrambled hastily to her feet again. She stared wildly about her, looking for evidence of her presence there, but could see none. She backed out through the door, leaving it open, then thought better of it, and went back to shut it, wiping the handle to obliterate any prints.

She was at the door of the workout room when she remembered the malachite block in the tub. She turned and saw that her jogging shoes had left a trail of wet prints on the hardwood floor.

She began to gag, deep and dry in her throat as though strangling on a bone. She could not go into that bathroom again; she could not.

She unlaced her shoes, pulled off her socks, went back through the workout room, and opened the bathroom door. The marble floor was slick with water, and the tub smelled like industrial waste. She could not look at what was in it. She rolled up her left sleeve, knelt, twisted her head away, and plunged her arm into the water. Her groping fingers touched smooth flesh, and she cried out. She felt it at last, wedged under his left hip. Finally she had to use both hands to yank it out from under him. She took it to the sink, rinsed it, and reached for a towel, but on second thought pulled a wad of Kleenex from a box and rubbed the block down with that. She pulled out another wad. There was so much water on the bathroom floor that she did not think she could leave footprints even if she tried, but the floor of the workout room was another story.

She closed the bathroom door behind her, wiped the handle again, stuffed the block into her pocket and her shoes and socks under her arm, and, squatting on her haunches, moved backward, swabbing the wet marks after her. They grew fainter as she progressed toward the

door. In the hall, she sat down to put on her socks and
shoes and a pair of gloves she'd had in her raincoat
pocket. Then she went directly to the library, wiped the
block again, replaced it exactly in the center of the
leather-bound blotter on the long table, retrieved the
pens from the drawer, and wiped them and inserted them
into their sockets. Next she went into his bedroom, where
she threw back the spread and blanket, rumpled the
sheets, and disarranged the pillows; anything to obscure
the time of his death. Then she walked quickly out of the
room and down the hall. At the top of the back stairs she
paused, clutching the post to steady herself. Her breath
exploded in little ragged pants as though she were sob-
bing.

She let herself out the back door and locked it behind
her, glancing quickly at her watch before dodging out of
the pool of light over the back door. She was surprised to
find it no later than eleven-thirty. She thought she could
not be observed as she hurried along the side of the house
and down the front walk, as she unlocked the gate and
shut it behind her, and set off down the street. The night
had turned misty, and she staggered once or twice on the
slicked pavement.

At the Wisconsin Avenue lights, she realized that she
had walked west instead of east, away from the Metro
stop at Dupont Circle. She realized too that underneath
her raincoat, her arms were wet to her shoulders, perhaps
stained as well. Her pockets bulged with damp Kleenex,
and a glance over her shoulder told her the tails of her
raincoat hadn't dried, though since the coat was black,
the wet hardly showed. After she stuffed the Kleenex into
a sidewalk trash bin, she didn't think she looked strange.
She decided to walk down Wisconsin to M Street, then

cut down to the Foggy Bottom station at twenty-third. It would not be wise to pass through Georgetown again. She laughed a little hysterically. It wasn't exactly wise to be walking the streets of Washington alone at night, either.

The quiet, dim, clean Metro station soothed her; she almost felt safe; the round eyes winking the arrival of the next train seemed friendly. Yet by a certain numbness in her head, by the way she observed her hands and feet doing the correct things without being responsible for them, she knew she was still in shock. The car was nearly empty, but the black woman with tight gray curls and a yellow plastic shopping bag chose to sit next to her.

"I'm going to my daughter's in Takoma Park to baby-sit," she confided. "My daughter just called. Lance, that's her nine-year-old, broke his arm tonight fooling around after dark with some rough kids in the neighborhood. I says, 'Why wasn't he inside doing his homework?' but she says, 'Mama, you're crazy, it's Saturday night. He don't even have homework *weekdays*.' Anyway, I said I'd come and help her out."

"That's very nice of you."

"I do what I can. I remember raising my own kids alone; nobody helped with them."

Theresa smiled.

"You know, you look awful pale. Do you think you're coming down with something? They say the flu is going around. I'd hate to bring anything into the house. Why, you're shaking!"

"Now that you mention it, I don't feel very well," said Theresa, teeth chattering. She closed her eyes.

"That's a shame," said the woman. She hesitated. "I

wonder if it's catching. Not that I don't like talking to you . . ."

When Theresa opened her eyes, the woman was gone.

She let herself into the house. Matt would be back from his camping trip sometime tomorrow afternoon. She had decided during the long waiting hours that she must give him up, that he must go live in the country with Dan and his new wife. She could not feel anything about it yet, and she did not know how Matt would react. She guessed that he would hate and then love the idea.

She wanted to strip herself, to stand for hours under a steaming shower; but the mere thought of the tub nauseated her. Instead she threw off her damp sweatshirt and lay down on the bed, pulling the comforter around her shoulders, pressing her knees to her chest. She still shuddered spasmodically.

She sat up, remembering that she had not wiped off the sink taps after rinsing the malachite block. A second later, she realized her fingerprints must be all over the place—the library and exercise room door knobs, the lid of the toilet seat in the bathroom next to Marty's room that she'd had to use on the way out. But that's all right, she argued feverishly, huddling under the quilt: I'm the housekeeper, after all. Except for the bathroom, my prints must not be in his bathroom. But my hands were dripping wet—surely I couldn't have left prints on the sink. . . . Yet what if I did? I clean it every day. But not on Saturdays. . . . She closed her eyes, and fingerprints swam behind her lids, millions of whorls and smudges, blurred, sharp, stamped incriminatingly on hangers, blotters, knife-edges, ceilings—her fingerprints staining his towels, his robe, his razor, his drowned flanks; her fingerprints floating like islands on the bloodied water that smelled like raw copper.

Just before unconsciousness, she remembered that Monday she would have to discover the body and call the police.

CHAPTER TWENTY

Two uniformed police officers waited under the portico. Across the street a young couple had paused and was eying the blue-and-white scout car at the curb while pretending to be absorbed in the excretory functions of their miniature black poodle.

"Mrs. Foley?"

"Yes. Come in." Last night she had almost decided to disappear, to vanish back into obscurity as though she had never existed as Edward Kaplan's housekeeper. Why go through the hell and the danger of calling the police! Then reason finally conquered madness. They would find her. Of course they would find her. The only way was to face it, to tough it out.

"Which way?" said the black officer curtly. They followed her up the staircase, holsters creaking, their feet noiseless on the rich pile. She opened the door of the master bedroom and stood aside as they passed through.

"In there."

They reappeared in a few minutes, and the black officer jogged heavily down the stairs. The other pulled out a

notebook and ballpoint pen from his breast pocket.
She'd seen them do that in the movies.

"Just a few preliminary questions, Mrs. Foley." His
Southern drawl was as slow as a terrapin crossing a highway. "Where can we talk?"

"The library," said Theresa automatically, then realized her error. The library, with the malachite block on
the table, was the last place to invite a police officer. But
it was too late. "This way."

Voices filled the foyer below, and three men appeared
suddenly in the upper hall. One was lugging photo-
graphic equipment; another carried a large black case.
Theresa stared at them numbly.

"Mobile Crime Unit," said the officer. "M'am, you'd
better sit down before you fall down."

In the library he chose a straight-backed chair and motioned her into the white leather opposite, as though he
were the host. But his back was toward the table. She
clasped her hands around her knees to keep them steady
and willed her eyes not to travel beyond his left shoulder
to the green block shouting its presence for all to hear.

Should she get rid of it? She could drop it into the
Potomac or the C & O Canal—or better yet, into Chesa-
peake Bay, first prying off the brass plate so that nothing
would connect it with Ned Kaplan. The plate itself she
would smash into anonymity with a hammer. Yes! She
would get it out of the house in her handbag this afternoon.

Immediately, though, she saw the danger. Mrs.
Sweeney had dusted the room for years; she would notice
that the block was missing. She would call it to Theresa's
attention, maybe to the attention of the police. They
would make the connection—

"You're the housekeeper, you said."

"Yes."

"Complete name?"

"Theresa Foley."

"Permanent address?"

"Four Knox Circle, Silver Spring." No use lying as she'd lied to Kaplan.

"Live-in?"

"No, I work five days a week, seven-thirty to four." So far she felt prepared.

"Your employer's name?"

"Edward Devereaux Kaplan."

"Age?"

"I . . . don't know. Fifty, maybe."

"This his permanent place of residence?"

"Yes."

"So you came in this morning—"

"Yes, a little early." The officer was waiting, so she battled on. "I let myself in the back door as usual, started breakfast, as I do every morning. Mr. Kaplan is usually down by eight. Sometimes later, of course; that's why I didn't think anything of it until I noticed how quiet the house was. There's usually a radio going upstairs or the shower or something." She shivered involuntarily at the memory of waiting below in the kitchen for the moment she would have to go upstairs; she prayed the officer would think her nervousness feminine and natural. "Finally I went up—"

"That would be what time?" His "time" had three syllables.

"Quarter past, I suppose. I was beginning to think Mr. Kaplan might be out of town and forgot to tell me. He travels a lot; he just got back from Japan." Her nails cut eight little crescent moons into her palms. She drew a deep breath. "I knocked at his door. I didn't hear anything, so I knocked again. Finally I opened the door. I didn't like doing it, but I thought something might be wrong."

"What could be wrong?"

"I guess I imagined a heart attack or—I don't know. Really, I just wanted to find out whether he'd be down for breakfast."

"Did Mr. Kaplan have a history of heart trouble?"

"I'm sure he didn't. He was very fit."

"But you assumed a heart attack?"

"I didn't assume anything," said Theresa sharply. "I didn't know what to think." She saw she must continue. "I just put my head in the room; I didn't want to intrude. When I saw the bed had been slept in, I knew he must be at home. I called his name several times. Then I looked in the bathroom. That's when I found him. I ran downstairs and called nine-eleven right away."

"How come you asked for police? Why not the ambulance?" A big man with a meaty face and eyes as expressionless as metal slugs stood in the doorway. He was wearing a belted raincoat and, incongruously, a red, yellow, and black plaid cap. Obviously he had been listening for some time. "I'll take over, Purdy. Have that typed up for me."

"Right, Sergeant."

The big man eased his bulk onto the chair Officer Purdy had vacated and relaxed the belt of his raincoat. He pulled a small tape recorder out of his pocket, set it on the table between them, and punched a button. "Well?"

She felt as though a wing had just dropped off the

flimsy aircraft she was so inexpertly flying. "Why not an ambulance?" she repeated stupidly.

"He might just have fallen. CPR has been known to bring people around. Did you think of CPR?"

"Oh, no," cried Theresa, sincere at last. "The water— the whole place— He looked so . . . *dead!*"

The big man contemplated this information, his breath whistling in his nose. Then he said, "Dead since when, do you figure?"

"But I've told all that to the other officer—"

"I'm asking you to tell it all over again to me."

"I know Mr. Kaplan's morning routine. He regularly showers about seven-thirty. So when I found him forty-five minutes later, naturally I thought—"

"But he didn't shower this morning."

"I can explain that. The shower isn't working. Merchant's fixed it once, but there's no water pressure. I have to call them again." But there was no need to call Merchant's now.

The big man chewed a hangnail contemplatively and whistled through his nose. "There's a phone in Kaplan's bedroom. Why not use it? Why go all the way downstairs?"

"I didn't think of it," said Theresa truthfully. Odd, but she hadn't. "I only thought of the phone in the kitchen that I always use."

The flat gray discs gave away nothing. "When did you last see deceased alive?"

Theresa blanked. Then she remembered the day it must be. "Friday."

"Friday morning?"

"No, late Friday afternoon. He came home unexpectedly."

"What do you mean, unexpectedly?"

"He was just back from Tokyo. His secretary told me that since his plane got in at one, he planned to make it a working day. That's very typical of him, at least I have the impression he was a hard-working man. So naturally I didn't expect to see him before I left at four." She felt she was talking too much, giving damning evidence, though she couldn't think what it might be. She could feel the silk of her blouse sticking to her wet armpits.

"He seemed normal? Nothing unusual?"

"I thought he looked tired and . . . strained. But after a flight from Tokyo, that *would* be normal, wouldn't it?" She'd said something intelligent at last.

"House has a pretty complicated security system. You got your own keys?"

"I do." Would the questions never end! Should she ask to have a lawyer present? She didn't know, but she thought lawyers were for the Miranda Act, when they were actually accusing you of something. This was more like the games played in the film when they'd separated Lana and her boyfriend and tricked Lana into selling him out. They were trying to trick her now into mixing up her stories. At least there was nobody to doublecross her.

Suddenly she felt more confident. Because there was, after all, only one player and one story. Every move she was describing she had actually performed. The Krups still contained coffee brewed this morning. Six squeezed orange halves had not yet gone into the garbage disposal. The table was laid for his breakfast in the morning room. She *had* gone upstairs at approximately eight-fifteen, *had* knocked at his door, *had* ventured in, *had* called his name, just as though she were performing for an audience.

"Who else has keys?" He broke off, swiveling in his chair. From downstairs came the whine of a vacuum cleaner.

"Oh, no!" Theresa jumped up. "It's the cleaning lady's day. Mondays and Thursdays. I forgot to call her. May I go down?"

The big man sighed and stabbed the recorder. "Send her up. I may have questions."

Mrs. Sweeney was in the dining room halfheartedly stroking the Aubusson with the big Hoover upright. When she saw Theresa, she switched off the machine and planted fists on bony hips. The two women faced each other across the gleaming expanse of table.

"I seen the police cars outside, but I'm not one to stick my nose where it don't belong. Maybe you'll have the goodness to tell me what's going on."

"Something very bad has happened," said Theresa, gripping the carved back of one of the tall chairs. She felt like a child who hasn't learned the big words. "Mr. Kaplan fell this morning in the tub."

"He's dead." Mrs. Sweeney's voice was eager.

"Yes."

"Why the police?" The nostrils quivered.

Again the sickening sense of ground dropping away beneath her. "I didn't think a doctor would be any use."

"Time for the Book." Mrs. Sweeney marched from the room, stripping off the ubiquitous Playtex gloves.

Theresa hesitated, not wanting to deal either with Mrs. Sweeney or her reading material, but the cleaning lady was wanted upstairs for questioning, and Theresa followed her into the kitchen. Mrs. Sweeney was seated at the table, her Bible open, lips moving in a sibilant whisper. Theresa noticed that three pink plastic curlers still nestled in the iodine hair.

"They want you upstairs. They have some questions."

Mrs. Sweeney's head jerked. "Want *me?*" she said indignantly. "Whatever for?"

Theresa shrugged. Does she know I'm afraid of her? she wondered. Does it show? She didn't trust her voice.

The face grew sly. "I wouldn't be so anxious for me to go talking to police, if I was you. I can tell them a few things, you know. I'm not blind, though you'd like it if I was."

Theresa stared at the red-rimmed eyes, the sharp pink nostrils. She hates me, she thought; she always has. "What things?" she said, anger freeing her tongue.

Mrs. Sweeney showed dead teeth in a smile. She patted her pink curlers coyly. "Oh, I don't know. Things like the nights you don't go home like you're supposed to. Things like two to a bed—"

The control Theresa had willed for the past two hours shattered like glass. "Go ahead!" she cried furiously. "Tell them anything you like! And when you do, *I'll* tell them you let yourself into this house this morning with a stolen key. Stolen, got that? I'll tell them I've noticed certain valuables missing. I'll tell them you've been crazy in love with him for years and jealous of anybody else who works for him. I'll tell them you finally went off your nut and killed him—you're plenty strong enough! I'll tell them you've been off your nut for years!"

Mrs. Sweeney's face shrunk like a drying sponge. She licked her lips with a sharp red tongue. "You can't talk to me like that," she said, removing her apron and folding it in neat quarters, "and I ain't giving you another opportunity. There's been something wrong about this house ever since you walked into it. I'm getting my coat and going home. I won't be back." Below the sleeves of her print housedress, her elbows were aggressive.

"But the police—"

"Never had nothing to do with 'em, never will. You don't need the law when you got the Lord." She jerked on black street pumps, thrust her work shoes and Bible into a plastic bag. "I'll expect you to send me what's due."

"The key, please."

For a moment, she thought Mrs. Sweeney would refuse to produce it. But she rummaged in a red handbag and flung it on the table. The kitchen door hissed with the outrage of her exit.

Drained and empty, Theresa picked up the abandoned feather duster and wandered aimlessly through the big rooms, flicking at a picture frame here, a lampshade there. She paused in the drawing room entrance as two sturdy-looking men came through the front door carrying a stretcher and slow-trotted purposefully up the stairs. She did not know what to do with herself. The big man probably had more questions, but she did not want to voluntarily put herself within his range. What would Mrs. Marty do under the circumstances? Probably offer the whole crew sandwiches and coffee. But then Mrs. Marty would have nothing to hide.

She returned to the kitchen. There was coffee—and she poured herself a cup and sat down at the table, cradling it in her cold hands. Presumably there was a great deal of activity taking place above in the master bedroom, but she could hear nothing. She turned on the small TV next to the sink, turned it off again. What *should* I be doing? she wondered. She sat still and waited.

When the phone rang, she jumped spasmodically as though she'd touched a bare wire. She got it before the second ring.

"Theresa? Dorothy Swerdlow. Good morning. Look, we've got a minor crisis here. I'm trying to locate Mr. Kaplan. They're waiting for him in the boardroom, but he hasn't come in yet and they're giving *me* hell about it! He's not at his Club and I'm wondering, did he leave the house at eight-thirty as usual?"

She had not only forgotten Mrs. Sweeney; she had entirely forgotten that Dorothy Swerdlow and Security American would be waiting for the boss. "Oh, Dorothy!" A dam burst inside Theresa at the voice of that loyal woman, and she felt grief for the first time. She couldn't hold back the flood of words. "He's had a terrible accident, upstairs in the bathroom. This morning. In the tub. The police are here. He fell. He's terribly hurt. He's dead!"

It was ten-thirty when the young officer with the deep drawl stuck his head in the morning room.

"Mrs. Foley?"

Theresa turned mutely. For the past hour she had been standing on a stepstool in the morning room, wiping down the dieffenbachias and fiddle-leaf figs in their big white jardinieres with a cloth and Green Thumb Leaf Polish. She estimated she had only a few hundred leaves to go.

"Sergeant Kilty wants you upstairs."

She followed him, sick with dread. She thought she had made it through the first round without catastrophe, but Dorothy's call had unnerved her. She felt naked, exposed. She wondered wildly whether they would make

her look at the body. She didn't think she could do it—
she'd faint or scream or get sick or something. Break
down and confess the whole thing. Though surely it had
been taken away by now?

The big man stood in the library with his back to her,
seemingly absorbed in the painting over the fireplace.
When he finally acknowledged her presence, the flat gray
eyes told her nothing at all.

"You wanted to see me?"

"Just to say we've finished up here."

"You mean I can go home?" She didn't want to go
home; she wanted him to leave the library because she'd
decided that after all she had to get rid of it, there was no
alternative. She could see it out of the corner of her eye; it
seemed to glow, like hot green fire.

"As far as MPD Homicide is concerned, you can go
anywhere you like."

She had no choice but to leave the room. She sat at the
little Sheraton desk in the small drawing room, staring at
the monthly account book open in front of her without
seeing it. Eventually, she heard voices in the foyer, then
the slamming of the big front door. When she looked out
the window, the police cars were gone.

She set the security locks, let herself out, and taped a note
for Mario on the back door. The block weighed so heavily in her shoulder bag that she had to cradle it in her
arms. She would drive to the Bay this afternoon.

The trouble was, she didn't want to leave. She had
scheduled part of the afternoon for polishing the brass
fittings in the dining room and Windexing the morning
room glass doors. She wanted to throw herself into the
simple jobs now, as though everything were just as

usual—to see brass gleam and glass sparkle. Mario was coming at two. A note was not the kindest way to break the news that he was out of a job, though she'd told him to put in his hours as usual until further notice. As usual, that's the way she wanted it to be.

The great, remote, hostile force against which she had been struggling for months with every muscle of her brain and body had suddenly collapsed, catapulting her in a free fall through the thin resistless air of space. She had lost outline, definition, purpose. Intent. Antagonist. She wondered what she was going to do now.

CHAPTER TWENTY-ONE

She arranged with Dorothy Swerdlow to stay on half-time with full pay at Ned Kaplan's residence for a week or two, "until things simmered down."

"Frankly," said Dorothy, "here at Security American we're still pretty much in shock. He was a tough boss, but he was fair. I've been his secretary for nineteen years. It's like God has died." She conquered the tremor in her voice. "What about you? Have you begun to look for another position?"

"Not yet."

"You can count on me for a recommendation if you need one, Theresa. I know Mr. Kaplan appreciated your work."

"Thank you. I'm very grateful."

She hung up the phone thoughtfully. She was aware—who more—of the irony of Dorothy Swerdlow's recommendation; yet, if she could ever pull her shattered life together, she did want to go on in this profession for which she had discovered a real flair. Housekeeping was all a question of orchestration, she had decided. You had to see the big picture, the grand plan. Q Street was this grand picture: If she hadn't achieved these heights before, it was for lack of the big canvas. And, though understanding the totality, you still had to have a head for detail, the thousands of infinitely fine brush strokes that finally created the domestic masterpiece.

This time she might even live in, she mused, thinking about the long and bitter argument she'd had with Matt about his going to live with his father, his tears, which had shamed him, and his final capitulation. They would see each other weekends, regularly at first—they had sworn it. Then would come phone calls excusing himself because of family outings, the horses, football games. Then dates with girls. He would grow away from her and prosper, the fates willing. And then perhaps some day he would come back, and they could be friends at last.

As she and Mary Jane were friends again at last. She had destroyed the diary—shredded it and burned the scraps in the little backyard fireplace. Not because it was evidence against her, but because the story it told had at last been given closure. For the first time, too, she had been able to go through Mary Jane's things, sorting clothes for the Goodwill and a cousin Mary Jane's size. And she had given Chris Stacio, Mary Jane's apartment mate, her daughter's amethyst ring. The silver sandals she kept. Perhaps one day they would be only objects to discard. But not yet.

As for Holly, perhaps her friend might be relieved to see the last of her. Monday evening at suppertime she had banged at Theresa's front door, bursting into the room when Theresa opened it, her eyes wide.

"Quick, turn on the news! You won't believe what's

happened!" She grabbed the remote and punched it frantically.

So Ned Kaplan's death had made television. "What has happened?" said Theresa. She was terribly tired.

"Jesus, Terry! Your boss—dead in the bathtub! Kaplan. Banker. It's got to be the same guy!"

"I know he's dead. I found him this morning."

Holly fell back onto the sofa, staring. "You're kidding! You *found* him?" Theresa saw the whole sordid episode flash like a horror film through Holly's head. "And you didn't tell me? Thanks a lot!"

"I was going to."

"Next week, right?"

"Holly, it hasn't been a good day."

Holly's pretty, plump face softened. "You poor kid. I'll fix us a drink. Bourbon? You've got to tell me *everything.*"

Theresa told, repeating the story by now automatically. Holly listened, full red lips parted, brown eyes wide.

"But why the police?"

Theresa began to laugh hysterically. "Not you, too! Why *not* the police, for God's sake. People call them when a damned cat's up a tree!"

"No, that's the fire department, only they don't come for cats anymore." Always vehement herself, she could be shocked at Theresa's ferocity.

"What's the difference! I called the police, that's all there's to it. No doctor could have helped, believe me."

Holly looked meditative, swirling bourbon in a glass. "You know," she said finally with awe in her voice, "in a way this is kind of like divine retribution or something, isn't it. I mean, first you suspect him of killing Mary Jane and then he goes and brains himself in the tub, just like that."

"I don't know anything about divine retribution," said Theresa brutally. "I do know he deserved what he got." She realized she believed the words absolutely.

Holly looked at her fearfully. "Theresa?"

"What?"

Holly gulped bourbon nervously. "Saturday night. You weren't home, were you? I rang the bell and then I phoned, but there wasn't any answer. I thought we were going to the flicks."

"I don't know anything about the flicks. I went to bed at seven. I was dead."

Holly looked at her doubtfully. "It must have been hell, finding him." Her face was expectant.

"I'm sorry," said Theresa, "but I can't." She sagged against the couch pillows, her arm across her face. "I don't want to talk about it anymore. Don't you understand? *I can't!*"

"Gee, Terry, I understand." Holly hovered a few moments, but when Theresa said nothing, she let herself quietly out the door.

The big man sat behind his desk studying his thumbs, his coffee cold in a thick mug labeled Soup 'n Crackers. His plaid cap hung on a coat rack just above his left shoulder like a defiant flag. It was his secret vanity, to everybody else an old rag, to him the badge of the clansman sweeping down upon the invading hordes. In fact he had never been to Ireland and had only the most rudimentary conception of its history. "So what have you got, Purdy?" he said morosely.

Officer Royal Purdy shuffled papers. "We still don't have the coroner's report."

"*That* I know. With stiff's stacked five deep at D.C. General, the Medical Examiner's Office can sit on a case forever. What else?"

"I interviewed the neighbors yesterday. She lives out in Silver Spring, 4 Knox—"

"That also I know." Kilty swallowed cold coffee, grunted in disgust, shoved the mug aside. Purdy lept to his feet.

"You need a refill, Sergeant." He disappeared, replenished the mug from the coffee machine in the bullpen, set it carefully on Kilty's filthy green blotter. "There's a woman lives next door, Mrs. Holly Bauer. She wasn't in, but Number 8 in the Circle said she owns a business called"—he glanced at his notes—"La Beautique. I have a transcript of her statement." He extended papers. "Want to read it, sir?"

"Just give me the highlights." Kilty's right hand went to his left pocket before he remembered he hadn't smoked for three years. He wondered again how a disgustingly preppy guy like Purdy had made it into MPD. A master's degree in Urban Environment from the U. of Alabama. Hell, you could learn all you needed to know about "urban environment" just taking a stroll three blocks east of the Capitol of the United States at midnight.

"Mrs. Bauer was at home Saturday night, the twenty-sixth. Decided to have a quiet evening, watch a movie on TV. Knows Theresa Foley well; they've been neighbors five years. Thinks Foley spent the evening at home, at least that's what Foley told her. Bauer went to bed after the news at ten. Slept soundly until past eight A.M., Sunday the twenty-seventh. Ate breakfast, read the *Post,* then took it next door to Foley."

Kilty leaned forward. "And?"

Purdy frowned at his notes. "Nothing, Sergeant. She hands her the paper, they talk for a few minutes, then Bauer leaves. Doesn't see her again until Monday evening when she catches the Kaplan thing on the local news. She runs over to tell Foley about it. Of course, Foley knows."

"Give me that."

Purdy put the report in the sergeant's hand deferentially and sat at attention while Kilty read, his lips moving.

She was upset, naturally, who wouldn't be! Still kind of shaky. Said the police had been there all morning. She didn't want to talk about it, especially since her son Matt was there. I fixed her a drink, she looked like she needed it. I also asked her if she'd like me to stay the night, on the couch, just for company in case she couldn't sleep or something. She said she'd be o.k. So I left, making her promise to call me if she needed anything—

Kilty threw the sheet down on the desk. "You believe this Bauer dame?"

Officer Purdy's baby-blue eyes grew earnest. "I found no reason not to, Sergeant. She talked to me in a perfectly straightforward way."

"You don't think it's strange that two single women, good friends, sit alone right next door to each other all Saturday night? Hell, I don't mean that"—Sergeant Purdy had colored slightly—"I mean why don't they

watch TV together, play cards, do whatever women do—
talk, for chrissake. Why do two good friends spend a Saturday night alone?"

Purdy looked perplexed. "I don't understand why Saturday night's important. The body—"

"I know you don't. What else you got?"

Purdy reconsulted his notes. "Five houses in Knox
Circle. People at Number 8 gone for the weekend, didn't
get home until Sunday evening after nine. The couple at
Number 10 went bowling Saturday night, home a little
before eleven. They thought they remembered Foley's
Honda in the drive."

"Going or coming?"

"They weren't sure. They didn't pay much attention."

"Nobody does. What about Sunday morning?"

"They slept in. Woman remembers seeing the Honda
in the drive when she went out after lunch."

"That all?"

"That's about it. Even though there's just a few houses
in the Circle, it's not exactly a chummy neighborhood.
Number 10 didn't even know Foley's name. Like you
said, they don't care. But I think there might be something interesting here." He handed Kilty another sheaf of
papers.

"What's this?"

"I had a printout made of the disc in Kaplan's computer in his study. You see the date, March twenty-
sixth—that's last Saturday" His voice was eager. "If
you'll look it over, sir, you'll see it's about some financial
takeover he was planning for Security American—"

"So?"

"So big wheels like Kaplan who try to muscle other

corporations can make big enemies. If you're thinking this is homicide—"

Wheels shrilled as Kilty pushed away from the desk. It was after six and the fluorescent lights made his eyes ache; he felt a beer coming on. He smiled at Purdy pityingly.

"Hell, Purdy," he said, not unkindly, "I know what you're thinking. International cartels. CIA. Drug money. Hit men. Payoffs. The trail leading right to the Oval Office. You're praying for a big international murder case with your mug on TV and the front page of every paper in America. Pretty soon the White House. The Secret Service. I know. I used to say the same prayers. Funny how it doesn't happen that way. Even when some nut shoots the President, he's nabbed with the gun in his fist. No, if anybody killed Kaplan—and I would bet money somebody did—it was small and personal. Something, say, a housekeeper would do."

Purdy seemed to find his thick sheaf of papers something of an embarrassment. "What about the Maynard woman?"

"What about her?"

"He paid her nine thousand six hundred and ninety dollars over the last twelve months. Suppose he says, 'That's it, I'm through.' Suppose she gets mad enough to do something about it?"

Kilty laughed mirthlessly. "Know who Diana Maynard is, Purdy?"

"No, sir."

"She's the highest paid whore in D.C. And the smartest. Not only demands big money but clients who can tell her how to invest it. We got a load of her bank account when we pulled her in on a drug charge two years ago.

Don't tell me a woman worth two million's going to get irate over a few thousand bucks."

Purdy's deferential expression didn't waver. He bitterly resented Kilty's eternal sneer, but he was ambitious. "Well, then, Sergeant, what's the next step?"

"Bring Foley in."

"What's the charge? We haven't got anything on her."

"We'll get something. Bring her in. Make her sweat." He heaved his bulk from the chair and reached for the plaid cap.

In some ways she was not surprised when she answered the front doorbell to see the polite young officer scraping his feet on the porch mat. It was pouring rain and his dark blue shoulders glistened. "Mrs. Foley?"

"Yes?"

"I wonder if you'd mind coming along to MPD Headquarters with me for a few minutes. We have a couple more questions we'd like to ask you in connection with Mr. Kaplan's death. It won't take long."

"But why? I've told you everything I know." Surely she could refuse. Didn't they have to have a search warrant, or something?

"I'm sure you have, m'am." He showed white, even teeth in an ingratiating smile, reassuring her that policemen were the nicest fellows in the world. "I'm just obeying orders."

She looked over his shoulder at the gray curtain of rain. "I'll have to get my coat and umbrella. And," she added firmly, "I have to make a phone call before I go."

"Yes, ma'm, if it won't take long. I'll wait here."

In the kitchen she dialed Stephanie Ruso's number. She didn't really think that Stephanie had returned to the boarding house, but there was a slim chance. A phone call might be incriminating, but if they were booking her for murder—and she knew they were—only Stephanie's story could help her now.

"Mel speaking."

"Is Stephanie Ruso there?"

"Hang on, I'll find out."

That seemed hopeful. Theresa doodled nervous arrows on the telephone pad.

"This is Stephanie."

"Thank God!" In her relief, Theresa forgot to identify herself. "Look, Stephanie, I'm being taken to police headquarters to answer more questions about Ned Kaplan's death. If I have to, I'm going to tell them your story. I'm going to give your name."

"Theresa? Why didn't you say so! I read about Kaplan—and you know, I was glad! Justice for once. Look, you don't need me, you need a lawyer."

"I can't discuss that now. I just want you to know I may need *you*. You ran out on me once. Don't do it again."

She hung up and got her black raincoat that was hanging in the back hall. Ten days ago, ignoring the DRY CLEAN ONLY label, she had thrown it into the washer; it would never look the same, but her careful inspection had discovered no traces of stains. Still, she thought wryly, it's not the coat I would have chosen to wear to police headquarters.

The young officer ran ahead of her down the walk to open the car door. She thanked him. He helped her in. They might have been stepping out for their first date, only he hadn't handed her a corsage.

Before they turned down Pennsylvania Avenue, she

realized that he was not taking her to the building at Wisconsin and Volta where she'd tried to meet Stephanie Ruso last November. So that had definitely been a wrong guess. "Where are we going?" she asked, disoriented by the flap of windshield wipers, the heavy traffic. They seemed to be skirting the White House grounds, and there was the Washington Monument, a blurred shaft in the rain. What was this, some kind of tour?

"MPD Headquarters, Indiana Avenue. Ever been there?" he asked without irony.

"Certainly not!"

Defensive, he noted. Might mean guilty, might mean nothing at all.

The Homicide Branch of the Criminal Investigation Division occupied the third floor of the enormous stone building. The friendly officer escorted her down several corridors to a room with fluorescent lighting, a table, two wooden chairs, and a large mirror. The table was bare except for a writing pad, and a calendar that she saw was two years old. "If you'll just take a seat," said the officer. "Can I get you a cup of coffee?"

She nodded, wanting to sound cooperative.

"Sugar or cream?"

"Black, thanks."

He closed the door after him. She tried to peer through the single small window but could not see through the glass. She tried the door, but it was locked. So this was the upshot of all that official courtesy! She sat down and looked at her watch. She had thought it must be afternoon, but it was only ten-thirty. The officer returned with coffee in a Styrofoam cup, nodded politely, and left.

At ten forty-five a woman in a smart navy blue suit, carrying a briefcase, put her head in the door.

"Adams?"

"No, Foley."

"Wrong room." She shrugged cheerfully and withdrew.

"Oh, wait, please wait!" cried Theresa, but she was gone and the door locked behind her.

At eleven-ten it reopened, and Detective Sergeant Kilty entered the room. He studied her, hands in pockets already strained by the heft around his belly. "We got a few more questions, Mrs. Foley. If you don't mind."

She should have known it wasn't over—that it would never be over. He suspected her of murdering Edward Devereaux Kaplan: She could see it in his cold eyes. When he maneuvered her into the chair facing the glass, she realized it was a two-way mirror, probably concealing a video camera. She'd seen that last week on a television crime show. So she was being recorded. They intended to make her crack.

Sergeant Kilty took a seat across the desk. He was tired: thirty-one cases of homicide on his desk that week; but he intended to break the Foley woman even while reason told him that Edward Kaplan might indeed have killed himself had he lost his footing in that tub. Reason also told him to wait for the autopsy report from the Medical Examiner's Office at D.C. General, though given the backup there, it might be next week before it came through. But Sergeant Kilty had always given more credit to hunches than to reason, and he leaned forward now with an unpleasant smile that he thought sincerely friendly.

"We'd like to establish your whereabouts the night of Saturday, March twenty-sixth and Sunday, March twenty-seventh." Would she talk? The big talkers were usually guilty, in his experience. Hell, they could keep you hanging on their gab eight hours at a stretch, bend over backward to let you know in detail how they spent every crucial minute surrounding a crime. But, they were usually guilty.

"I don't understand. I found Mr. Kaplan Monday morning—"

"Just answer the questions, Mrs. Foley. Saturday night—where were you and what were you doing?"

"I was at home, I think. Yes, at home. I went to bed very early with a book. About seven o'clock."

"Isn't that kind of unusual?"

"Yes, rather unusual. But I'd had a fairly strenuous week."

"And you were alone the whole evening? No one with you?"

Was it a trap? Had someone from the Metro identified her? Someone arriving at a Georgetown neighbor's for a party? She could not believe it. "I was alone," she said. "My son, Matt, was on a camping trip with friends for the weekend."

"What about your neighbor, your good friend, Mrs. Bauer? You didn't hear her knocking at your door?"

The police must have talked to Holly. Had she told them about their movie date, that she'd telephoned and rang her doorbell? Stupid, stupid that she should have forgotten to cancel Holly! Yet she could not see Holly as an informer. "I heard nothing," she said evenly. "I must have fallen asleep over my book rather quickly."

"How about Sunday?"

She shrugged. "An ordinary day. As a housekeeper, I don't often get a chance to clean my own place, so I did some vacuuming. I made a casserole and some cookies and froze them since I don't usually get home weekdays until five. Matt—my son—got home from his camping trip about four. But I don't understand why you're asking me all this." She tried to keep the panic out of her voice.

Before Sergeant Kilty had a chance to reply, an officer stuck his head in the door. "Things are breaking fast on the Foggy Bottom case. You're wanted."

Kilty sighed. The Foggy Bottom case, involving as it did the brutal murder of two blacks by a suspected white vagrant, had been simmering for weeks. But he'd hardly started tightening the screws on Theresa Foley. He stood up. "Don't walk out on me," he said, wagging a fat finger in her face. "I'll be back."

She waited until twelve-twenty, her heels beating an increasingly impatient tattoo on the floor. Then she got up and attacked the door. It was finally opened by a black woman officer, her gun and holster riding incongruously, noted Theresa, on pear-shaped hips.

She did not try to control her anger. "My name is Theresa Foley and I have been *held* in this locked room since ten-thirty without explanation. I insist upon being released immediately. You have no right to keep me here like this—"

The officer was laconic, unimpressed. "Hold on a minute, m'am. Just you go sit down again, and I'll find out what's going on."

But it was twenty-five minutes later before the door opened and still another officer put in his head. "Foley? Follow me." She hurried after his lean, noncommital back.

In a secretarial area outside a door labeled COM-
MANDER OF CRIMINAL INVESTIGATION stood a short man
with small, shrewd eyes whom Theresa did not recognize.
He wore the inevitable businessman's tan belted raincoat
and carried a briefcase large enough to hold two bowling
balls.

"Thanks, Sam," he said to the officer, who nodded and
sat down behind a computer. He looked at Theresa ap-
praisingly. "I hear they've been letting you cool your
heels awhile."

"For hours—in a locked room!" She did not know
who he was, but she was too indignant to watch her
tongue. "I thought there were laws against this kind of
thing in America!"

"Never mind, it's over now. Come on, I'll buy you a
cup of coffee."

"But who are you?"

"Bob Cohn's the name. Lawyer. Let's get out of this
place, shall we?"

She pushed ahead of him through the glass doors out
into the afternoon and saw that the sky had cleared. She
gulped spring air into her lungs as though she had been
suffocating.

George's, in the ground floor of an office building across
Indiana Avenue in Judiciary Square, was a cafeteria with
chrome tables and black chairs crammed with bureau-
cratic types wolfing yogurt and salads. Robert Cohn
grabbed a tray. "Hungry? Lunch is on me."

"Maybe later. Coffee's fine for now." She pretended
interest in the menu printed on a board while she studied
Bob Cohn discreetly as he moved along the line. She had
known him only as a name on a placecard, the guest next

to whom she'd tried to seat Elsa Frazier before her own good sense and Franchot intervened. A man Elsa Frazier hated, she wondered why. She guessed he was a hard man, tough and cynical; yet he had just done her a good turn. She could not fathom why or with what powers he had rescued her. Or even what she had been rescued from. When he had set two coffees on the table, pulled out a chair, and seated himself opposite, she said, "Are you going to tell me about it, Mr. Cohn, or leave me guessing for the rest of my life?"

He was twitchy, creasing his paper napkin into triangles, rearranging cutlery, shooting sharp glances right and left. A man, thought Theresa, used to perpetual motion and conflict.

"I guess I owe you an explanation," he said at last. He locked his eyes on the glass wall behind her so intently that she had to resist turning around to see what he was staring at. "Let me start this way. Every four or five years I teach a law course at G.U. Why? To keep an eye on the talent coming up and because, let's face it, once every five years it's rather refreshing to be in touch with comparative innocence in this sadly evil world. I know I have a reputation as a hardnose"—he smiled, definitely pleased with the repute—"but I'm not quite as cynical as people think.

"Last semester I taught a course in criminal law, small-ish class for once. At finals I corrected a certain exam that I had no option but to fail: The student had answered less than a third of the questions. I didn't like that—first because I don't like failure, second because, on the basis of a first exam, I could have sworn this student had real brains. Cream or sugar? Coward! I called her in. Ah, a reaction at last."

"I expected you to say 'him.' "

"Then you're hopelessly behind the times. More than half the law students at G.U. these days are female. As I was saying, I called her in. What chiefly impressed me was her emotional state. She was jumpy, evasive. She looked and talked like a person who'd had a bad shock. Now shock is not all that uncommon in law students, but it's usually connected with the grade on their last exam. Hers wasn't."

Theresa was suddenly sure she knew who this law student was. Funny, she had always assumed Stephanie Ruso was getting a graduate degree in English or Education. She had never thought to ask.

"I questioned her ruthlessly about the exam she'd just flunked," Cohn went on. "She made excuses, asked to take it again, then burst into tears, and the story came out. I think you know the story. No—don't answer that.

"The story was that she'd had a bad experience the night of last September twenty-first when she signed on to work as kitchen help for a housekeeper named Mrs. Marty, who was employed by a Washington banker named Edward Kaplan living at 3001 Q Street. A girl fell down the back stairs that night and died. Mishap. Accident. Unfortunate tragedy. One of the most prominent doctors in Washington ruled it so. But my student had evidence to the contrary. She related it to me, at length. I happened to believe her story—first because she's got her head screwed on straight and second because it jibed with a few skeptical observations I'd made myself about that evening. She rang true. Even though I happen to be Kaplan's lawyer."

"I didn't know that."

Cohn stirred the sugary sludge at the bottom of his

cup. "No reason you should. Anyway, I reassured this student, who shall be nameless, that I believed her and that I would look into the matter. I also told her that she should pull herself together, take an incomplete, and make up the work in the spring semester. She had panicked over bad grades and was thinking of dropping out of G.U. altogether."

"I know."

"Ah." Cohn threw her a sharp glance. "At any rate, I had moved the District Court to look into the case of the girl who fell, when Kaplan died himself. That settled matters, at least in my book—I don't believe in prosecuting beyond the grave. Until this morning when the student telephoned to say that you were being taken down to MPD in connection with Kaplan's death. She begged me to intervene."

So Stephanie, thought Theresa with a surge of gratitude that stung her eyes, had come through after all.

"All I could do on such short notice was pressure certain pals in the Medical Examiner's Office to come up within the hour with the lab report they'd been sitting on for two weeks. Not their fault, I might add parenthetically; they're radically overworked. Fortunately I've got connections. And the result, from your point of view, was satisfactory. Even Kilty had to admit it."

"My point of view?"

"Death by misadventure, as they call it. Going to pass out? Bend over and drop your head between your knees."

"I'm all right," whispered Theresa. She realized that her knees were locked together under the table, that she had been holding her breath like a swimmer under water. "I'd like some more coffee, please."

Cohn signaled a waitress. "Want to hear more?" He flashed a look at his watch and she realized he must have another appointment. "Then brace yourself. At first Forensics didn't like the look of the head injuries. There were two wounds, a deep gash across the forehead and another about two inches higher on the scalp. But they finally decided that he probably fell once, picked himself up, slipped, and fell hard again. They also, don't ask a layman like me how, decided the second blow—the deep gash across the forehead—was the killer. That is, though we're talking seconds, even nanoseconds, he was dead as he went under. And it didn't happen Monday morning, Mrs. Foley. Autopsy says he'd been dead at least twenty-four hours when you found him, maybe more since it's hard to fix time when a body's in water. I'm sorry for the details, but you seemed to want to know."

"I did—I do." This was the reason for Sergeant Kilty's questions. And this man had saved her. She raised her steaming cup to her lips with both hands to steady it. She was free, not innocent but free, at least that's what Robert Cohn seemed to be saying. "But I still don't understand," she managed to say, "why they took me to Headquarters this morning."

"I couldn't get much out of the Commander, but it seems that the good Sarge didn't like the look of the setup. He wanted you in for more questioning. If he'd waited for the lab report, you probably wouldn't have been bothered. Though I don't know: He seems to have it in for you."

"You mean, I could still be—"

"As a lawyer, I can assure you there's not enough evidence to charge you." He glanced at his watch again. "I've got to run. You're the girl's mother, aren't you—

no, don't answer that, I don't want to know." He stood up, extracted three dollar bills from his wallet, and shoved them under his coffee cup.

"I don't know how to thank you," said Theresa, rising and offering her hand. She hated to see him go. Not only had he undoubtedly saved her life, he had been kind in his brusque, overbearing way—and there were so many questions she still wanted to ask. "You don't know me, Mr. Cohn, and after all, you were Mr. Kaplan's lawyer. Why did you bother?"

Cohn smiled for the first time. "Let's just say that I happen to have a soft spot in my heart for my law students. Besides, conflict of interest is nothing new to me. Good-bye, Mrs. Foley. Good luck."

CHAPTER TWENTY-TWO

T heresa opened the security lock to the front gate with the key no one had thought to ask her to return and went up the walk. An imposing FOR SALE BY APPOINTMENT ONLY sign dominated the green lawn. Overhead pink buds on the huge beech were springing into leaf and along the front of the house the sun had already coaxed open the magnolias' waxy cups. She took the walk along the side of the house and pushed open the gate giving onto the patio. Mario was filling the pool.

"Hello, Mario."

He turned and grinned, hitching up his baggy pants with his free hand. He still sported the fake safari hat, and she realized he was absurdly proud of it. "Theresa! What you doing here?"

"I was going to ask you the same thing."

"The real estate agent, she tell me the house sell better if it look 'lived in.' So I bring out all the chairs and tables and umbrellas, rake the beds, sweep the patio, and now I fill the pool. What do you say?" He grinned at her engagingly. "I would like you for my boss. Will you buy?"

Theresa laughed. "Yes, if you'll lend me a couple million. Actually I'm here to collect my how-to-run-a-house books. They cost a lot of money and I'll be needing them. I think I'm going into this business permanently. I'm pretty good at the job—and it pays."

"Good pay I don't know about." Mario scratched a tan patch of bare belly mournfully. "My cousin, Luciano, he send me money to come to this country. He say, 'Mafia will take care of you.' I come, I ask, 'Where is this Mafia that will take care of me?' He say, 'Wait, you see.' I still wait. Sometimes on Sunday he give me a ride in his big black car."

"Someday I'll give you a ride in mine. After I find a new job. Everything's going to be sold at auction, so I won't be back after today."

The big red-and-white kitchen looked the same, burdened with the gleaming appliances that had squeezed, pulverized, toasted, brewed, baked, broiled, chopped, frappéed, blended, frozen, and nuked a vast assortment of expensive meats, shellfish, poultry, grains, and produce for Ned Kaplan's solitary meals. It would be the same wherever she went; it was the same with the rich everywhere. Rich and poor, masters and servants. At the thought of servants, John Franchot and his words, "Us working classes have to stick together" sprang into her head. They had galled her at the time, but now she smiled a little at the possibility of gravitating into John Franchot's orbit again. Now that he no longer had her guilty secret as a weapon, he was going to discover that the working classes did not necessarily stick together, at least in the matter of cheating their employers. She had her scruples, after all. But perhaps they could still be friends.

At any rate, she would know how to deal with him better this time.

She had brought a canvas carryall into which she now stowed her aprons, her precious telephone list, her leather notebook of household accounts, and the five or six household management books that had been, she believed, almost totally responsible for her cachet. Because she did have it, cachet. The few notes from the Fraziers, the Meiers, and an unknown city banker in need of a housekeeper, along with Sarah Cohn condoling her upon the abrupt termination of her employment with Edward Kaplan, assured her of that. She looked around. There was nothing more to take away with her. It had all been his.

On her way out, she walked deliberately to the bottom of the back stairs and looked for the last time up the narrow well. Wildly, she had thought of leaving some token—a plaque, a white stone, a spray of roses—at its foot. But that, she realized, would have been an empty, sentimental gesture. Her task had been accomplished. The real tributes you bore within, close to the heart, like a child.

She let herself out the back door, setting the lock. Mario had abandoned his work and was smoking a cigarette, his bare feet decorating one of the patio chairs. She waved and he grinned and waved back, swinging his arm broadly like a flag.

For the last time, she went down the wide brick walk flanked by carriage lights. Could she forget what had happened here or, if not forget, survive the memory? She did not know. She knew that she must try. Just as she knew that someday she would have to pay, as he had paid.

She had left the front gate unlatched. She tried to close it now behind her, but for some reason the lock wouldn't catch. She grasped the iron bars and clanged the gate back and forth a few times, but something had gone wrong with the bolt, it didn't give. She had always hated that gate; it didn't matter now. She walked away, leaving the great spiked barrier standing open behind her.